EIRIK'S OATH

VIRGINIE MARCONATO

OLIVERHEBERBOOKS

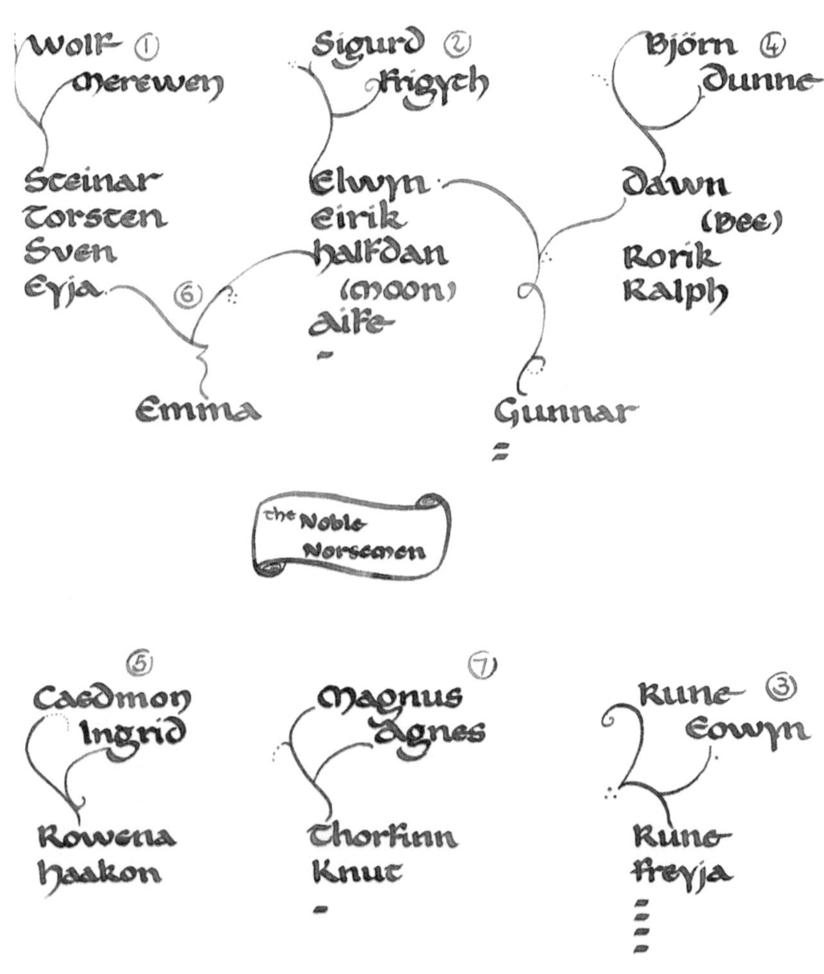

Wolf ①
Merewen
Steinar
Torsten
Sven
Eyja
⑥
Emma
Sigurd ②
Frigyth
Elwyn
Eirik
Halfdan
(Moon)
Aife
Gunnar
Björn ④
Dunne
Dawn
(Bee)
Rorik
Ralph
the Noble Norsemen
Caedmon ⑤
Ingrid
Rowena
Haakon
Magnus ⑦
Agnes
Thorfinn
Knut
Rune ③
Eowyn
Rune
Freyja

PROLOGUE

Freyja held on tight to Asta's little hand as she followed Eirik through the village.

In truth, it had been a stroke of luck to find someone whose name was familiar immediately upon her arrival. All her life she had heard about her Saxon mother's friend who had married a Dane called Sigurd. She knew he and Frigyth had adopted a son when they'd gotten married, then later welcomed another together, as well as two daughters. She also knew that their second son had been raised by Sigurd, though he'd been fathered by a man called Olaf, who had raped Frigyth and left her to deal with the child on her own.

That son was none other than the man who was now leading her to Wolf's hut. Her parents had told her the Icelander would be able to help her when she'd decided to leave Denmark. Were they right? She could only hope so, as she knew he helped people in need, especially women like her, who were fleeing dangerous or painful situations.

"Here. I will leave you to it," Eirik said, stopping in front of one of the largest huts.

"Thank you."

The man was rather curt but it was no wonder. He probably had better things to do than escort strangers around. Still, gruff or not, he had helped her. She watched him go with the impression that she'd lost her only ally, then finally knocked on the door.

"Come in."

Inside the hut, there was only a woman, busy making dough on the biggest table Freyja had ever seen. Merewen, Wolf's wife, by all accounts. She matched the description her mother had given her exactly, even if the beautiful auburn hair was now streaked with silver.

"Can I help you?" she asked in heavily accented Norse, her gaze darting from her to Asta, who was huddling by her side, impressed by all these new people.

"I hope so. I'm Freyja, Rune and Eowyn's daughter. You might remember them?"

The woman beamed as she wiped her hands clean. She seemed delighted to meet her. "Indeed, I do! And I have to say, you're the image of your father."

"I am." Freyja touched her braided hair. It was flaming red, just like his was. All six siblings had hair tinged with copper, but her sisters' was subdued, more like a reddish gold. Her brother, Rune, was the only one who could match the fiery hue flowing in her locks.

"Is Rune here as well? And your mother?"

"No, they didn't come with me." She cleared her throat and decided to go straight to the point. Merewen, just like Eirik, was busy. "They told me Wolf might be able to help me."

The Saxon nodded but didn't press her further. Evidently, she was used to people coming to see her husband for some purpose or other. Freyja was grateful for her discretion because she didn't want to have to tell her story in front of the little girl, who had no idea why they were here.

"Come, let us go find Wolf. He will be in the garden."

1

EAST ANGLIA, SUMMER 1074

Eirik was skimming the froth off the surface of the amber-colored mixture bubbling over the fire when a knock on his door made him stop with the ladle in midair. Sighing, he wiped his hands on a piece of cloth and went to open the door. Why was it that people always visited at the most inconvenient of moments? Or perhaps they didn't, and he just resented the interruptions. Having left his family's hut almost two decades ago, he was not used to having to take into account other people's wishes.

The door opened on a grim-looking Wolf—an unusual sight, and one that didn't bode well.

"Wolf," he said, bracing himself for bad news.

The Icelander nodded, eyeing the inside of the hut as if expecting someone to be there. As if that were an option. Everyone knew Eirik lived alone, and rarely welcomed people inside.

"Do you have a moment? I have a favor to ask of you."

"Of course." Who would refuse the Icelander a favor, when he was always the first to help others? Not him. "But you'll have to come in. I was making mead, and I need to stir the pot before the liquid starts sticking to the bottom."

"Please. Don't let me spoil your mead."

The door was closed and the two men walked inside.

Eirik concentrated his attention back to the simmering liquid but indicated that he was listening. After a while, Wolf started talking.

"It's about Freyja, the woman who arrived in the village earlier today."

Ah, yes.

The fiery-haired little Dane with her shy daughter clinging to her, her entrancing accent, and her altogether inexplicable allure. Not that he would ever admit it to anyone, but he had thought of little else all afternoon. How could he not? She had been like a ray of sunshine appearing in the midst of a rainy day, utterly unexpected, illuminating the scene and leaving a rain-bow-shaped memory in his heart.

Eirik stilled, ladle hovering over the pot.

A rainbow-shaped memory in his heart?

What the fuck was that? Since when did he think things only skalds skilled in the art of poetry and imagery would dare say out loud? Next he would think that Freyja had smelled as heady as the liquid bubbling under his nose, or that he wanted to lap at her folds to check if she was as sweet as the honey he'd poured into the pot a moment ago. He swallowed, because, well, he *had* just thought that.

And now it was all he could think about. A woman made of honey for him to taste and devour.

"What about her?" he asked, glad to have something to justify not having to face Wolf when there was a sizeable bulge tenting his braies.

"She needs a place to stay in the village. I was wondering if she could stay with you, at least for a few days, while we decide what to do." Wolf sighed. "I would welcome her but we have Rothgar, Sanna, and Liv with us at the moment."

Yes. The children's parents, Steinar and Cwenthryth, had gone to take their eldest son, Ulf, to a distant fair. The boy had expressed the wish to learn a new trade a few weeks ago, and everyone had agreed this would be the best way for him to meet people able to introduce him to what was available.

Eirik slowly stirred his spoon through the thickening liquid, pondering his answer. What did he think of the idea of welcoming a stranger under his roof? Not just a stranger, but a woman whose sensual appeal he had not missed? Their encounter had been brief, and yet he could feel even now the ripples of it in his body, a highly unusual occurrence. He rarely felt uncontrollable desire for a woman, especially one he had seen for such a short time.

This unprecedented reaction was precisely why he would prefer her not to come anywhere too close.

It frightened him.

"Couldn't she stay with Inga, the butcher's daughter?" he asked, naming the first unmarried person who came to mind. "It might be more appropriate."

"She could, but I would prefer if she were with a man I trust, someone able to protect her and little Asta if need be, so I thought of you."

Yes, of course, he had, Eirik thought somewhat dejectedly. There were not many men his age living alone in the village. They all had families of their own and full houses. The few that had left their parents and not yet married were notorious lechers who could not be trusted to keep their lust in check, unlike him, who had made a habit of it. It galled him that his father's closest friend thought him—

Eirik froze when what Wolf had said finally registered.

Slowly, he turned around. "Protect her? From what?"

From whom?

There was a silence, too heavy for his liking. This would be bad.

"I will leave Freyja to explain the situation to you if she wants," Wolf eventually said, crossing his arms over his chest. "I feel it is not my place. Suffice it to say that there was someone on the ship who brought her from Denmark who might want to come after her. I cannot allow that to happen."

"No."

Every muscle in Eirik's body had tensed. If one thing was guaranteed to rouse his ire, it was hearing that a woman was under threat, which was little wonder, given his past.

The bile in his stomach soured, as it always did when he thought about what he'd learned on his sixteenth birthday.

That day, on the day he'd become a man, he'd been told that he was the product of a rape.

To say that finding out about what his mother had endured at the hands of a stranger had been a shock would be putting it mildly, and knowing the truth about his origins had turned his life upside down. The man who was raising him, a strong, well-respected Dane called Sigurd, was not his real father. His father was a man named Olaf, who'd been beaten to within an inch of his life and banished from the village for what he had done by none other than Wolf.

No.

Eirik clenched his fists. That vile man he had never even seen didn't have any claim on him. He had used his mother like a rutting animal, he had never repented for it, he had never come back to enquire about a possible child born of that forced coupling. Forget blood ties that didn't mean a thing, his father was, and would forever remain Sigurd, the man who had loved him and offered him the happy childhood he had not had himself.

He had known from birth that his eldest brother, Elwyn, had been adopted at the death of his drunken father and he had thought that admirable enough. To be told later on that the Dane had not only offered a poor orphan a home, but also welcomed the child imposed on his wife by another man, had humbled him. Sigurd was a good man, who'd striven to make a good man out of him. Eirik would not let him down now. He would do what needed to be done.

His decision was made in a heartbeat.

If the little fiery-haired Dane was in danger, then of course, he would welcome her in his hut, he would do what he could to protect her and her daughter. Making sure no woman ever had to endure what his mother had endured was the sole aim of his existence, and here was a chance to do just that.

The unfortunate, unexpected desire Freyja had stirred in him earlier was a complication, undoubtedly, but Eirik hoped it would be gone the next time they met. It had been based on little more than a glance, so it seemed unlikely that it would linger. If it was still there, then it would simply have to be ignored. It shouldn't be too difficult for a man who was used to negating his feelings. Doing so had become a way of life.

The day he had received his arm ring and become a man—the same day his parents had told him about his origins—he had sworn a solemn oath to himself.

He would never allow himself to possess a woman.

The blood of a rapist ran in his veins. What if it came out when he least expected it? What if blood did matter, more than he knew? What if he was, deep down, like the man who had sired him, rather than the one he called his father? From the moment he'd learned what had happened to his mother, Eirik had been afraid of his nature, afraid he would one day lose control, ignore a woman's refusal because his lust needed to be slaked. There was an easy way of preventing this. He would never try to bed anyone—it was just too risky.

As he'd become older, however, he'd seen that there was a flaw in his plan, something he had not taken into account when he'd made his decision. Desire. He did feel desire for women, and as much as he hated it, his body responded to it. Realistically, he would not be able to live the life of a Saxon monk.

His solution had been to allow himself to give pleasure, and still stop himself from taking any in return. Physical satisfaction he could have on his own later, in the privacy of his house, away from the temptation a woman's soft body offered. And the compromise had worked.

Years of constant vigilance had ensured his self-control, so Eirik was confident he could welcome Freyja in his house without being overcome by his desire for her. It had never happened before, there was no reason it would happen now. Besides, there was no guarantee that he would appeal to her, so it was unlikely she would think of seducing him.

If she did not initiate anything, it would be easy to ignore whatever lust she stirred in him.

He nodded at Wolf, masculine understanding passing through them.

"Bring her when she's ready."

"I'M sorry to cause you such—"

"Don't be sorry. And you're not causing me any trouble. As you can see, there's plenty of room in my hut. You might as well make the most of it."

Freyja arched a brow at Eirik's gruff tone and scowling face. She had already had a chance to see that Sigurd's son could have quite abrupt manners, but he seemed mightily aggrieved for someone who was telling her she was welcome. He was barely meeting her gaze, as if he could not bear the sight of her.

She had gone along with Wolf's suggestion and accepted Eirik's hospitality because she didn't have much choice, but she would have loved to have another alternative. Not that he was making her feel like a burden, exactly, but still, they didn't know one another and he was now having to provide for both her and Asta. It was awkward.

"Are you hungry?"

"Yes!" Asta piped before Freyja could even open her mouth. "Very."

To Freyja's surprise, because she had imagined he would find this brazenness unwelcome, Eirik gave the little girl a broad smile. Mmmm. Maybe he was not really aggrieved, maybe there simply was something weighing on his mind.

She allowed herself to relax.

Eirik gestured to the table, indicating that the three of them should sit.

"If you're hungry, then you're in luck, as I roasted a whole leg of boar this morning and I cooked onions to go with it. I also bought a big loaf of bread, and we can add cheese if that's still not enough."

The little girl's eyes went as round as coins at the description of the feast awaiting them. "I haven't eaten since this morning, and it was only a hard piece of bread. Freyja didn't have anything, as she gave me her share. And anyway, the food aboard the boat was not as good as roasted meat and onions. We only had—"

"Asta!" Freyja chided gently. The girl's initial shyness had vanished after the warm welcome Wolf had given them, and she had turned into a rather chatty little thing. She found it endearing, but the formidable man used to living alone might not agree with her. "Eirik doesn't need to know all that."

"I do," he contradicted, looking displeased, though not at her or Asta. "Knowing that you haven't eaten for a whole day, nor adequately for the best part of a week, is of the utmost importance. Sit."

He reached out to the platter at the far end of the table. A whole leg of boar was lying on a bed of sliced onions and wild herbs that had cooked in the dripping juices. It did smell good, she had to admit, and she was famished. As Asta had said, it had been days since they had eaten sufficiently, and this was food fit for a banquet.

"Thank you," she said, when he placed in front of her a wooden bowl filled with juicy onions on which rested a generous chunk of meat.

Asta had been served first, her portion almost as big, and been instructed to start eating without waiting for the others, which she had done with no hesitation. Once Freyja had been served, Eirik filled all three cups with ale and handed out thick slices of bread. Finally, he helped himself to food, heaping his own bowl high with onions and meat, before cutting a wedge of cheese. This he sliced into slivers he scattered evenly over the steaming onions.

It looked so appetizing that Freyja asked if she could do the same. "I have never seen anyone eat cheese like this."

"Try it. The cheese will melt over the hot food and coat the onions," Eirik explained, nodding at his bowl. "Like a sauce, I suppose."

"Yes. It's delicious," she said when she took her first bite, amazed at the flavors exploding in her mouth. "And this cheese is nothing like I've ever had."

"Thank you, but I didn't make it. It's made by Ingrid, a friend of my mother's, who is married to the goldsmith, the only Saxon man living in the village. It's his grandmother's secret recipe, and

I was lucky enough to be given a wheel of cheese in thanks for my help the other week."

"Well, whatever you did, you were certainly rewarded for it."

"As you say. That cheese is popular around the village."

Freyja couldn't help arching a brow when Eirik cut himself another slice of the boar a moment later. The first one had been enormous.

"I know," he said with a side smile. "My sister Aife always jests that even the chef of the gods Andhrímnir himself would not be able to sate my hunger."

"I don't know if I would have put it quite like that," she said, pleased to see that his earlier gruffness had dissipated. Perhaps he had simply been hungry. "But I suppose a man your size will not thrive on half portions."

Sorðinn! Freyja thought when the words passed her lips. Why did she have to mention his size when she was already too aware of it? It was not exactly that he was bigger than average—though he was—it was more that he seemed to contain so much unleashed energy in that big body that he felt twice as big as he actually was. This, at a time when she felt more fragile than she had ever felt. Months of strain had left their mark on her body. She knew from the way her clothes hung on her that she had lost a lot of weight.

And Eirik had to be the strongest, most impressive man she had ever met. It could not fail to make her feel inadequate.

"Time for bed, I think," she murmured.

It had been a long day. A long few months, to be more precise. Now that she had eaten, she felt the fatigue and the tension she had accumulated over the last three weeks weigh her down.

She was ready to fall into oblivion.

Eirik nodded toward the corner to her left, and a spacious pallet piled high with furs and blankets, the perfect bed for a large man. Freyja was not surprised he should be so well organized, she had not missed how clean and welcoming his hut was. And the meal he had offered them had been perfection.

"You two girls will sleep here," he announced, standing up. "I will go get a few more furs from my brother Moon's house and sleep in the other corner."

Before she could protest and point out that he didn't have to surrender his bed when he had already done so much, Asta cried out and ran to the nest of furs.

"Thank you, Eirik. This is the most comfortable bed I've ever slept in, and it even smells good."

Freyja knew she should have chided her but she didn't have the heart. It was good to see the little girl happy after what she'd been through. Besides, once again, Eirik didn't seem to mind her reaction. For a man on his own, he seemed used to children.

"Good. I'm glad," he said with a wink. "Close your eyes then."

2

———

The first thing Freyja saw in the morning when she woke up was Asta curled by her side, the familiar length of woven wool bunched in her hand as if in protection. Then she saw that Eirik's makeshift pallet was empty.

Was he up already?

Before she could wonder further, the door opened and he entered, carrying a bucket of fresh water and a loaf of bread. The fire was burning bright in the fire pit and a pot was suspended over it. It was obvious he had been up for a while, and little wonder.

She disentangled herself from Asta's hold and sat up, guilt burning in her chest. Judging from the light pouring in through the only window, it was late already, more than she was comfortable with, at least. She shouldn't be still in bed, she should be helping Eirik getting ready for the day.

"No need to rush, Freyja," he whispered, his brow creasing in what looked like concern. Did she look so bad? "You will be tired after your travels."

She was, even more than she had realized the previous night.

Her whole body ached after days spent being tossed about in a boat on high seas, but that was no excuse to be idle, not when he was generous enough to have her and Asta under his roof.

"I'll be fine," she whispered back, careful not to wake the little girl who needed her sleep when she left the pallet. "I'm awake now anyway. What can I do?"

He didn't answer at first, then understood she would not be deterred. "You could maybe crack these nuts open and slice some bread while I go get fish from the smokehouse? We can break our fast with this and some honey."

"Of course."

It didn't take Eirik long to come back. Freyja had cracked open two dozen nuts, and was cutting the third slice of bread when he entered the hut, four fillets of fish in hand. They looked plump and shiny, and her mouth instantly started to water. Despite her lavish meal the evening before, she was famished again.

"Here. Do you want one fillet or two?" Eirik asked, sitting down. "I can always go back for more when Asta wakes up if you want two."

"One will be fine, thank you. They are quite big."

He nodded and, as she could have predicted, placed two pieces of fish on his own plate. They ate in silence, exchanging the occasional glance.

Then there was a loud snoring sound. Freyja stole a glance at Asta, who had flung her arms to the side and was occupying the bed with as much ease as if she had been living here all her life.

"Your daughter is not shy around strangers, is she?" Eirik asked with a slanted smile.

"Asta is very outspoken," she agreed, returning the smile.

Though she didn't know the little girl very well yet, that wasn't in doubt. Freyja was glad of it. She thought it might only help her overcome her terrible loss.

She bit her lip, looking at Eirik, wondering what to say next. Should she explain what the situation was while they were alone? Yes. He deserved to know who he was welcoming in his house. Besides, it would be best if she were honest. He was bound to find out the truth sooner or later and would likely feel annoyed to see she had not trusted him with the information.

"She is not my daughter, though."

"Oh?"

Eirik arched a brow at this utterly unexpected answer. When he'd asked him to welcome them in, Wolf had not told him that the two of them were not mother and daughter. Then again, perhaps he didn't know either.

It was then that he remembered. The girl had called her "Freyja," not "*Moðir*" last night. He had thought it rather odd, but perhaps calling one's parent by their name was the norm in Denmark, he'd reasoned.

Apparently, it was not, and there was another explanation. He waited for Freyja to elaborate. Surely after such a declaration she wouldn't stop there?

"Can we go outside?" she asked, after another glance at the sleeping Asta.

"Of course."

She was right. It would not do to discuss what was bound to be a sensitive topic within the girl's hearing. Though she was asleep right now, Asta could wake up at any moment.

Eirik led Freyja to the bench facing the river, one of his favorite spots in the village. The water's soothing babble filled the air, preventing the silence between them from becoming awkward. Without quite knowing why, since they were about to discuss a little girl who was nothing to him, he had the feeling that he was about to have one of the most meaningful conversations of his life. This, with someone he had only met the previous day. But that was the strangest thing of all. He felt as if he had actually known Freyja for a year rather than a day. Why was that? It had never happened to him before.

"'Tis much warmer here than in Denmark," she observed, leaning the back of her head against the hut and closing her eyes to the sun. "Have you ever been there?"

"No." Though he had wanted to go to his father's country for years, he had not found the opportunity to do so yet.

Because they weren't here to talk about his reasons for not going, he didn't elaborate. But neither did he press her to get on with her story. He knew she was steeling herself for something that would be painful to tell.

After one big inhale, she started. "I have always wanted to visit my mother's country, as you can imagine. And finally, last month, I decided it was time. My parents helped me find a ship. It took a couple of weeks to find people who accepted me to take me along."

Eirik frowned. She was making it sound as if she'd merely come for a visit, to see Eowyn's native country once in her life. But Wolf had given him the impression she was here to stay.

Which was it?

"When I boarded the merchant ship, I was surprised to see a family on board as well. A man, a woman, and a little girl. Asta. We soon got to talking. The father was fleeing for his life, having become involved with the wrong kind of people. He was badly injured and though no one dared say it, we all feared he might not survive the crossing. And indeed, on the third day, he died." Freyja's eyes closed, as if remembering the awful moment. "His wife, unable to bear the grief, begged me to take care of their daughter. I promised, not quite sure what she meant but worried at the urgency in her voice. She removed the woven belt she was wearing at her waist and handed it to me. Before I could understand what she had in mind or do anything to stop her, she threw herself overboard. No one looked twice. It would have been folly to jump after her in the icy sea, I know, but..."

The shrug she gave betrayed such helplessness that Eirik placed a hand on her arm. The impulse surprised him. He was not given to such gestures, usually keeping himself to himself, especially where women were concerned.

"Did Asta see this?"

He couldn't imagine the horror if she had. And how had her mother chosen to make an orphan out of her so easily? His own father having suffered after losing both his parents in a boat accident, ironically enough, Eirik could not imagine anyone willingly abandoning their child to their fate. Freyja had been a stranger, and yet the woman had entrusted her daughter to her without hesitation, without knowing what kind of woman she was or what care she would take of the little girl. It was shocking, but perhaps he shouldn't be so surprised. He had heard of couples like this, who lived for one another, to the exclusion of others, even their own children.

After a while, Freyja opened her eyes and looked at him.

"Asta didn't see anything. She had been sleeping at the time, mercifully. When she woke up, I had to tell her what happened. I explained I would be looking after her now and I gave her her mother's belt, the only memory she would have of her parents and her old life. I'm sorry to say that she didn't seem overly affected by the loss. I got the impression her parents had never lavished much attention on her. And yet she is such a lovely little girl."

By the gods. What a dreadful start in life. But Eirik sensed that this, as awful as it was, was not the worst of it. Wolf had said there was a man after her. Who? Not the father, who was dead.

"That's not all, is it?" he said softly, when he wanted to growl his indignation.

"No. Asta's uncle was on board with us, one of the

merchants. That was the reason the family had been allowed to travel on the boat. Unlike my parents, who paid handsomely for my passage, Asta's parents had been accepted purely because Harald was her father's brother. I suspect he had a hand in the dangerous dealings that got the man injured." She made a grimace, as if she preferred not to think about it. It was hard to blame her. Anything that caused a mortally wounded man to flee by sea was bound to be unsavory. "Anyway. When we finally landed, one rainy evening, Harald told me he would take his niece with him. He was—is—a rough man, so I was surprised he would want to look after her. He barely said two words to her during the crossing, and she seems to barely know him."

"Aye, it is odd," Eirik agreed. Rough men who regularly took to the sea were not the kind to want to burden themselves with children, much less little girls. He must have had a purpose in mind, one that would not meet his or Freyja's approval, no doubt.

"He told me he knew a Saxon merchant who had been after a Norse bride for a while. He said that Asta would be perfect. He would look after her until his next crossing, and next time he came, he would offer her to the man."

"Next *time*? She must be ten summers at the most!"

The outrage in Freyja's eyes matched his own. For a moment, small as she was, she looked like a fierce opponent one wouldn't like to cross.

"Exactly. I refused, as you can imagine, reminding him that her mother had asked me to look after her, not him. Perhaps the woman knew he couldn't be trusted, which was why she entrusted her daughter to me instead. But, being her uncle, and related to her by blood, he has a stronger claim on Asta. His friends, at least, agreed that he was the best person to raise her. Alone against a dozen men, I knew I was fighting a losing battle."

The hand that was still resting on her arm gave a light squeeze. Had the men turned violent when she refused to hand over the little girl? It was all too possible. What had they done to her? Her face was unmarred, but that didn't mean she hadn't been harmed.

His guts tightened at the thought. "What happened?" He had to force the words out.

"That night, while everyone was asleep, I left the harbor. I had already decided to come to Wolf's village to seek refuge, but it was now doubly important that I found him without delay."

Refuge? Was it just a turn of phrase, or had she just hinted that she was not here on a mere visit? Had she, like the unfortunate family, fled Denmark and a dangerous situation?

A long silence followed the declaration.

Now Eirik understood who the man in pursuit of her was. Harald, the merchant. Not someone looking to rape her, as he had first feared, but someone intent on putting his hands on Asta for just as nefarious a purpose. Not much better, admittedly, and it still meant that the two of them needed his protection, but he felt somewhat relieved. Freyja was not the prey being hunted.

As to the merchant uncle, if he ever dared show his face in the village, he would be sent away in a manner that made it clear there would be no second chances.

"Look at me, Freyja. You agreed to take care of Asta when her mother asked you. That was very brave of you and I would understand if it scared you, because it means you have to face a rough bastard intent on getting her back. Well, I need you to know that Harald is not getting anywhere near you or Asta. You're not on your own. Wolf entrusted you to me when you arrived, and that means you're my responsibility now, no one else's."

She stared at him with wide eyes. "But I shouldn't be, you don't—"

"You are." In that moment, Eirik felt like taking yet another oath, as important as the one he had taken on his sixteenth birthday. "I'm telling you. Just like Asta can rely on you, you can rely on me. I care not who that Harald is or what he wants with his niece. He will not hurt her or you, you have my word on it."

"Thank you." She actually sagged on the bench, as if relieved to have someone on her side.

And she did. Him.

He had been right earlier to think that his life was about to change, because it was. At least for the next few weeks.

Eirik sat back in turn, and fell in deep in musings. Now that he had two people under his roof, he would have to go hunting more often. He had to look after them, take care of their well-being as well as ensure their protection. The two girls both looked too thin for comfort.

He afforded himself a smile.

He had sworn never to get married and now he was about to live a family life.

How ironic was that?

~

"Can I go and see the children now?" Asta asked, once she'd finished her mid-day meal. She had not been awake long, and still bore the traces of sleep on her adorable little face.

"What children?" Freyja asked, replacing the lid on the pot of honey. They had only just arrived and the girl had been asleep most of the time. When had she had the opportunity to meet anyone?

"Rothgar, Sanna, and Liv."

Of course. The day before, while Freyja had talked to Wolf, Asta had played with his three grandchildren outside the hut. Apparently, it had not taken them long to create a bond. Good. Having friends in the village would help her settle faster.

"Yes." She smiled. "I'm sure they'll be pleased to see you too. Just make sure to greet Wolf and Merewen first, and thank them for having you."

Once Asta had bounded out of the door with the energy of a young puppy, Freyja put the plates in a pile and followed at a more sedate pace. The fog in her brain had still not completely cleared, and the sweet-smelling furs in the corner were beckoning. She shook her head. No matter how tempting it was to lie back down, she would just have to ignore it. The day was half gone already; she could sleep tonight.

"Where do you think you're going?"

Eirik suddenly appeared in front of her, blocking the way to the door. Though he'd mellowed during their conversation outside this morning, he now sounded as gruff as he had the day before.

"To wash the dishes at the river?" she answered, blinking. Wasn't that obvious?

"No, you're not, not when you look about to collapse from lack of sleep." Before she could protest, he had taken the plates from her hands.

She was not surprised to hear she appeared about to collapse. It was how she felt. Though she had spent a good night, she felt drained of all her strength. She sat on the stool in front of her. "I do feel weary," she admitted in a small voice.

"Well, then, if you're tired, you need to go to bed."

He made it sound so easy. But perhaps it was that easy.

So she burrowed under the furs and was asleep in moments.

The next day she felt better, even if her body was still stiff, and on the third morning, she was relieved to see that she was restored to her usual state and able to help around the house. It would not do for Eirik to think he'd been saddled with a lazy woman.

By the time the sixth day dawned, she was starting to hope that Harald had given up on finding his niece. He had to, for surely it would not take him six days to conclude that the two of them had taken refuge in the nearby Norsemen village?

But perhaps there were other Norse settlements she was unaware of, and he had gone to the others first?

Needing to know where she stood, she went to find Eirik, who was, oddly enough, collecting mud in a basket. She had never seen anyone do such a thing and she had no idea what he might need it for. But she quickly stopped wondering, as there was something much more important she needed to ask.

"Are there other villages with Norsemen around here?"

He frowned, as if unsure why she would ask such a question without preamble, then nodded, understanding. "There are three others along the coast, closer to the harbor. Perhaps Harald went there first. It would make sense. In any case, it matters not. When he comes, we'll be ready. I've warned my two brothers, Wolf's sons, and a few trusted friends about a possible visit from the man."

"Thank you." She couldn't have asked for more.

Relieved, she raised her head to the skies. Above them the dying day had thrown a thick blanket across the sky. Foregoing their usual fluffy appearance, the clouds had bundled together to form a coarsely woven cover of dappled pink and mauve. The effect was most peculiar, and a little bit unsettling, as if something unusual was brewing.

"Do clouds always behave thus in your country?" she asked, looking back to Eirik.

"Behave?"

She reddened when he arched a brow at her odd choice of words. Of course, clouds did not "behave" in any way; they just were. And why had she felt the need to ask such a stupid question in the first place?

"What I mean is that I am more used to seeing them on their own, scurrying away in the wind or heavy with rain."

He threw her a blinding smile, a smile the likes of which she had not expected from such a formidable man. "So am I. Tonight's sky is unusual indeed. But I don't think you will find our normal one very different from the one you're used to."

Used to. Yes, she was indeed in a new place, with people she didn't know and yet felt familiar with. She wasn't sure how to handle that.

"Because of all I've heard about your family from my mother, I do not feel as uncomfortable in the village as I would have in a completely strange place," she admitted. The same went for him. He was a stranger, and yet he was not, not really. "But it is odd staying in your hut when we don't know anything about one another, apart from what our parents told us."

He nodded, as if he understood the feeling exactly and sat down on the bench behind him.

"Let's see. I have a black horse called Fenrir, which was given to me ten years ago by Wolf. I make pottery when I feel the need to stop thinking." He glanced at the basket at his feet and Freyja was glad to understand what he intended to do with the mud. "I cannot fall asleep if I'm not lying on my side, preferably the left, but the right will do as a last resort. I do not like raw eggs, and I've never owned a shirt that reached above my navel, not since I was a child, anyway."

Freyja couldn't help a smile at this list of inconsequential details, because oddly, it did make her feel better to hear them.

Those were exactly the sort of things she would know about the people she was close to, the people she shared a home with.

She sat down next to him and started to talk.

"I don't have a horse, but we had a white dog called Tǫnn when I was a child. I am quite skilled at embroidery, as this is what I do when I need to think and solve a problem." She showed him the hem at her cuffs, decorated with a pattern of suns and stars. "I can fall asleep in any position, but I often wake up during the night. I cannot abide eggs, whether raw or cooked. And all my shifts reach well past my knees."

He tilted his head in appreciation of her choice of information that mirrored the ones he had given her. Then his face became serious once more and Freyja knew he was about to tell her something far more personal. The atmosphere had gone from teasing to tense in the blink of an eye. She swallowed.

"And I fear I will never be able to accept the fact that I was fathered by a man who raped my mother."

Oh.

She had heard the painful story and she was not surprised Eirik had difficulty dealing with the knowledge that he was the product of such a monstrous coupling, but being told this about someone she had never met and actually hearing it from the person's own mouth while witnessing the despair in his eyes were two very different things. His anguish tore at her heart.

"I'm sorry," Freyja mumbled, the words a very poor response to what he had revealed.

"You have nothing to be sorry for. This is none of your doing."

Was he annoyed at her comment? Amused? She couldn't tell. "No, of course not, but..." But she could still be sorry, even if she understood he didn't want her pity.

"Because of what happened, and though I do love and respect my father more than I can express, once I'd been told the truth, I found myself looking for father figures throughout the village, as many as I could identify with. By being with them, I wanted to chase away the image I had built in my mind of the bastard who hurt my mother."

Yes, this thinking made sense. Reminding himself on a regular basis that men could be trusted helped him see that Olaf had been the exception—and that he didn't have to follow in his path. Blood was nothing compared to care.

It was like with Asta. Though the girl had not been born of her body, Freyja's care of her would ensure that she blossomed, better than she had at the contact of the woman who had actually carried her and the man who'd barely paid her any attention.

Freyja waited. She would have taken Eirik's hand in hers but she didn't dare initiate such an intimate gesture.

"Fortunately, it was not hard to find good men in the village," he carried on. "Wolf has told me many times that he sees me as a fourth son. My uncle, Björn, spent a lot of time with me, teaching me how to make mead and ale. I often helped Magnus and Caedmon at the forge, listening to their stories. And it worked. Surrounding myself with people who knew what it meant to be honorable helped. It proved to me that it was possible, as a man, to be something other than a monster who—"

His voice broke. It was more than Freyja could bear. Forget what she dared or not, what was intimate or not. In that moment Eirik needed her. Just like he had done the day before, she placed a hand over his forearm.

"Yes, it did work. These good men who took care of you shaped you into the reliable, honorable man you are. They have ensured you grew up into someone who could never hurt a woman." Though their acquaintance was short, instinctively she knew this was the case. "Your parents must be so proud of you."

"I hope so. I certainly try to be a man they are not ashamed to have raised. To that end, I decided to stay away from women. The risk my bad blood will come rearing to the surface is too great. I cannot bear the idea that I could hurt anyone, much less a harmless woman. I'm strong. It wouldn't take much. If I lost control..."

"You are strong," Freyja agreed. There was no doubting the power in that body. Anyone could see it. "But you are also strong mentally. I'm certain you—"

"But I'm *not* certain of anything—I cannot be, considering how I was conceived," he snarled. Though she knew the anger was not directed at her, she recoiled. She couldn't help it, considering how impressive he was. When he saw her reaction, he stilled, knowing he had frightened her. "Forgive me. But that is precisely the problem. I cannot know how I will behave if a woman starts to pull away for whatever reason while she is in my arms. I cannot trust my reaction. So I swore to myself on my sixteenth birthday that I would never bed anyone. The risk is just too great. I cannot allow myself the opportunity to be overwhelmed, to hurt a woman when my wretched nature reveals itself, and leave her to deal with the child that might result when I cannot find the will to spill outside her body. I could not live with myself if any of that happened."

The revelation left her stunned.

Eirik, the most masculine man she had ever met, was a virgin. He'd consciously decided never to allow himself any pleasure so as to ensure he didn't hurt anyone. What a sacrifice to make. And how could anyone live such a lonely, unfulfilling life?

Freyja took in a shaky breath. A moment ago she had bemoaned the fact that she didn't really know anything about Eirik. Now she feared she had gone in too deep for her peace of mind. What a burden he was carrying, too heavy for anyone.

I'm sorry.

The words were not allowed to pass her lips. He would only snarl at her if she spoke, tell her she had nothing to be sorry for.

"I'm sorry, I don't know why I told you all this," Eirik said, leaning the back of his head against the wall of the hut. "And I'm sorry for snapping at you. You really have done nothing wrong. It's only…"

Yes. It was only that after more than two decades of bearing all this on his own, something had to give. Why not with her, a stranger who still somehow knew what had happened to his mother?

When he left, Freyja remained a moment alone on the bench, thinking back to everything Eirik had told her. It was a lot to take in. As a young man he had made a decision that would affect the rest of his life and he had stood by it, no matter how difficult it was. He had decided to punish himself for something he was not responsible for. The unfairness of the situation bothered her greatly. Because of what this Olaf had done all those years ago, Eirik would never find love. He would never have a family.

Cruelly, this was something the two of them had in common. She was probably unable to have children—and he was unwilling to even try.

As if to taunt her and remind her of her barrenness, all around her, nature was blooming. Trees had unfurled their greenest leaves, flowers were dotting the ground, birds were sending their sweetest songs to the skies. In front of her, a spider had started to spin its web between two posts on the pigpen. The ingenious animal was scurrying back and forth, creating breathtaking work in moments. Freyja watched on, fascinated, until the web was complete. Such timeless beauty, yet so ephemeral, so strong yet so vulnerable to destruction.

Just as she was about to stand back up, a gnat landed in the middle of the new construction. Immediately, the spider pounced, preventing it from escaping, and started to wrap the tiny body in silken strands. Mmmm. Of course. Beautiful and delicate as it was, the web was destined to be a weapon of death.

Freyja nodded to herself, humbled by the reminder.

Nothing was as it seemed in life.

3

———

"Steinar and Cwenthryth are back from the fair with Ulf, they took the children back with them. So we can have Freyja and Asta if you want."

Eirik stared at Wolf, wondering what to answer. Should he accept the offer? A few days ago, he might have. Indeed, when the Icelander had first asked him to welcome the alluring Dane and the child he'd thought to be her daughter under his roof, he'd suggested Inga instead, wanting to protect his tranquility.

But now...now he was wondering why he had valued it in the first place. What he had called tranquility had in fact been solitude. He knew it because he saw the difference. Now he had someone to wake up for in the morning, something to look forward to when he got back home at night. Asta brought life to the hut, Freyja brought hope. It would be hard to go back to silence and despair.

Besides there was no way he would entrust them to anyone else, even a man as competent as Wolf. He'd told Freyja that she was his responsibility and he'd meant it.

"No, it's all right. They can stay with me," he answered as calmly as he could, doing his best to hide his panic at the idea

31

that Freyja could be gone before the day was over. "You have your wife to look after and you're often called away on some business or other. I don't have anyone, and I'm always around, so it's easier for me to make sure Harald doesn't get to her or Asta."

At the mention of the merchant, Wolf lifted his head. "She told you her story then?"

"Yes."

And he would make sure to protect her. It was personal now. A few days ago, when she'd arrived, she'd only been a woman in need of protection, his mother's friend's daughter, someone Wolf had entrusted him with. She was now...Freyja. A woman who could sleep in any position but woke up often in the night and didn't eat eggs.

And he wanted her in his house.

He didn't know the sleeping habits of any other woman, because none had ever slept in his hut. He had never had to cook for any other person so he had no idea what food to avoid. He did now.

He loved the company. He loved that Freyja didn't expect anything from him. She knew their arrangement was not based on attraction and didn't expect him to behave in one way or the other. She and Asta brought joy to his solitary life without asking anything in return. The least he could do was to look after them.

"I will keep them as long as they need."

"Thank you. I knew I could rely on you."

Wolf walked away, looking satisfied. Eirik put his axe down and went inside to have a drink. He felt like a man who had just avoided some disaster or other.

A moment later, Freyja entered the hut, a bunch of parsnips in hand. From the way his body leaped at the mere sight of her, Eirik knew he had made the right decision. This woman belonged here, by his side.

As long as she didn't ask to leave, he would keep her and Asta with him.

"Did I see Wolf outside just now?" she asked, closing the door behind her.

His heartbeat picked up. If he told her why the Icelander had come, she might ask to go live with him and Merewen. It was a risk, but of course he could not lie to her. He might have kept Wolf's visit to himself for now if she had not seen him, but she had.

"Yes. He came to tell me that Rothgar's parents were back from the fair."

His hut is empty once more. You can go stay there if you want.

He didn't add this detail and mercifully, she didn't pick up on it. It seemed that the thought of leaving had not even crossed her mind. He allowed himself to breathe again.

"That's good," she said instead. "I wanted to see them and thank them for what their son has done for Asta, so I will go introduce myself. Unless you think I should wait, give them time to rest?" she added, pursing her lips.

"No," Eirik assured her. "They will be delighted to see you, and very happy to hear that Rothgar has a new friend. Come, I'll show you where their hut is. I was on my way to the forest anyway. Just, maybe..."

Before leaving, he handed her a piece of linen with which to cover her distinctive fiery hair. Even if Harald chose this moment to appear, he would not immediately identify this villager going about her business as the woman he was looking for.

"Thank you," Freyja said, placing the covering over her head and tucking her hair inside it. Then she followed him outside.

He picked up his axe from where he'd left it earlier and led the way to the opposite end of the village. Freyja followed him, looking around with curious eyes. In the three weeks she'd spent here, she had rarely left the hut, keeping mostly to the vegetable patch and the chicken enclosure. It had been sensible to stay close to people who could help if need be, people who knew Harald might be looking for her.

"Here," he said, knocking on the door. "I'll say hello and leave you, if that's all right? I need to go cut some more wood for the fire."

"Of course. Thank you."

After exchanging a few pleasantries with Cwenthryth, Eirik left for the forest, accompanied by Steinar, who needed to replenish his own stock of wood after being gone for so long.

Freyja was left alone with a dark-haired Saxon woman who reminded her of Merewen, Wolf's wife, a Saxon, evidently.

"Will you have a drink with me?" she offered, gesturing to a pot of water where fragrant leaves were brewing. "I just made a tisane."

"I don't know... If you're busy—"

"Not really, I was only going to shell these few nuts for tonight. And you can always help me, can't you, while we talk? I suspect you will do a better job than Steinar, who more often than not reduces the kernels to a pulp."

"Yes, I suppose I am not half as strong as he is." Freyja smiled, grateful to be given a way to be useful. And the tisane smelled too good to be refused.

Having reached an agreement, the two women sat at the table. While Cwenthryth poured two cups of yellow-green liquid, Freyja reached for the second hammer, the one Steinar probably used. In the pile in the middle of the table were walnuts, hazelnuts, and beech nuts. She selected a hazelnut first, the easiest of the three to open, so as to give herself time to learn how to handle the hammer before she started in earnest.

"So you are Asta's mother," Cwenthryth said, sitting next to her and taking her own hammer, a smaller one that would no doubt be easier to use. "Rothgar has been telling us so much about his new friend that I feel I know her already."

Should she correct her assumption, Freyja wondered? Yes. After all, there was no shame in her situation. "Actually, I'm not Asta's mother. I only met her on the boat that brought me here from Denmark. Her parents were making the crossing as well." She explained what had happened to them, but kept to herself the part about Harald wanting to sell his niece to a man three times her age. Eirik was probably telling his friend about it as they cut wood. Let the man tell his wife tonight when he came back. She didn't have the stomach to talk about the possible fate awaiting the little girl. "So you see, I had no choice but to take her in."

No. Even if the mother had not made her swear to take care of her daughter, Freyja could not have left her in Harald's hands, knowing what he had in mind.

"That is awful," Cwenthryth murmured. "Poor little girl. I'm surprised Rothgar didn't mention any of this."

So was Freyja. But perhaps there was a simple explanation for his silence. "Perhaps he doesn't know. Perhaps Asta wants to pretend none of it happened. Sadly, I get the impression that she was not particularly close to her parents."

"Yes, and it would make sense that she would rather not mention such painful events to a little boy who can do nothing about it."

For a moment the two women worked in companionable silence.

"You know, I'm not Rothgar's real mother either," Cwenthryth said after a while, selecting a particularly fat walnut from the pile. "Or Ulf's. They were birthed by Steinar's first wife and I only married him four years ago. From the start, however, I was lucky enough to form a bond with the boys."

Yes, Freyja did know that, which was another reason she had

been honest about her relationship with Asta. Eirik had told her only the night before about how Steinar had met his Saxon bride thanks to his first wife, Astrid. After years of making his life a misery, the woman had planned to leave him for her lover and arranged for someone else to take care of their sons when she was gone. The odd circumstances of their meeting had made it hard for Steinar to accept his feelings for Cwenthryth at first, but he had soon seen that resisting was pointless. The two of them were made for one another.

There were many such fascinating stories in the village, and Freyja enjoyed spending her evenings talking with Eirik about the people he knew and loved. It helped to compensate for the fact that she was not able to move as freely as she would have liked around the place.

It also gave her a fascinating insight into a man who was becoming more appealing by the day. He had a talent for making people come alive through his descriptions. And of course, it never hurt that while he talked, she could look at him without appearing rude.

"Was it not too difficult to be accepted as a second mother?" she asked Cwenthryth, her gaze on the walnut she was prising from its shell. She didn't mean to be indiscreet, but she was curious, and this was an unhoped-for opportunity to talk to someone who'd been placed in a similar situation. Steinar's wife might have some good advice for her.

"No. With love and patience, I believe any family can be created. Look at Eirik. His eldest brother, Elwyn, was adopted, but you wouldn't know it from the way he and the other boys behave toward one another."

Freyja had never seen them together, but she knew Sigurd's family was as close as any could ever be. And, yes, she agreed. Love and care were more important than anything else. So perhaps all would go well for Asta, who, by all accounts, had known little of that love or care up until now.

"You also have two daughters, I take it?" she asked, feeling lighter than she had since she'd stepped off the merchant boat.

Cwenthryth beamed. "Yes. Sanna and Liv. You might have seen them?"

She had, two adorable little girls, as different one from the other as their parents were. Sanna had the same dark hair as her mother, while Liv was the image of Steinar.

"I did see them in Wolf's hut the day I arrived. They both played with Asta, even if she has since developed a marked preference for Rothgar, who is old enough to climb trees, chase her through fields, or do whatever else she wants to do." Freyja laughed, remembering all the mischief the two children had gotten into. "I'm afraid she is taking advantage of his good nature."

"Oh, I know. Don't worry. He's delighted to have someone with whom to go in the tree house. Now that Ulf is becoming a man, they spend less time together, and I think he misses that bond. Having an intrepid friend his own age is just what he needs."

There was another pause, during which Cwenthryth refilled their cups.

"Eirik told me you have become the village midwife?" Freyja asked.

"One of them, yes. Helga is still teaching me. But I enjoy the work, I like knowing I'm helping." She shook her head, as if contemplating a mystery. "I'm a woman and I've had two children myself, but every day I make new discoveries about what our bodies can do. It's fascinating."

"Yes. I can well imagine."

Freyja took another sip of her drink and fell into deep

musings. Perhaps she could ask Cwenthryth if she had any explanation as to why her womb had not quickened once in fourteen years, despite an active love life? No, this was too personal a question, and would bring about a discussion she was not ready to have—with anyone. Besides, what would be the point? The explanation was obvious. Either she or Arvid had been barren, and she wasn't sure it would help in any way to know which one.

Once the tisane had been drunk and all the nuts shelled, Freyja stood up, surprised to see that the sky had already started to turn a deeper shade of purple. It was time to go.

"Thank you. It was very nice meeting you."

It had been, so why did she feel like crying? Perhaps, she reflected, because when she had set off on that boat, she had not dared hope to find half of what she had found in the Norsemen village. Support, protection, friendship—a daughter. But she now knew she could easily build a new life here. The relief was immense.

"And you. Come see me whenever you want."

As soon as he saw the horse in the distance, Eirik knew who the rider would be.

He knew all the Norse people living in the area and the man atop the sorry nag he'd evidently borrowed from a local farmer was not one of them. He had to be a merchant. And not just any merchant.

Harald.

He fit the description Freyja had given him, from the rather greasy hair to the beard streaked with white. Eirik seized the axe he had discarded only a moment ago. How lucky that he should be the one seeing the visitor first. He would send him on his way if he truly was Harald, and that would finally put an end to the threat hanging over Freyja and Asta.

Yes. And then what? Would they decide to leave the village, safe in the knowledge that no one would come after them? Would they move into their own hut, since they no longer needed protection? How would he bear it?

Well, these questions would have to be addressed later; for now, he had a stranger to deal with.

"*Heill ok sæll.*"

Eirik didn't return the greeting. If the man thought him rude, it mattered little. He considered pretending he didn't speak Norse, but quickly concluded that would not serve. If the two of them couldn't talk, the man would go speak to someone else.

So he waited.

"I'm looking for a woman."

His instinct had not failed him. This was indeed Harald, coming for Freyja. Eirik's fingers tightened around the axe handle.

"Aren't we all, my friend?" Perhaps the best way to convince him Freyja wasn't here was to pretend he didn't even know what he was talking about.

The man let out a snort. "Yes, well, I don't mean it like that, though I could certainly do with a fuck. Do you have any accommodating women in the village by any chance? Ones that are not opposed to demanding lovers?"

Eirik's body tensed further. Had he not already been predisposed to hate the man, this unwelcome comment would have ensured he didn't want to have anything to do with him.

"We don't, I'm afraid."

"Oh well, it matters not. The whores in town are willing enough to take it rough, once they see what's in my purse—and in my braies." He gave a smile that managed to be self-satisfied and sinister at the same time. "Anyway, the woman I'm looking for is small, very thin, red-haired, and she is accompanied by a little blonde girl."

Eirik shook his head, hoping his disgust was not too obvious. But he was finding it hard not to throw the man to the ground and show him what rough meant. "I can't say I've ever seen anyone fitting that description. What do you want with her?"

The smile was replaced by a frightening scowl. It made no doubt that the man was dangerous and should not be allowed anywhere near Freyja or Asta. "She abducted my niece. I need her back."

It was only then that Eirik realized he had no reason to believe Freyja's version of the story rather than Harald's. He didn't know either of them and neither had produced any proof of what they were saying. But his heart told him Freyja was telling the truth. Even if she weren't, he couldn't in all conscience send a little girl away with a stranger who talked so blithely of women taking it rough and looked so angry. The risk that he would hurt her was too great. Here, at least, and even supposing she had been abducted, Asta was looked after and happy.

"The woman abducted your niece, you say?" he repeated, infusing as much scorn as he could into his voice. "How did that happen? Didn't you just say she was tiny? Surely she shouldn't have had the upper hand over a brute like you? Or did she outwit you, perchance?"

Just as predicted, the man didn't like the questions. "Never mind how it happened!" he snarled. "I just didn't expect the bitch to be so wily. Have you seen her or not?"

"No. I already told you."

Eirik crossed his arms over his chest, indicating the conversation was over. Harald didn't take the hint. He looked past him and over to the other huts.

"I will go and ask—"

"Everyone here will tell you the same. Do you think we don't know who we welcome in our village? And we would not harbor criminals, anyway."

"Well, she would not look like a criminal to you, would she? She would look like a woman traveling with her young daughter, hardly a suspicious sight."

"True. But as I said, we haven't seen any woman arriving out of nowhere in years. And if she really has abducted the girl, she would be in hiding, not coming to the first place you'd think of searching, would she?"

Finally, Harald nodded. "Well, if you or anyone here happens to see her, will you send word to me, Harald the Tall, at the harbor? I'll be staying for another couple of months, I should think, for the rest of the summer."

"Will do." Though he would have liked nothing more than to tell him to go to hell, Eirik thought it wiser to appear as if he were on the side of the slighted uncle instead of the fugitive he wasn't supposed to know. That was what Harald expected of him. "Perhaps you should go ask in the nearest town. If the woman and child are as distinctively Norse as you seem to suggest, the Saxons will not have failed to notice them."

"I hadn't thought of that. I went to the other Norse villages before coming here and they haven't seen them either. But perhaps, as you said, she stayed clear of the obvious hiding places. Aye, it would make sense."

At long last, the man turned his horse away from the village. A moment later, he was heading toward the forest. Eirik waited until he had disappeared between the trees before putting the axe back down. Then he took his first real breath in what felt like a day.

That had been too close for comfort but fortunately, Asta hadn't been anywhere for her uncle to see. As she did every day, she'd been playing with Rothgar. And, as they'd agreed, Freyja had stayed hidden inside. So disaster had been avoided.

Once his breathing was back to normal, he entered the hut and found Freyja standing by the window, trembling.

"Harald," was all she said.

"Harald," he confirmed.

What would be the point of lying? She had evidently heard their conversation and even if she hadn't, he would have told her who the visitor had been. This was about her, she had the right to know what she was up against. Except that now, she might no longer be in danger.

As far as the man was concerned, the woman he was hunting was not in any of the villages he'd searched. He would have no choice but to conclude that she had not sought refuge in the Norse community, and go back to Denmark empty-handed at the end of the summer, before the weather turned too bad for sailing.

"Thank you for what you—"

"No need to thank me," he cut in. "I told you the man would not get his hands on you or Asta. I meant it."

"I know. That doesn't mean I cannot be grateful for your protection."

"No. I suppose not."

There was a pause.

"You've never wondered if I was telling you the truth? For all you know, Asta's parents entrusted her to her uncle and he has every right to get her back." She bit her lip as if regretting putting such ideas into his head but wanting to be honest. "They might not even be dead for that matter. You cannot know for certain what happened on that boat."

Yes, everything she had told him could be a lie, he'd thought that just now, during his conversation with Harald before concluding that it was hardly relevant. Asta needed to be with someone who would take good care of her, and that was not her uncle.

Besides, Freyja would hardly point out that she might even have made up the part about the Danes dying, if that were not true.

"Even if you had really abducted Asta from the man supposed to look after her, I wouldn't care," he told her honestly. "I'm not letting her anywhere near that vile man. I may have no proof that Asta's real mother is dead or that she entrusted her to you, but come to think of it, I've no proof either that Harald really is her uncle."

He was, however, certain that he was not a man to be trusted with little girls—or grown women.

Freyja's body softened, as if she'd heard all the reassurance she needed. "Thank you. And for what it's worth, I am telling the truth."

"Yes. I think I know it."

She hugged her middle, which made her appear even more fragile than usual. Though she had lost some of the gaunt look she'd had when she'd arrived in the village, her clothes didn't really fit her properly, indicating she still had not gained the weight she'd recently lost. He would do what he could to remedy that. Starting from now.

He knew his brother had killed one of his goats that morning. He would surely give him a leg in exchange for a bucketful of oats.

"I'm going to see Elwyn," he announced, untying the rope holding the sack closed. "I won't be long. Stay inside, just in case Harald decides to come back."

Freyja only nodded.

4

———————

The rest of the day was spent without any incident. To Eirik's relief, Harald had not been seen again. Of a common accord, he and Freyja had kept silent about the man's visit, not telling Asta what had happened. He wasn't even sure the girl knew her uncle was after her. Well, she didn't really need to know what fate the man had in store for her, did she? It was best to wait it out.

Before the winter, Harald would be gone and they would finally be assured she was safe.

In the morning, armed with his two biggest buckets, Eirik set off for the well. When he came back a moment later, he found Freya sitting on the bench outside. She was staring at a spider web spun between two posts on the pig enclosure. Morning dew had strung pearls along its delicate frame, transforming it into a veritable work of art.

"Beautiful, is it not?" he murmured.

"One of nature's most awe-inspiring creations," she answered back.

Mmmm, yes. And he was staring at another one. In the pale

morning light, Freyja's profile was perfectly chiseled, her eyelashes as delicate as the glittering web.

"I'll start preparing the meat," he said, already making his way to the hut. If he carried on staring at her, he feared he would do something neither of them wanted him to do. "The pheasant has been hanging for six days now. It should be ready."

Freyja nodded and followed him back inside. Immediately, she started to cut turnips into cubes for the pottage. Without ever consulting with one another, they knew how to work together. Doing his best to ignore what this made him feel, Eirik took the bird from its hook and headed back outside to pluck it.

"Will you please keep the best feathers for Asta?" he heard Freyja call out. "She was talking about decorating the tree house as a surprise for Rothgar the other day, I think she would like to use some of the bright-colored ones."

"Good idea."

He smiled to himself as he plucked the pheasant he had killed the previous week. Steinar's boys had been using the tree house for years and never once had they thought to decorate it. Only a girl would think of doing something like that. Which went to show that Rothgar would benefit from Asta's presence in his life, as much as he himself was benefiting from Freyja's.

When he came back into the hut, the plucked bird in one hand and a bunch of feathers in the other, he found Freyja sitting at the table, looking intently at her palm. Why? What had happened? Had she hurt herself? He leaned over her shoulder, wanting to make sure she hadn't burned or cut herself while he'd been out. She hadn't, she was simply observing a strange little object.

Cradled in her hand was a piece of wood, the shape and size of a large, dried broad bean. It was dark and polished to a smooth finish but there seemed to be scratches at one end. Eirik's eyes narrowed. Was that a human face? With closed eyes?

"What's this?"

She looked up at him and gave a small smile. "My most precious possession, made by my father. You know he is a boat builder?"

"Yes."

"Well, unsurprisingly, he's very skilled at carving wood." She brushed a loving finger over the wooden bean. Eirik could tell this gesture was familiar. "When he understood that he had fallen in love with my mother all those years ago, he knew he had to woo her and make her forget the hurt he had caused her, so he carved a little statue of himself. He added tiny swaddled babies to represent the family he wanted to have with her."

"I don't have to ask if it worked since they ended up marrying?" he asked, as he put the pheasant on the spit and set it over the fire to roast.

"No. And he could have saved himself the trouble. My mother was already in love with him anyway." She snorted, as if to say that the two of them could have spared themselves weeks of suffering if they had simply accepted what they felt for one another from the start. "Each of us girls got one when we were older, and grown up enough to look after them. By an odd coincidence, my father had made five bean babies and they ended up having five girls."

Eirik was amused at the story. Were they really talking about the man the Saxons had called Devil? This seemed more like what a lovestruck youth would do. "And your brother? Didn't he get anything?"

Having heard the story from his parents many times, he knew Freyja had an older brother. Eowyn, her mother, had fallen with child after a night with a Norseman she had not thought to see again. When he'd unexpectedly returned a year later, she'd been afraid to let him know about the little boy who had resulted from the fiery encounter, and wanted to hide the child. To give her time to think of a way of breaking the news to him her friend Frigyth had pretended that the red-haired babe, little Rune, was Moon's twin brother.

The deception, of course, had not lasted long. Her father had eventually found out the truth and understood that he would never be able to be parted from his son and the woman who was soon to become his wife. A few months later the three of them had left for Denmark.

"My father made him a small boat in the image of the one that had taken him to my mother the year he was conceived. And the arm ring they gave him when he turned sixteen had an image of a fiery devil carved on it." She paused, as if considering. "Do you know what I mean? Or this is not something you do here?"

"We do. The older generation like to keep traditions from their country alive and the younger one is proud to take part in."

Freyja was about to ask Eirik what his ring looked like when, without warning, he removed his tunic and shirt together in one fluid motion. Muscles bunched, skin rippled—and all the air left her lungs.

In front of her was a vison of strength and beauty such as she had never seen. He was raw, uncompromisingly male, and she remembered thinking the day she had arrived that he probably appeared twice as large as he was because of the restrained energy he exuded. Well, now she could see that he appeared large because he was.

"Here," he said, twisting to the right to show her the arm ring wrapped around his left bicep. He seemed perfectly at ease, much more than she was, despite being the one fully dressed.

She stood up to have a better look at the seven thin strands of metal twisted together in the middle of the broad ring. All were silver, like the band itself, but one appeared to be gold.

"What's the meaning behind it?" she asked, running her

finger along the beautiful piece of jewelry when she actually was itching to touch the skin underneath.

Eirik swallowed, visibly too moved to answer. Freyja's heart seized in her chest. What was it with a man at ease with his vulnerability? Why did it affect her so?

"The seven strands represent the seven people in our family," he said eventually, his voice hoarser than usual. "I'm the gold thread in the middle, mingling with the others. It was my parents' way of reminding me that, whatever our different origins, we were all inextricably linked by love if not by blood. They guessed I would need the reminder more than anyone else."

"It's beautiful," Freyja murmured. It really was. The ring, and the symbol.

The man.

By the gods, but he was stunning. Not that she was surprised but... There was a difference between knowing something and seeing the evidence with your own eyes. She wasn't sure how she would ever get the sight out of her mind.

"And...this?" she asked, pointing to dark markings peeking from under the wide band.

"My father told me one day that some men had marked their bodies thus in his native village. His own father was among them. He would have done it too, once he'd reached adulthood, only he became orphaned at a young age. When the time came to have it done, he found it too painful to do it without his father being here to witness the result. I thought I would honor him, do what he had not—"

Freyja thought she understood what he meant even if he stopped talking abruptly. He'd thought he would do what Sigurd had not been able to do. It was a beautiful gesture and it made sense. Of all men, Eirik would have felt the need to belong, to have a connection to the man who'd given him the life he could all too easily not have had, and the grandfather who was of his spirit if not really of his blood.

Fascinated, she traced the series of symbols cutting a line across his left pectoral and blooming over his muscular shoulder. It gave him a dangerous, wild edge that suited his gruff exterior.

"I saw such markings on men in my village too," she said in a breath.

Yes, she had, but never had she thought anything of them, or felt the urge to stroke them. On Eirik, though, it was the most wonderful thing, and it made her want to do more than trace it with her finger. She wanted to go over them with her tongue, slowly, until he rolled his head back and asked her to stop if she didn't want him to rip at her clothes to lick *her* skin.

Freyja stilled. Since when did she have such scandalous thoughts? First she had almost swooned at the sight of his chest, and now this? It had to stop. Most likely Eirik would be horrified if he knew that she was imagining licking him. And not just on the chest.

He had told her he would never bed a woman. In the circumstances, he wouldn't want to hear about what lewd acts she was imagining.

"Did women in your village mark their skin too?" A corner of his lips lifted. "Are you hiding a marking anywhere on your body, my little vixen?"

Vixen?

Where had that teasing come from? And how was she supposed to handle it?

Freyja sat back down on the stool so clumsily that she almost fell down. Then she retrieved the bean-shaped baby to put it in the purse at her belt, as if by doing so she could recapture what she had inadvertently allowed to escape by asking about the arm ring. Had she guessed that Eirik would take half his clothes off to show her, she would never have opened her mouth.

Behind her, she heard him turn the pheasant over the spit, then she watched him get the bowls from the shelf opposite her.

She swallowed when she saw that he had not put his shirt and tunic back on. Was he going to remain bare-chested for the rest of the day? Didn't he have any idea what this would do to her? He didn't seem to think his body in any way remarkable, or that the sight could affect her.

Oh, but it did, it definitely did.

"When I left, my brother was about to have another child," she said to prevent an uncomfortable silence from settling between them. Then she cursed herself for this choice of conversation because now all she could think was that she might never meet that niece or nephew, and that made her sad.

Well, if she were sad, at least she might stop thinking about licking Eirik, she thought ruefully. That was the main thing.

"I wish I could meet your brother," Eirik said, sitting down opposite Freyja.

He had always been curious about the boy who was almost the same age as his brother, Moon. Without knowing why, he felt the two of them would get on well. Perhaps because Rune's start in life was unusual as well. He'd been conceived in a night of passion that should have had no consequences, and his father had refused to acknowledge him at first, before falling in love with him and his mother when he unexpectedly returned.

"It is not inconceivable that you should meet him one day," Freyja answered, keeping her gaze averted. Why was she not looking at him? She usually wasn't so shy. "Being the only one of us who was born here, he's often said he wanted to visit with his wife and children. My parents visited a few years ago with his two eldest sons. You might have seen them?"

"I did. By coincidence they arrived in time to take part in the banquet given to celebrate the birth of my niece Emma, Moon's first daughter."

"Oh, yes, they did tell us about that when they came back. I remember." Finally, she met his gaze. "It really is odd to think we know so much about one another's family, don't you think?"

"Yes."

Usually when you met a stranger, you didn't know how many siblings they had or how their parents had met. But he did know that about Freyja. That and more.

He also knew she woke up many times in the night. Not because she had told him, even though she had, but because he also woke up during the night, and as she was staying in his hut, he had seen it for himself. He knew things about her he knew of no other woman. He knew she liked to linger in bed on occasion, but no matter how early or late, she had to see to her needs as soon as she was up. He knew she didn't like honey in her gruel first thing in the morning, but lavished it on her bread after a meal. He knew she always smelled good, regardless of the time of day or what she'd been doing.

He knew…too many things, really. And not all of them appropriate. Like the hungry way she had of looking at him at times.

Like she was doing right now.

Why had he not put his clothes back on, he suddenly wondered? He was not like his friend Sven, who liked to wander around bare-chested when the weather allowed it. The answer hit him like a blow to the back of the skull.

Because, you fool, you want to feel Freyja's hands on you again, this time all over your chest, not just over your markings. All over your body.

Yes, that was exactly what it was.

"Are we almost ready to eat, do you think?" Freyja asked, cutting the loaf of bread into the thick slices he favored. This time he knew why she was averting her gaze. For the same reason he was averting his.

Because looking at one another right now was too dangerous.

Eirik shot back to his feet. Eating. Yes. That should help cool down his blood. Especially that Asta would be in the hut with them then. With her around, there would be no time for lewd thoughts.

He tore one wing off the pheasant roasting on the fire. "Yes, I think the meat is cooked," he said when he saw that it came away easily.

Freyja stood up. "Thank you. I'll go and get Asta then."

IT TOOK Freyja a moment to locate the little girl, who had gone to the river with Rothgar, and some new friends, little Gunnar and his sisters, to test out their new raft. She only managed to drag her away by promising she would tell her all about her boat-building father. The girl seemed to have found a fascination with boats, which surprised her somewhat, considering she had lost both her parents during the crossing. The more she thought about it, the more she believed Asta had not really known love and would be happier in her new life.

When they entered the hut, Eirik had placed everything on the table. He had also put his shirt and tunic back on. Ignoring the deflating sensation in her stomach, Freyja told herself that it was better that way.

They sat down to eat the pheasant and turnip stew she'd prepared to go with it, talking and laughing as any family would do.

"Where's your cat, Eirik?" Asta asked after a while, reaching for another piece of bread. "I haven't seen it yet."

"That's probably because I don't have one," Eirik answered, sliding the pot of butter toward her. He already knew she liked nothing more than freshly churned butter on her bread, just like he did. The two of them really had a lot in common, including a solid appetite.

Just like a real father and daughter would.

The thought hit her like a bolt of lightning. She was still adjusting to the fact that she was Asta's new mother, and here she was, already finding the little girl a father.

"You don't have a cat?" Asta carried on, providing a welcome distraction from the disturbing musings.

"No."

From the way Asta's eyebrows shot to the roots of her hair, Freyja could have sworn Eirik had just admitted to never having eaten a single piece of bread in his life. "Every house should have a cat. Who catches mice for you?"

"No one." He frowned, as if only realizing now that he'd been missing something. "You mean that is why I sometimes find holes in my braies?"

Freyja bit her lip. The gruff Norseman was playing along, indulging the little girl. It was something she had never thought to see, endearing and silly at the same time.

"Of course, that's why!" Asta exclaimed, oblivious to what was going on. "Mice eat everything. You should have a cat. We had two at home. Two black ones."

Here, her voice wobbled. For the first time since they had arrived, she looked about to cry. Freyja's chest squeezed. It seemed that the two animals had provided her with the affection her parents had been unable to give her.

From the way Eirik stilled, it was obvious he was thinking the same thing.

"I'll tell you what, Asta," he said before the silence became too tense. "Tomorrow we'll go see my cousin Bee. She loves animals and has many cats. She'll be able to find us one, I'm sure."

"A black one?" Asta's eyes lit up in hope.

"A black one if you want. You're right. It is better that way. No man wants braies that are full of holes, and I don't want to have to ask you to start chasing mice, do I?"

"I couldn't do that, silly! I'm a little girl."

"Yes. That, you are. So, a black cat it will be."

Freyja already knew she would never forget the look of pure joy on Asta's face—or Eirik's kindness. Earlier, she had wanted to lick at his skin in lust, she was now itching to hug him in gratitude.

They were finishing the meal with a bowl of fresh berries coated in honey when the door burst open on Rothgar.

"Asta! You have to come, quick."

He headed straight to the end of the table, and the little girl sitting with her spoon in midair.

"Rothgar, where are your manners?" Eirik chided gently. "You could have knocked. And you'll have to wait for Asta. We are still eating, as you can see. Besides, you were together all morning, were you not?"

"Sorry, but, I didn't know this morning..." The little boy looked about to burst with happiness. "I have another cousin! And it is a boy, at last! I wanted to tell Asta, show her."

"Sven's baby is born then?"

Eirik beamed and ruffled Rothgar's hair. Freyja stared at him, fascinated. He was truly stunning when he allowed himself to express the joy he was feeling. His eyes gleamed and his face was transformed.

"Yes. He was born last night," Rothgar explained, his words running one into the other in his excitement. "*Faðir* told us just now, while we ate. His name is Espen. I haven't seen him yet, I wanted to wait for Asta because I know she'll want to see him too."

Asta had already left her stool and was looking at her friend with wide eyes, as excited as he was. Freyja knew the girl loved babies even more than she loved boats, and she would have waited for this piece of news with impatience.

"Oh, can I go, please, *Moðir*? I've finished my meal."

Freyja stared at the little girl, stunned. Had Asta just called her "Mother" so naturally?

Eirik saw her shock and cleared his throat. Then, when it became clear she was not going to be able to utter a word, he answered in her stead.

"Yes, I think your mother doesn't mind you going to see the baby." He turned to Rothgar, behaving as if nothing momentous had happened. "You two be calm about it, though, and make sure you don't stay for too long. Eahlswith will be tired and you will not be their only visitors. Tell Sven I'll go see them in a few days, when they've had a rest."

"Yes. Thank you!"

The two excited children shot out of the hut, leaving the two adults alone. Freyja still hadn't moved, had hardly taken a breath.

"Are you all right?" Eirik asked her softly.

"Yes. Did you hear that?"

"I did." He smiled at her. That smile was stunning, yet another reason he should allow himself to express his feelings more. "But I'm not as shocked as you seem to be. You're taking such good care of her that it is no surprise she should consider you as her mother now, especially if, as you suspect, her parents paid little attention to her."

Yes, she had thought the same thing only a moment before.

She wanted to nod, and found that she could not. She was still frozen, in relief as much as in shock. Asta had adopted her as her new mother, she had a group of friends and a safe place to be. She would be happy, away from her scheming uncle.

"Eahlswith," she croaked eventually. "Is that the woman I saw the day I arrived in the village, the one who was nearing her term?"

"Yes."

Eirik could tell Freyja wanted to change the subject and give herself time to deal with what had happened, so he indulged her by explaining how his friend and his wife had met.

"She's a Saxon, as you've probably guessed. They got married back in January." Sven had saved Eahlswith from being murdered by her twin sister, but that would be a story for another day. "His wedding was rather a shock for many, but I always suspected there was more to him than the carefree seducer. That man was made to have a family."

He and his friend were opposites in that regard. People had taken the fact that Sven had bedded many women as proof of his unwillingness to settle down. By the same token, because there were many stories linking him to women, they assumed Eirik had a normal love life. He did not. But people only saw what they wanted to see. Men would never believe that he never took his pleasure with the women he caressed, and women probably thought he was just a lover who was more generous than most. It was enough to establish him as a man like any other. All this went to show that no one knew what was happening in a person's heart, and appearances could be deceptive. It was best not to try and guess what people's lives really were like.

"I'm glad all went well. Eahlswith seemed rather uncomfortable when I last saw her and I know Sven was getting worried."

He smiled, delighted for his friend. He and Wolf's children had grown up together, they were almost as close as brothers, and he felt like this new little boy, Espen, would be like a nephew to him.

"I will give them a few days before I go to see them. As I told Rothgar, they will not want to be invaded by too many visitors at this time."

Eahlswith would be tired, and they needed time to get to know their son in the privacy of their home. How wonderful it would be to welcome a new babe with the wife you loved, get to know him or her and feel you had—

Eirik stood up with decision, bowl in hand.

No need to start imagining such things. This, just as the welcoming heat of a woman's sheath, would be a joy he would never know.

5

———

"Well, with all that black hair, Espen must be the loveliest baby I've ever seen," Eirik announced as he walked into the hut, an enormous root cradled in his arms. Freyja recognized it as the one she had tried to lift earlier before giving up and settling on two more reasonably-sized logs she could actually carry to feed the fire.

That morning, Eirik had gone to see his friend Sven's new baby. Feeling it was not her place since she didn't know either parent, Freyja had not dared to go with him. To make her refusal less obvious, she had argued that she needed to take in the dress Merewen had given her for Asta. That was true, but it had only been a ready excuse. In reality, she would have felt like an intruder in Sven's house.

"Don't people say that every time they see a new baby? That he or she is the loveliest they have ever seen?" she said, putting her needle and thread on the table. She had just finished the hemming of the skirt.

"Perhaps, but perhaps they mean it every time," Eirik answered, not in the least perturbed. "Until the next one comes, and they see that it is even lovelier."

59

"Yes, perhaps," Freyja conceded, amused by the explanation, as she closed the door behind him. "Either that or they don't know what else to say to not offend the parents."

"Are you calling me a liar?"

Eirik stopped in his tracks and turned to look at her, a scowl on his face. Heavens, as her Saxon mother would say, with the gnarled piece of wood in his arms and his eyes ablaze, he looked utterly menacing. Had she misjudged the situation? She'd thought they were enjoying easy banter together and he would welcome the teasing. Had she been wrong? What would he do now? Hurl the root in her face? Cast her out of his house?

"N-no. I'm sorry, I only meant—"

Before she could finish the sentence, Eirik burst out laughing. "Don't look at me like that! I'm only jesting. Did you really think you'd angered me?"

"I don't know," she admitted, still not quite certain she had not. After all, despite the unusual easiness they had found from the start, they hardly knew one another.

"Believe me, Freyja, people who have angered me can be in no doubt about it. I make sure to let them know they've gone too far."

Yes, she didn't doubt he did. "I suppose I will see the difference if I do, then, one day."

He shook his head, a smile still playing on his lips. "Anger me, you? Never. You will never coax that particular beast out of me."

No, but coax another kind of beast—lust—she might well do.

Freyja swallowed when Eirik's nostrils flared. Her insides fluttered in response and his eyes immediately darkened, as if he'd felt the quivering in her core and approved of her reaction. Yes, this was lust indeed, burning bright between them. In that moment, he wanted her. And she wanted him.

Should she—

From somewhere behind them, the fire crackled and popped, recalling her to her senses. What was she thinking? Of course, she could not throw herself at him like a wanton! Not only was it demeaning, but he had sworn an oath never to possess any woman. She should respect it.

It was only when Eirik turned to place the root on the glowing embers that Freyja realized there were no flames left in the fire pit. There had been no crackling or popping in the room. The sizzling tension had been all in her body.

She willed herself to calm.

"Oh, by the way, I saw my sister as I was leaving Sven's hut," Eirik said, stirring the flames back to life under the root he'd placed in the fire pit. They wouldn't have to worry about being warm for the rest of the day. Big as it was, the piece of wood would burn until the night. "She invited me to eat with her tonight. Would you and Asta like to come with me?"

Freyja's heart leaped at the thought of meeting more people from the village, people who were connected to Eirik. This time she felt she could agree to go because she would not be an intruder, exactly. Aife would have heard of her through her mother and might be curious to meet her. Besides, being surrounded by other people seemed a good idea right now. It might help her forget the inappropriate feelings she'd been battling with since the moment Eirik had bared his chest to her.

"I would love to come, if it's no inconvenience."

"Of course not." He brushed the comment aside with an elegant gesture of the hand. "She's married to an old childhood friend, one of Wolf's sons, Torsten, and they have a little girl."

Oh. Freyja hadn't known that. Of course, the news reaching Denmark was few and far between. She made a note to find out all she could and put it in a letter to send to her parents at the earliest opportunity. She would have to find someone to take the missive to the harbor and locate a boat of merchants heading home, though, as she couldn't go herself. The risk of running into Harald was too great. Perhaps one of Wolf's sons or Eirik's brothers wouldn't mind doing that for her?

She would prefer not to mention it to Eirik himself, as he had actually met Harald and she feared a confrontation between the two men if they ever crossed paths again.

"Do both your sisters live in the village?" she asked.

She'd heard him mention Moon the other day and she had seen Elwyn from a distance once, but though she knew that Eirik had two sisters, she had yet to meet either of them.

"No, Hedda left for Denmark a few years ago and married there. Oddly, her husband is called Thorsten also. It is Aife we'll see tonight."

Freyja nodded, feeling as if she already knew the woman she had heard about all her life and who was only a couple of years younger than she was.

Asta soon came running, and together, they made their way to Aife and Torsten's hut when the sun disappeared behind the horizon.

"Here," Eirik said, stepping to the side to let her enter first. "This is Freyja," he told his sister, a woman who was just as small and slender as he was tall and imposing.

"Welcome!" Aife exclaimed, drawing her into her arms as naturally as if they were old friends. "I'm so glad to finally meet you. I feel like I've known you all my life. Had you been born here, I think we would have been raised together, like we were with Wolf and Merewen's children."

Yes, they most likely would have, so Freyja gladly returned the embrace.

Once the presentations had been made, the four adults sat down and partook of the mead Eirik had brought along with him. Freyja had never tasted anything as delicious, sweet and floral, and she had to force herself not to gulp it down. She guessed it would be quite strong and she didn't want to make a fool of herself.

"Was there a reason you wanted to invite me tonight?" Eirik asked once his cup was empty.

Judging from the smile floating on his lips, he thought there might be. And if the color on his sister's cheeks was any indication, he was right. Aife took her husband's hand and nodded. Freyja thought she had guessed what she was about to reveal and her own heart melted. The woman looked so happy and in love, it was hard not to be envious.

"I'm expecting another child. We told *Faðir* and Mother last night, and I saw Elwyn this afternoon, when I went to the well. Moon told me about a week ago that he was certain I was expecting and I didn't have the heart to lie, though I have no idea how he could know when I had only just seen Cwenthryth to have it confirmed." She let go of Torsten's hand to take Eirik's. "I invited you tonight because you were the only one left to tell."

"Congratulations!" He beamed, before standing up and drawing her into a bear hug. "I'm so glad for you."

Freyja had seen earlier that the couple had a little girl, Thyra. She was just over a year old, and currently playing spinning tops on the floor with Asta, who never tired of launching the wooden toy and retrieving it for her. Freyja remembered being told on the boat that Asta had wanted a baby sister for ages. It seemed that was no lie, and her love for babies ran deep.

"Shall we eat?" Aife asked, still looking flushed from sharing her happy news with everyone.

Eirik sat back down and poured everyone a cup of ale while Torsten started to ladle cabbage soup into bowls. Once everyone was served, Aife handed Freyja a dish of omelette flavored with sorrel leaves. Eirik smiled, took the plate in her stead and placed it to one side.

"No eggs for Freyja, sorry," he said, guessing she would be ill at ease refusing the food that was so generously offered to her. The comment would be better coming from him. "I will have her share of omelette and give her my chunk of smoked eel to compensate, if it's ok with both of you."

"Of course." Aife said easily, handing her a slice of rye bread. "Here. Try the bread with it. They go well together."

"Thank you," Freyja murmured, grateful he had spared her any embarrassment. This really was just like being among friends, easy and natural.

"Tell me, isn't it too hard living with my brother?"

"Aife, please!" Eirik said between his teeth, while Freyja went a beautiful pink color. What had possessed his sister to ask such a thing?

But in truth, he had expected such curiosity.

"I'm sorry, but it is a valid question," Aife insisted, not in the least ashamed. "For all I know, you've turned into a bear. After living for so long on your own, your manners might well have become less than graceful." She leaned in toward Freyja who was sitting opposite her. "He swears a lot, you will have noticed. He gets that from our father, I'm afraid. I don't know why, because my two other brothers are not as rough. And he eats enough for two. I hope he leaves enough food for you and Asta at meal times. If not, come here, we'll always have something for you. It's not—"

"Sister, that's enough!" Really, she had to stop talking now. Would she paint him as a coarse, selfish pig who could not look after guests properly in front of the only woman he had ever wanted to impress? It was humiliating.

Torsten threw him a sympathetic glance and turned to his

wife. "I think there's no cause for worry. We're talking about Eirik, not Arne. Now, *he* might well have the manners of a bear."

"Mmmm." Aife appeared somewhat chastened.

"I am very grateful to Eirik for having us, and I don't mind the swearing at all," Freyja flushed but she stood her ground. "And if he eats a lot, it is no wonder, given how tasty the food he prepares is. Truly I've never known a better cook."

Relief swept through him. She didn't seem to think his manners were lacking in any way. She was grateful to him and she loved his food. It was the best thing he had heard in a while, and so he helped himself to a second cup of mead.

The rest of the meal passed without incident, and soon he, Freyja, and Asta were making their way back to the hut under a sky strewn with thousands of stars. The beauty of the night never failed to enchant Eirik, and he was pleased to see that Freyja seemed just as awed as he was. She was walking with her face turned up and he had to grab her elbow on more than one occasion for fear she'd stumbled over a root hidden in the dirt or stepped into a hole. She was not like him, who knew every inch of the village and could have walked with his eyes closed.

The third time she stumbled, he didn't release her and just kept hold of her. She didn't protest or even pass any comment. Why would she? It felt right.

As soon as they reached the hut, Asta ran to the pallet, declaring she was exhausted. She was asleep in moments, holding the belt she always slept with. Eirik fully expected Freyja to follow her under the furs but to his delight, for he felt restless and wasn't ready for bed, she asked if he had more mead in the hut. It seemed she was not ready for bed either.

Good.

"You like it then?" he asked, pouring her a large cup of the drink. Many people had praised his mead over the years, but hers was the compliment he most appreciated.

"Yes. It's nothing like I ever tasted."

"Thank you. I experimented a lot, perhaps that is why."

"Yes. Perhaps. The best things often happen when we least expect them."

The words seemed to acquire a deeper meaning and they looked at one another a long, tension-filled moment.

"Let's go outside," Eirik eventually suggested, raising his cup. "'Tis warm enough, I should think." They would be better able to talk without the risk of waking Asta.

Freyja nodded and followed him out of the door.

"I was surprised you remembered I didn't like eggs," she said, as she sat on the bench.

He snorted, taking his place next to her. "You told me as much only the other day. Do you think I have a sieve for a brain?"

"No, but you could have forgotten. It was hardly important information."

Perhaps it was unimportant, to someone else. But he would not forget anything she'd told him so easily.

"Are you telling me you forgot what I told you that day?" he asked throwing her a sideways glance he knew would be lost. Not only was it dark but she had buried her nose in her cup and she was looking at the ground.

"No."

"Well, then. And I thank you for taking my defense earlier, when my sister went out of her way to make me appear like a self-centered boor. I have no idea what possessed her to say such things."

He would have to have a word with Aife at the earliest opportunity. This could have gone very badly. Fortunately, Freyja had not let his sister's comments rile her.

"It was nothing. Rune would have done the same to me, I'm sure. It's what siblings do, and no cause for concern."

Perhaps. Still.

"You truly don't mind the swearing?" he insisted, feeling self-conscious.

Did she think him a coarse, selfish pig who could not look after guests properly? She might have lied to spare his feelings and be polite. And Aife was right. He had never lived with a woman before, so he might well behave in a manner that was offensive to them, especially in his most unguarded moments. How had he not thought of this before?

"Truly." She gave a small smile, as if it surprised her as well. "Does your mother mind your father swearing?"

"I think not." In reality, he had never thought about it. Heat started in the pit of his stomach at the idea that she was comparing their situation to that of his parents, who had a loving marriage. "I've never heard her berate him for it, in any case."

"I'm not surprised, if it's just part of who he is and how he behaves. She married him, didn't she, knowing how he was?" There was a silence. In the darkness, Freyja's eyes glittered like gems. The color was completely different than when they were bathed in sunshine, almost dark. "And as I said, you do feed us some of the tastiest foods I have ever eaten, so I suppose I cannot complain."

The glow inside his chest expanded. She hadn't lied earlier. She was truly glad to be staying with him. "Thank you."

The silence stretched, became almost tangible, and the air around them grew thick with tension. It was just like when he had removed his shirt in front of her. Eirik felt himself leaning toward Freyja. Why, he wasn't sure. Surely he was not about to kiss her? He never kissed women, if he could help it.

And yet...

"I think I will go to bed now," Freyja murmured, standing up.

Though he would have loved her to stay longer, he had no

choice but to nod. He already knew he would stay out here long into the night, trying to coax his blood back down to its usual slow flow.

"Good night, Freyja."

6

———

"Who made this?"

At the question, Eirik turned to face Freyja. She was holding one of his latest creations, a pitcher of unusual proportions he still wasn't sure he would keep.

"I did."

Taking it from her hands, he poured himself a cup of ale. Yes. It was rather awkward to hold.

"And the cup also?" she asked, nodding at the earthenware vessel he'd just filled, one of the first pieces he'd ever made and his favourite.

"Yes. I'm going to save you some time." The corner of his lips lifted. Why was it that he loved her questioning? As someone who'd led a solitary life, wasn't he supposed to value peace and quiet above all things? "I did all the pottery you can see in this house. And most of my friends', actually. My parents', too."

She seemed to ponder this, then lifted the pitcher once more. "Mead, and now this? You're very talented, you know."

He shrugged. "Thanks."

Was he talented? He didn't know. He liked doing it, that was

69

for sure, which accounted for the time he'd spent perfecting the art. And that, in turn, had made him quite skilled. Yes, it was not talent so much as perseverance and an eye for proportions.

And those of the pitcher were definitely off, he decided. It bothered him every time he looked at it, so he would throw it away at the earliest—

"Another experiment, I suppose. Well, I like it," Freyja declared, nodding in approval. "It is very unusual. Not many people would have dared make such an unconventional object and gotten away with it. But you did. I'm impressed."

She replaced the pitcher on the table and Eirik could have sworn he saw the object smirk at him. As well it might. The wretched, top-heavy pitcher knew it had just been guaranteed a long and happy life under his roof.

"I've never tried to make pottery," Freyja mused, oblivious to the fact that she had just saved the object from destruction just by loving it, flaws and all. "I always imagined it would be too difficult. Is that the case?

She lifted her head up to him. Fuck, she was so beautiful... Those eyes. They'd captured a mysterious color he thought he had never seen.

It was when she arched a brow that Eirik realized he'd been losing himself in the swirl of her irises instead of answering. It was not the first time it had happened, though how could he stop himself when she had the most entrancing eyes he had ever seen? He remembered his mother telling him that her Saxon friend had black eyes, a gift from her unknown father come from a distant land. Perhaps that was why Freyja's eyes were of an unusual, darker blue than most people he knew, utterly fascinating. As to her hair, it was pure Norse, a living flame, vibrant with life and energy.

Would her intimate hairs be as fiery, he wondered? He was burning to find out, bury his face between her legs and delve into her soft petals, explore her with his tongue, learn what made her melt. This was something he had never done before, guessing that it would test his control to its limits. Kissing was relatively safe, and so far he had been able to hold on to his control when feeling a woman spasming around his fingers. It had been enough for him to know he was giving her pleasure. His mind usually managed to convince his body that they could stop there. When he felt particularly aroused, he stroked himself to release while his lover watched on and smiled at his selflessness.

After all, despite his oath, he was still a man, with men's desires. He could not deny himself every satisfaction and remain sane.

"I'm sorry, what did you say?" he said, when he realized he still hadn't answered Freyja's question.

She looked at him strangely. Damnation, had she guessed that he'd been thinking of tasting her intimately? He hoped not.

"I asked you if pottery was difficult."

"Not really. With practice, I believe anyone can make a pot."

"Yes, perhaps. But not everyone would think of making one like this, as I said." She brushed a finger around the rim of the pitcher and smiled.

He cleared his throat. Why did her appreciation please him so? He usually did not set much score by what other people thought. He did not understand how he behaved around this woman, and he wasn't sure he liked it.

"I will have to go into town sometime this week," he announced, instead of dwelling on it.

Every year he met with a group of Danish merchants come to sell their furs. The products were very different from the ones he could get here, and buying from them was his one luxury in life. He'd put off the visit for as long as he could, not wanting to leave Freyja alone with Harald lurking about, but now seemed as good a time as any. Mayhap a few days away from her would help restore some sense into him, restore him to his usual self. He remembered how he'd thought that there was little risk in having her under his roof. It seemed he'd gravely underestimated the danger the little Dane posed, with her deep blue eyes and endearing manners.

He had never felt less secure in his ability to uphold his oath.

"I told Wolf and his sons to look after you and Asta while I'm gone, as well as my brothers," he added, not wanting her to worry. "They can guard you as well as I can."

This was true, even if he was loath to leave her.

She nodded, doing her best to look brave. He could tell she didn't want to add to his burden. "Of course. In any case, I think Harald may have given up looking for us."

Mmmm. He wasn't so sure that was the case, even if it was true they had not heard from him since his visit to the village. Still, Eirik wouldn't breathe easily until he'd found out for certain that the man had gone back to Denmark. He didn't tell Freyja what he thought, though. There was no point in worrying her further.

"I will be gone two days, perhaps three. No more." He would take this opportunity to ask some of his friends at the harbor to keep themselves aware of Harald's whereabouts and inform him the moment his boat left.

"Of course," Freyja said again. "Go. We'll be fine."

It was when his body started to ache with the restraint needed not to draw her into his arms that Eirik knew he did indeed need to take some distance from her.

FREYJA DREW in a deep inhale to savor the feeling of peace spreading through her.

She could almost fool herself that she lived here, in Eirik's hut, that she had a new life, and everything would be all right. The pain of the past year was beginning to fade away, just as her mother had predicted.

Leaving had definitely been the best choice, the one that would allow her to heal.

She was much better off here, with Eirik. His hut was welcoming, very different from the one she had left behind in Denmark, which was a relief. She would have hated to be constantly reminded of her old life. Not for the first time she reflected that the unexpected barrenness of her union, which had caused her so much pain, had turned out to be a blessing.

How would she have borne the idea that her children would grow up without their father? That she had taken them away from all they knew, from their loving grandparents? No, in the circumstances, it was much better that she had never fallen with child during her marriage. It would only have added to her distress.

Besides, she now had someone to look after. She was, in effect, Asta's mother.

And the little girl was happier than she had ever been. True to his word, after their discussion about the cats, Eirik had taken her to his cousin Bee, who was married to his adoptive brother. The kind woman had given them not just one, but two black kittens from her latest litter, to replace the ones Asta had been forced to leave behind in Denmark. Seeing the little girl draw them into a fierce hug had melted Freyja's heart. The two little bundles had promptly been named Pepper and Coal and brought home.

Home.

Yes. This felt like home.

Pensively, Freyja took a cup from the shelf by the window and allowed her fingers to brush the smooth surface.

It was one of Eirik's finest pieces, she thought. How could a man so powerful produce something so delicate? He'd claimed it was all down to practice, but she wasn't sure it was that simple. Some people didn't reach any ability in any endeavor, no matter how long or how hard they tried. Her youngest sister Solveig had never managed to embroider a single shift without making it look like the work of an eight-year-old. Arvid's mum had cooked all her life, yet the food she made never failed to be uninspiring and bland. She, herself, despite her father's guidance, had never been able to carve anything that resembled what it was supposed to be.

As she looked through the window, Freyja's mind started to wander to Denmark and the people she'd left behind. What were her sisters doing? Had Rune met his new baby yet? How were her parents bearing her absence? Then her mind crossed the sea again and she came back to the village. Was Asta playing dice with little Sanna or running in the fields with Rothgar? What did Moon look like?

When would Eirik be back?

She berated herself for that last question. He'd only been gone for a day. Surely she didn't miss him already? They had only met in the flesh a few weeks ago, even if she had heard about him all her life.

As she kept looking toward the forest, she saw a man appear in her field of vision. At the well he veered right and started to walk straight to the hut. It was obvious he was coming to see her. Eirik had told her that he would tell a few trustworthy men to keep an eye on her during his absence, but this one she didn't know.

A moment later, there was a knock on the door. She opened it to reveal a man with longer hair than most and a neatly trimmed beard.

"Good morning. I'm Moon, Eirik's brother."

Freyja smiled. Only a moment she had been wondering what he looked like, and here he was, as if he'd heard the question. "Good morning," she said warmly.

"I'm the one my mother passed off as your brother Rune's twin all those years ago." He let out a laugh, incongruous in its spontaneity. A moment ago he had looked like a fierce warrior, and in the blink of an eye, he had become something more akin to a mischievous little boy. "You might have heard that story?"

Her smile broadened. The man seemed utterly charming, less intense than his brother, but still formidable, and strong as an ox. It was impossible to imagine him as the fragile baby he had once been. "Yes, I do know that story," she confirmed.

She was sure everyone in the village knew it.

"I'm happy to finally meet you," Moon said, nodding. "Eirik told Elwyn and me that you were being pursued by a Dane merchant who wanted to steal your daughter away?"

"Yes." She didn't bother to correct the slight distortion of reality because that was exactly what it felt like.

"Don't worry. With the help of Wolf's sons, we'll make sure you're not on your own if anyone dares to come to you."

"This is very kind of you." She gestured to the inside of the hut. "Would you like a drink?"

"No, thank you. I just wanted to say hello and make sure that you were safe. My friend, Sven, kept an eye out for you last night, as he was up with the baby anyway. Tonight it will be my father." Freyja didn't answer, so stunned was she. Was the whole male population being put on watch for her sake? "Mayhap I will ask my wife, Eyja, and her friend Cwenthryth to visit you later this afternoon?"

"Some company would be good," Freyja agreed. "I already know Cwenthryth. I visited her to thank her for all her son has done for Asta."

Moon nodded. "I'm guessing the boy's friendship has helped her get used to her new situation."

"It has. And I am beyond grateful for what everyone has done for me."

"Think nothing of it. I'm sure you would have done the same for us."

~

EIRIK LET OUT A BIG SIGH. The day had been taxing, physically and emotionally, and he was relieved to be home at last.

For a reason they had failed to explain, the merchants had wanted a much higher price for their wares than usual, and haggling with them had quickly turned unpleasant. They kept pushing for unrealistic prices. As if all that were not enough, there had been a new man among them, a man in his sixth or seventh decade called Olaf, who had been more unreasonable than the rest of the group put together and the two of them had almost come to blows.

It had almost pushed Eirik over the edge.

Every time he met an older man called Olaf, he wondered if he was the bastard who had assaulted his mother. Could the Dane trying to sell him deer hides and bear furs at an extortionate price be the one who had fathered him in this horrid parody of lovemaking? He was old enough, and he could have gone back to Denmark after being banished from the village. How would Eirik have behaved if he'd known for certain that this was who the man was? How would he feel if he ever met him? Would he be able to stop himself from throttling him?

Would he ever be free from the strain of wondering if he would one day have to make that decision? How soothing it must be for his brother, Moon, to know where he came from, to know that he shared his blood with a man who was all that was honorable and kind, to not fear his nature and allow himself to share his beloved wife's bed.

Eirik would never know that peace.

He looked around him and sighed. Why was he feeling so dejected? It was not the first time had he come back to an empty hut and he'd never thought anything of it. Yet, today he shouldn't have found the hut empty. Today, he had hoped to see Freyja, or little Asta. At the very least, Pepper or Coal, the new kittens. But they weren't anywhere near to see. Well, he would just have to wait. They had not left, that much he knew. He could see their bag in its usual corner. And they wouldn't have left without saying goodbye, of course.

He was so weary that, though it was only mid-afternoon, he lay on the pallet and piled furs over himself. If he closed his eyes just a moment, he might feel better. If he just allowed himself to drift off and not think of...

The next thing he knew, Eirik was blinking away sleep and darkness had descended into the hut. He stretched, satisfied with his decision. He'd been right to allow his body the rest it needed, as it had also cleared his mind of his maudlin thoughts.

He was about to stand up when Freyja entered.

From the way she lit a tallow candle and stirred the fire back to life he realized she hadn't seen him, ensconced as he was in the dark recesses of the hut and hidden under the pile of furs. Of course, she wouldn't be expecting him so soon. He had told her he would be gone for three days. But he had hurried back home at the earliest opportunity, unable to bear the uncertainty of not knowing whether Harald had tried anything, unable to bear her absence. Somehow, in just a few weeks, she had become an essential part of his life.

He could not resist observing her a moment. She was so graceful. For a while, she busied herself with the tidying up of the dishes left on the table. Then she positioned the wooden tub he used to wash his clothes in the middle of the room, next to the fire pit and started to remove her shoes and stockings. Did she want to wash them?

No, she wanted to do much worse than that, he realized when she pinned her hair in place on top of her head to make sure it wouldn't get wet. She was going to wash herself. Eirik swallowed. If she really was about to do that, he should speak out, make his presence known.

Freyja took the pot that had been placed over the fire embers and still he didn't move. She grunted in satisfaction when she dipped a finger in the water and apparently found it pleasantly warm, ready for her. And then...then she started undressing.

Heart in his throat, Eirik watched every gesture. Under his fascinated gaze, she reached for the two brooches holding her dress and allowed the bodice to fall to her waist. After that, one tug was enough to make it fall to the floor. She folded the garment and placed it on the table. And then, finally, she lifted her shift above her head, before putting it next to her dress.

She was now naked, facing him, utterly oblivious to the fact that she was not alone and she was...

Glorious.

She stepped into the wooden tub. With a sigh of pleasure, she lifted the pot and slowly poured the contents over herself. All the air left Eirik's lungs as he watched the water sluice down her body, caressing each curve, leaving a shiny trail in its wake, a trail he wanted to lick away. Had there ever been a more beautiful woman? He didn't think so.

Feeling like the worst lecher but unable to avert his gaze, he watched everything Freyja did, wishing he could take part in the action, be the one tending to her. First, she dipped a piece of linen into the water at her feet and scrubbed her face clean. Then the true torture began. Eyes closed, she tilted her head to wash the crook of her neck, where he wanted to nuzzle her. She lifted a graceful arm to run the cloth along the underside, where he wanted to bury his nose. She rubbed one tender breast, then the other, where he most ached to kiss her.

Bloody hell, he was harder than steel and his tongue had gotten stuck to the roof of his mouth.

She turned, offering him a glimpse of her perfect backside, and reached out to get the bigger piece of linen she had put on a stool by the fire pit to warm. No! Everything within him rebelled. He was not ready for the moment to end. So, at last, he spoke.

"You are so fucking beautiful."

7

———

Freyja let out a gasp when a growl sliced through the darkness.

You are so fucking beautiful.

"Eirik?" she called out tentatively. It could well be him. The swearing was one indication, the gravelly voice another. And they were in his house, after all, it would make sense for him to be here. Except that she'd thought him still at the harbor and the hut empty.

She stilled, very aware of her nakedness. It would be bad enough if the man in the corner were Eirik. If it weren't...

"Aye. It's me."

She swallowed, both reassured it was not someone she didn't know and breathless at the idea that he was seeing her naked. "You're back."

And he'd been watching her. All the while, as she'd washed, he'd been here, hidden in the lurking shadows. Not expecting him to be back and not hearing or seeing anything when she had entered the hut, she had not thought to check whether she was alone before undressing.

Now that she knew she was being watched, she should be

covering herself, but she was frozen on the spot. A moment later, she felt a huge, masculine presence behind her. Then the piece of linen she'd prepared was wrapped around her, its warmth wonderful on her skin. Yet she shivered at the feel of strong hands on her shoulders.

"Are you cold?" Eirik growled in her ear.

"No."

Though on the surface she was chilled, her insides were burning. How could it be otherwise with such a man touching her?

His hands remained at her shoulders, the pressure of his fingers increasing with each heartbeat. She could tell he wanted to remove the piece of linen and run his bare hands all over her body. Had he ever done that? Was that why he seemed reluctant to let go of her, because this was new to him? Did he want *her*, or to find out what it felt like to touch a naked woman?

She heard a deep inhale and he took his hands away at last. Freyja shivered.

"Have you ever touched a woman?" she asked, before she could think of the wisdom of the question. He had never bedded anyone, he'd told her as much, and why, but perhaps he had experimented, at least kissed a few willing conquests.

"I've touched more women that you can count," was his shocking answer. She hadn't expected him to be so honest—or to have so much experience, considering what he had told her. Apparently, though he had sworn never to possess a lover, he had allowed himself some sensual gratification. She was glad. "There's nothing I like more than to give a woman pleasure."

Envy caused Freyja's chest to tighten. Who were these countless women who'd enjoyed his caresses? She wanted to be one of them.

"Would you like to touch me?"

Where had this brazenness come from? But perhaps it was

inevitable she should be unable to resist temptation. He had called her beautiful, he was looming over her, talking in her ear and she was...melting.

It had been so long since she had been with a man, and Eirik was more man than she could handle.

"I would like nothing more than to touch you," he answered. "But I'm not sure it would be a—"

"I am. Touch me, Eirik, please." She rolled her head back, leaning against his strong shoulder, willing him to put his hands back on her. "I'm burning."

If she were honest, she would tell him that she'd been desperate to feel his hands on her ever since the day they'd met and he'd told her that he would defend her and Asta against Harald. His masculine strength and good looks had overwhelmed her. Then his thoughtfulness had completed what his beauty had begun. At first, she had wanted the handsome lover, then she had hankered after the beautiful man he was on the inside.

Sensing that she would have to take the first step and prove that she was willing, she tugged at the piece of linen wrapped around her. It fell to the floor in a soft murmur. There was a growl at her ear and before she knew it, a hand had slid over her left breast, cupping it. She shivered in delight when a hot mouth landed on her neck. It seemed she wouldn't have to beg for his attention.

"Here," he said softly. "I'm touching you, Freyja. Do you want me to pleasure you too?"

Well, yes, that was what she'd meant when she'd asked him to touch her. How could he tease her so?

"Yes. Please." She needed this. "I haven't been touched in tenderness in so long."

"I will touch you in tenderness, but make no mistake about it, I will also touch you in lust. I will make you moan, I will make you writhe, and I will not stop until you have drenched my hand."

If he thought to frighten her or make her change her mind, he would be disappointed. This was exactly what she wanted.

"I will moan," she promised. "And I will writhe. But I'm not sure I'll...drench your hand." She wasn't even sure what he meant by that. "I've never—"

"You will, I'll make sure of it." The lips still at her throat started to nibble at her skin. "Let me take care of you. Just allow yourself to feel."

With those words, he snaked his hand down her stomach, his touch light and yet scorching. His thumb lingered around her navel a moment, circling it in tantalizing brushes. His other hand started to stroke her breast with slow and sensual gestures, then his fingers plucked at her nipple, which instantly went as hard as a pearl. She moaned, and moaned again when he covered her mons, warming the folds with his long fingers, ruffling the soft hairs with his palm.

Sorðinn, he had barely begun and she was already trembling. As if he'd sensed what was happening within her, he kept her pressed tight against his chest, warming her, supporting her, engulfing her in his much larger frame, making her fall apart.

"Yes," she breathed, "yes, yes, *yes!*"

Would she be able to utter even this simple word in a moment? She had no idea. She could already tell this would be different to what she was used to.

"Yes," Eirik groaned, lifting her right leg and placing her foot on the edge of the tub, spreading her wider for his caresses. "Open for me. Just like that. Let me feel how wet you are, how hot, how beautiful, how perfect."

His voice at her ear, combined with the action of his fingers at her breast and core conspired to make Freyja melt. Something swelled inside her and suddenly she had an idea of what he might mean by "drenching his hand." It did feel as if she were about to dissolve in a flood of pleasure. It frightened her a bit.

"Eirik..."

"I know. But it's just me giving you pleasure. Let it come."

And she did. Knowing she was standing in a tub of water helped her not worry about the consequences of her lack of control. She did let go, and allowed pleasure to gush out of her in a shocking release.

"Beautiful," she heard Eirik say. "Fucking beautiful."

Just when she wondered how she was going to find the strength to stay upright on one leg, she felt him lift her into his arms and cradle her against his chest. Grateful for his thoughtfulness, she burrowed her face into the crook of his neck, barely resisting the urge to sob.

Beautiful, he'd called it. Yes, it had been.

And he had called *her* beautiful. In this moment she certainly felt it.

"Come."

He brought her closer to the pallet and deposited her on the floor. After wrapping her in one of the blankets, he lay her down and piled furs high above her trembling body. She wasn't cold, exactly, but she couldn't stop shivering. She suspected it had something to do with the intensity of the release she had just experienced, a release unlike any she had felt in Arvid's arms.

Without her asking for anything, Eirik took his tunic and undershirt off, settled next to her, and drew her into his arms as naturally as if they had shared such intimacy a hundred times. But though they had not slept together before, she didn't protest.

It felt right.

"I take it that Asta is sleeping with Steinar and Cwenthryth tonight?" he asked, holding her tight against his chest. Her hand was resting on his pectoral and she was bathing in his wonderful woodsy scent. It reminded her of home, of her father, who worked with wood, and therefore always smelled just as good.

"Yes." For the first time, the little girl had asked to sleep in Rothgar's home. His parents had agreed and Freyja had not had the heart to refuse. And now, selfishly, she was glad, as it allowed her to nestle in bed with Eirik without worrying about being seen.

"I'm glad for her."

A kiss landed on the top of her head. Oh, the comfort of that simple gesture... She had missed it just as much as she had missed the pleasure a man's touch could bring her.

Eirik tightened his hold around Freyja, then forced himself to relax it. He didn't want to smother her, but the comfort it brought him to have a woman lying in his arms was like nothing else. Because of his situation, he had never had the chance to lie in bed with anyone. He had never missed it, as no one missed things they had not known, but now he feared he would want to sleep with Freyja every night for the rest of his life. His cock, so hard while he had pleasured her, was lying limply against his thigh. Lust was not what this was about.

After the day he'd had, this proximity was exactly what he needed.

For a long moment, they didn't speak. He thought Freyja had fallen asleep. Then she spoke, her voice hesitant.

"Those women you touched..." she started.

Eirik tensed, knowing this would be a very personal question, one that might well cause his dormant cock to wake up with a vengeance. "What about them?"

"Did you ever allow them to touch you in turn?"

Her hand, which had been resting on his chest a moment ago, had slipped to his stomach without him noticing. He caught her by the wrist, anticipating her next move. He was still wearing his braies but it was better not to play with fire. "No. I've never let them pleasure me."

And he wasn't about to start now.

Feeling Freyja's spasms of pleasure on his fingers had been one of the most satisfying and erotic experiences of his life. He had not lied when he'd said that he had pleasured countless women in that manner, but it had been different.

Every time he'd touched a woman, it had been for her benefit, not his. He had felt as if he was righting a wrong, as if a part of his soul had been restored to him. So he'd reasoned that if he pleasured enough women in his lifetime, he might leave this world with his soul, if not intact, at least less damaged than it had been at first. He would erase some of the taint he'd been born with.

So far it had not worked. Pleasuring women who meant little to him had not made him feel much better. He was starting to suspect that the only way he would feel at peace with his nature was to do what his father had done—find one special woman and give her the life every woman deserved. Caedmon, the village goldsmith, had once told him that he'd become a master at his craft by focusing on perfecting one single item, the dog rose, and creating it over and over again, in dozens of different ways. He could make delicate rings and beautiful chains, of course, but his true masterpieces were the flowers he could infuse such life into. He put his heart in those pieces, because they reminded him of his wife, and that made all the difference.

For the last two decades, Eirik had pleasured women because he could. And then Freyja had come. With her, everything had been different. He had pleasured her because he'd been dying to do so. His heart had definitely been in it.

She had undressed in front of him, not demanding anything, and she had stripped his soul bare at the same time. Stroking her had brought her pleasure, of course, but it had been just as much for his benefit.

"I—"

"No, please," he cut in, giving her wrist a light squeeze. "Don't make this more difficult than it already is."

Surely, pressed against him as she was, she would feel that he was hard. She would also know that he would not let such a state sway him, and why.

"I'm sorry," she murmured against the skin of his shoulder. "Forgive me, I didn't mean to make you feel bad. Only, it's hard to accept the gift you gave me without wanting to please you in turn."

Yes, that was the way it worked in a normal relationship, but this was not normal. He was not a man free to behave like another would.

"A gift can be accepted without compensation being given."

"Yes, but don't you see? You have given me so much already. Your protection, your understanding, a roof over our heads, hope for the future..." She touched her chest in emotion—or arousal, he wasn't sure. At the gesture, he almost rolled her under him to suckle the nipples he had not allowed himself to taste earlier. He suspected they would taste like honey, or fruit preserve. Sweet in any case. "And just now you gave me indescribable pleasure. I don't know how to handle it."

"There is nothing to handle. I'm happy to give you what you need."

"Thank you, Eirik. Truly." As she spoke, she nestled herself closer to him. He barely resisted the urge to draw her atop him and enjoy the intimate contact to the full. Considering how much bigger than her he was, her weight would barely register, only her warmth and the wonderful closeness he had never been able to experience before. "Can I stay here in your arms to sleep?"

Her voice was already slurred.

"Of course." He'd been about to ask her the same thing. There was no way they would sleep separately tonight, not after what had happened, not when Asta wasn't there, not when it gave him so much satisfaction.

"Then you will have to roll to your left side, won't you?" she asked, already moving to offer her back to him. Apparently she wanted him to engulf her from behind. If that was the case, he would be only too happy to oblige. "You can't fall asleep in any other position, if I remember correctly."

"Mmmm, no," he said, wrapping her in his arms. "Usually not."

But with Freyja tucked inside his body, Eirik had a feeling that tonight he might be able to sleep in any position—and have the sweetest dreams of his life.

8

———

"Eirik, please, come!"

Eirik was woken by a panicked Asta shaking him by the shoulder.

"What is it?" he asked, instantly alert. Though he'd been in the middle of the best dream of his life, the urgency in the little girl's voice had brought him back to reality in the blink of an eye.

"It's Freyja. She's dying. You have to come!"

Ice crystallized in his veins with a rapidity that left him breathless. Dying. What the fuck? Only the night before she had been tucked in his arms, safe and warm. What had happened? He jumped to his feet, thankful he was still wearing his braies. He wouldn't waste any time getting dressed.

"What do you mean, dying?" he asked, shoving his feet into his boots. He'd already understood he would have to go outside to see Freyja. She was not in the hut, and no wonder. Judging from the light pouring through the window, it was already well past dawn. He had slept past his usual time. "Where is she?"

Before panic flooded through him, he forced himself to

remember that the girl had a tendency to drama and she had seen her father die recently. It would be playing on her mind, making her see things in a warped, grim light.

"Just outside. I saw her being sick all over the ground as I was coming back from Rothgar's hut. It's just like what happened to my father. I'm scared she will die too."

Fucking hell.

"Stay here," he instructed the little girl, giving her a quick hug he meant to be reassuring. "I'll go see her."

With those words, Eirik rushed outside. At the back of the hut, by the bench, he found Freyja, pale and trembling, trying to sit down. He was instantly by her side.

"What's wrong?"

It was clear from her pallor that she had indeed been sick. As soon as he'd drawn her into his arms, she burst into sobs. Alarm spiked through him. What the hell had happened? Was she ill? Had she been frightened out of her wits by something she had seen? Someone? Had Harald come to the village while he slept?

"Freyja, please, tell me," he urged, unable to wait any longer.

"I-I'm with child."

Everything within Eirik stilled. This was the last thing he had expected to hear. The last thing he's *wanted* to hear. "You're...with child?" he repeated, his voice hollow.

She started sobbing again. "Yes."

Freyja could not believe what was happening.

She had noticed her courses had not come, of course she had, but she had not for a moment thought that a babe could be the cause. How could she have imagined that after so many years of being barren, she would bear a child? Having heard of such things, she had told herself that the upset of the recent months was responsible for the drying up of her courses. Her body was simply responding to the upsetting events in her life.

Now she knew different.

Arvid had made her with child that terrible night, when he'd taken advantage of her feelings for him and assaulted her. How cruel.

And what would she do now? How would she deal with the revelation? How would she welcome this child imposed on her? She had always wanted children. But not like this, not alone.

"The father..." Eirik started when her sobs finally subsided. It was obvious he didn't have any idea how to ask the question but he persisted. "Was this... Is he someone you know? Did you go to him willingly?"

Mayhap his own experience was influencing him and making him imagine the worst. Mayhap her distress was showing on her face. She didn't know. Whatever the case, he had immediately assumed this baby was not the product of a loving union.

And he was right.

"I..." Her voice trailed. How could she explain what had happened? It was too complicated, too terrible, too shameful.

"It's all right. You don't have to talk about it if you don't want to." Eirik's face had gone as black as thunder. "I think I have my answer, anyway."

Yes, he would have concluded from her reaction that this was not a child she had desired.

He tightened his hold around her and she melted into the embrace. Once again, just like when he had welcomed them under his roof, he was offering reassurance and understanding without asking for anything in return, without even understanding what had happened.

"How did you know I had been sick?" she asked when she finally drew back.

"Asta came to find me. She saw you as she came back from Steinar's hut," he explained. "She said you were dying, because you had been sick, like her father had been right before dying."

By the gods. This was terrible. After losing both her parents, the poor girl would have been terrified of losing her also. "Yes," she said, as understanding dawned. "Her father was terribly seasick from the moment we set off and he spent his time throwing up overboard. But that had nothing to do with what killed him in the end. As I told you, he died of his injuries."

Eirik nodded. "Yes, but if that happened it's easy to see why she would have made the link between being sick and dying."

"It is. I have to go to her, reassure her," Freyja said, already making her way to the hut. She could not let the little girl worry.

"I'll come with you." He paused before they could enter the hut and drew her into his arms again. She melted, again. "Wait. What will you tell her?" he whispered in her ear.

Freyja bit her lip. Should she tell the little girl what was happening? It wouldn't be long before her stomach started to swell since she was now more than two months gone. It was not hard to know precisely when she had fallen with child. There had been only one night it could have happened, and unfortunately, she remembered it all too well.

"I will give her a few more days to settle in before I tell her anything," Freyja decided. She, too, needed time to adjust to the situation, accept that she was to give birth in a few months' time. "She's had a lot to deal with recently. I will just say that I ate something that didn't agree with me."

Eirik nodded and opened the door.

After her shocking revelation, things reverted to normal between Freyja and Eirik. They behaved as if he had not pleasured her most scandalously, as if she had not revealed what was happening deep within her.

As if they could carry on with their odd arrangement.

But surely they could not. In the space of one day, everything had been turned on its head. For a brief moment they'd thought they could share something based on desire, even if it could not lead to anything. Then the following morning, even before they'd had a chance to talk about what he'd done to her and why, Freyja had been forced to accept that what she had dreaded would happen after the assault had come true—she had fallen with child.

As much as the oath Eirik had taken all those years ago, if not more, this prevented anything from ever evolving between them. Even if he'd felt desire for her before, he would no longer. Who would want a woman carrying another man's child? How long before he told her that their arrangement was over?

No, on that account at least she had nothing to worry about. She knew that Eirik would keep her and Asta safe until they found out for sure the threat Harald represented was lifted. Until the winter, and the departure of the last merchant boat, she was assured of a haven in his hut. Then she would be nearing her term, and would have to find a solution to her predicament. She would have to go see Wolf again. With his connections, he might have an idea of where she could go.

To Freyja's shock, in that following week, her stomach started to expand. She now looked unmistakably like a woman with child. Even if she had not been sick for the last few days, she would have known something was not quite right. Unsure what to make of this development, she went to see Cwenthryth. A midwife would know what was happening.

"I see nothing odd in the way this is going," her new friend explained, probing around her stomach gently. "It sometimes happens like this. Once the mother has realized or accepted that she is with child, it starts to show."

Yes, she had certainly realized it. How could it be otherwise when she was sick every morning and her breasts had grown so tender? Had she accepted it? That was another thing, and remained to be seen.

"It also helps that you feel more relaxed. Your body is allowing itself to grow."

"Do I feel more relaxed?"

In truth, she felt far from calm. In just a few months, she would have to give birth to a child she hadn't planned. She wasn't sure she knew how or where she would welcome it, and the idea was enough to send her into a flurry of panic.

"I mean, you are not worried about being pursued any longer," Cwenthryth specified when she saw her reaction. Of course, by now Steinar would have told her all about Harald and the threat he represented. "You know you're safe in the village, that the men will look after you and Asta."

Yes, this much she knew at least.

"Thank you, you have put my mind at rest." As much as it could anyway.

"No problem. Come back whenever you need to."

Freyja left the hut in a pensive mood and decided to go for a walk to put some order to her thoughts. Because she wasn't sure where Harald was, she didn't dare go into the forest, which was the place she most wanted to go. A wander around the village would have to do for now, until she knew for certain she was safe.

She placed a hand over her swollen stomach. Apparently, there was nothing extraordinary in the fact that her body showed what it had kept secret until then. It was perfectly normal. Still, Freyja could not help but marvel at the difference. Hidden under her clothes the bulge might pass unnoticed but that morning, as she'd lain in bed in the early hours, she had taken the time to explore her changing body, to touch the proof that she was going to be a mother.

She was going to be a mother.

How did she feel about that?

Torn would be a good way to describe it. Unquestionably, she could not rejoice, because this babe had been imposed upon her. But on the other hand, she had always wanted to bear children. And the man who had planted his seed inside her had not been a stranger who'd pounced before she understood what was happening, like Eirik's father had been.

Eirik...

He had increasingly been in her thoughts of late.

Living with him had brought back some of her peace of mind. It was not just that he was seeing to her comfort by day, giving her a bed to sleep in at night, and a safe place in which to get to know Asta. It was all the rest. She never had to justify herself with him. He was enjoying listening to her stories of her homeland, he laughed when she attempted a jest, he made her feel worthy and beautiful.

How had she ever thought him dour and gruff?

She stilled when she understood why she was feeling so content, despite the admittedly upsetting circumstances.

Eirik was giving her back what she'd once had with Arvid. What she had missed so much. What she had thought never to have again. How could that be? They had only known one another for a month, and she was with him not because she had wanted to be, but because Wolf had suggested she should stay with him. The Icelander could have sent her to anyone else in the village but he had chosen Eirik. She could only be grateful for this decision.

She shook her head and made her way back toward the hut.

As she drew near the pigpen, she looked at the spider's web, which had become an automatic gesture. But today there were no translucent droplets clinging to it, nor was it quivering in the breeze. It was gone. Only tattered remains clung to the posts. The sight tore at her heart. So much effort, ruined, so much beauty, gone.

Was it an omen? Was everything she was trying to build in the village destined to be ripped from her? Freyja shivered and all but ran into the hut.

9

———

"Ah, Eirik, there you are." Ketill, his neighbor's son walked straight over to him, an uncertain smile playing on his lips. "I realize now that I forgot to tell you something. The other day I met a man in the forest as I was coming back to the village. He was looking for the Danish woman and her little girl, the ones who are staying with you, you know. I told him they had arrived about a—"

"What the fuck?" Eirik exploded, before remembering that Ketill had no reason to suspect foul play, no reason to lie. Of course, he would have answered the man's question honestly, why would he not? He had no idea of the danger Freyja was in, no reason to be suspicious of Harald. Still, Eirik couldn't help but allow his anger to burst out of him. This could have potentially devastating consequences. "Why the hell didn't you keep your mouth shut?"

"I-I...well she's here, is she not?" The youth seemed panicked by his reaction. "He said he was the girl's uncle, so I didn't think he—"

"What else did he say?"

"Nothing. He nodded and headed toward the town. I

99

thought it odd, because I thought he might want to go see his niece, but he—"

"Yes. Thank you for telling me, Ketill."

The boy hastened away, only too glad to escape unharmed after angering him.

When he was alone again, Eirik kicked the fence post next to him. Damnation, now Harald knew he'd been lied to. Worse, he knew where to find the girl he was looking for, and the woman who had thwarted him. It would not be long before he came back to the village, seeking retribution. Why hadn't he done so already? It had been more than two weeks since he'd spoken to Ketill. There had been more than enough time for him to get organized and mount an expedition. He would want to get Asta back and take his revenge on Freyja. So why hadn't he come?

Eirik slammed his fist into the post by his side. Should he go to the harbor now with a group of friends to make sure Harald understood he was in no way to try and even see his niece? Should he tell Freyja that, unlike what they had thought, the man knew where she was? They had allowed themselves to believe that she was safe, if not permanently, at least for now but this news changed everything.

His question was answered when he turned and saw her standing in the door frame, looking at him with wide eyes, fear etched all over her face.

He rushed to her side, barely resisting the urge to take her into his arms. Then there was no need to resist it, because she threw herself against his chest.

"It's all right," he soothed, closing his arms around her. "I'm here. He's not getting to you. Ketill made a mistake but we won't let it matter. I won't leave the village again. I'm here."

She was trembling against him and he hated it. In her state she should not get agitated. "This is too dangerous. Asta and I should leave, we should—"

"No." Anything but that. They were not going anywhere. "You are safe here, with people who know they should protect you and why."

With me. I won't let anyone ever hurt you. They would have to kill me first.

He wouldn't allow her to flee again and put herself in danger for doing nothing more than helping a little girl and giving her a good life. She was protecting Asta, and he would protect her and her baby.

"Come. We need something to drink."

THE FOLLOWING MORNING, Eirik came back from the forest laden with mushrooms and herbs. He had promised Freyja he wouldn't leave again, but he had to feed her and Asta. Before leaving he had asked Sven, who could see his hut from his own, to keep an eye out for Harald or anyone acting suspicious. But when asked, his friend reported that nothing had happened.

Reassured, Eirik headed back to his hut. It had been a good morning. He'd even found a rabbit caught in one of the snares he'd set the evening before. Life had taken a turn for the better of late, since Freyja had arrived in the village.

In his house, to be precise.

Having never lived with anyone before, or even considered it, he could not believe the comfort and happiness it brought him. He'd always feared any such arrangement, and now he was wondering why. It was the best thing that could have happened to him.

As soon as he entered the hut, however, his good mood evaporated.

Freyja was pacing around the table, looking frantic. Why? She was not the sort of woman to get flustered easily, it had not taken him long to establish that. What had happened? Unbeknownst to Sven, had she received a visit from Harald while he was out in the forest, gathering food? Damn it all, he should never have left her alone, even for a moment. He should have known the merchant was not going to give up so easily.

"What's wrong?" he asked, taking her by the elbow. If anyone had hurt her or Asta, they would pay. In blood.

She looked at him, her eyes dazed. "I...I lost my baby."

He froze and thought for a moment that he might retch. What the hell? She had lost the child she was carrying? His gaze raked her. She appeared whole, and as healthy as usual. Surely if she had gone through a miscarriage that morning she would be lying on the pallet, pale and wan? Instead she looked flushed and agitated.

Freyja saw his reaction and placed a hand over her stomach. "No, I'm sorry, it's not... It's not that, don't worry. No, I mean, the little wooden bean baby."

Eirik finally allowed himself to breathe. Of course. The memory of her parents.

I lost my baby.

That sentence had sounded awful in the mouth of a woman who was actually with child, but thank the gods, she was only talking about the little carved bean baby. Not that he couldn't see how affected she was, but still, he couldn't help being relieved. At least her life was not in danger, or her sanity.

"When did you realize you had lost it?" He would help her find it.

"I saw just now that there is a hole in my purse. It must have fallen through there..." She was doing her best not to cry, he could tell. The little object meant the world to her, the last link she had to her family and her home. "I went to feed the chickens earlier. What if it fell out there, in the pen, and one of them swallowed it?"

It was not impossible. The creatures would eat anything. But he could not kill them all and check their innards, could he? Even if he had taken the possibility seriously, he guessed Freyja would not have let him do it.

"Oh, it's lost."

Freyja dropped onto the stool, hiding her face in her hands, realizing she had lost her most precious possession.

Though she knew it was ridiculous, she couldn't help but see it as a bad omen. Ironically enough, in the same week she had lost the fake little baby she loved, she had been told that she was going to have a real one.

What next?

Would someone come to take Asta from her, a loving aunt who would take good care of her and have every reason to be reunited with her? Would a letter arrive from Denmark to announce that her sister-in-law had died in childbirth?

"We'll find the bean baby, don't worry," Eirik soothed, as if sensing she was near tears. "Come."

They retraced her steps outside the hut, keeping their gazes on the ground for the little piece of wood that meant so much to her.

But by the time night had fallen, they still had not found anything. Freyja resigned herself to the fact that she would never see it again.

10

Another week passed, and still there was no sign of Harald. Dare Freyja fool herself he'd finally given up, aware he would have a battle on his hands if he tried to get his niece back while she was staying in a village of fierce Norsemen? One could only hope.

Having finished washing the dishes, she made her way back to the hut. Her waist was growing thicker by the day, or so it seemed. The bulge at her stomach was now very noticeable. She would have to find another dress soon. Perhaps she could ask Aife or Cwenthryth if they had some fabric or an old dress she could modify. Fortunately, her parents had insisted on giving her silver before she left, so she could purchase what she needed.

At the hut, Eirik was waiting for her. There was a gleam in his eyes she couldn't quite place and that made her nervous.

"What happened?" she asked cautiously. That gleam was not dissimilar to the one he'd had on the few occasions she'd thought he would kiss her. Was that what was on his mind? Was he about to kiss her? Asta was nowhere to be seen. As usual, she had fled to Rothgar as soon as she had finished eating, so she would be no deterrent.

"I have something for you. Give me your hand."

Oh. Evidently she'd gotten it completely wrong and she was the only one thinking of kisses. The idea was not reassuring.

She held out her palm and watched as he placed an object on it. Freyja gasped when she saw what it was. Encased in precious, shiny metal, the little baby bean was looking at her. Above its head was a small loop, through which a delicate, beautiful metal chain had been threaded. The modest wooden sculpture had been transformed into the most beautiful piece of jewelry. She stared at it a long moment then lifted her gaze to Eirik, who shrugged, as if it was nothing extraordinary that he should have restored it to her in such an unexpected manner.

"I found it in one corner of the hut, where it will have been kicked, the day after you told me you had lost it. I wanted to tell you immediately, but then I thought there might be a better way... I asked Caedmon, the village goldsmith, to fashion it into a pendant. It seemed the best way to ensure you didn't lose it again. I hope you don't mind."

Mind? No, she didn't mind. It was beautiful. And the most thoughtful thing anyone had ever done for her.

"I don't know what to say."

"No need to say anything. Just let me."

Eirik held out his hand in much the same way she had done earlier. She understood he wanted to place the chain around her neck himself. Oh. Should she let him? When she gave it to him, he gestured that she should turn around. Heart beating hard, she did as she was asked. Unwise as it may be, she could not refuse him. The feel of his knuckles on the sensitive skin of her neck when he brushed her hair to the side was enough to make her close her eyes. So sensual... A memory of what he had done to her the other night brought heat to her loins. Surely he would not start stroking her now, here, in the middle of the day?

No. He took his time, and he reduced her to a puddle of need in the process, but finally, the chain was fastened around her neck.

"Here. You will never lose your baby again," he murmured, his voice rich and deep in her ear, before taking a step back.

A hand over the pendant, Freyja turned around. Knowing that her precious possession was now as safe as it could be was a wonderful feeling. Eirik had done that for her. How could she express her gratitude? Lifting herself onto her tiptoes, she kissed him.

It was a sweet kiss meant to be a thank you but that turned into an inferno as soon as Eirik put his hands on her waist. It was as if someone had brought a torch in contact with a sheaf of straw—their bodies just caught ablaze and desire took over, wiping away everything that was not them and their need to touch. Their tongues started a slow, wanton dance, little grunts escaped their lips and their hips ground one against the other in search for more friction.

When Eirik's hands landed on her buttocks and lifted her to him so she could feel the strength of his arousal, they moaned at the same time, then drew back, shock etched all over their faces.

"I'm sorry," he whispered, "I didn't mean..."

"Me neither."

She hadn't meant to kiss him as if her life depended on him, as if they were, or could be, a couple. He had touched her intimately once, but this had felt more significant somehow, not a call of the senses but a cry from the soul.

And yet, it was a mistake. They could not kiss ever again. It was too personal. She was having someone else's baby and he had sworn never to bed a woman. It was obvious they could never be together.

"Your lips are so soft," he murmured, looking as dazed as if he'd made a discovery.

Absurdly, she felt like telling him his were as well. But it didn't sound like a very masculine thing to tell him, even if it were true. "You...taste as good as your mead," she said instead, before berating herself.

What a ridiculous thing to say! She would have cringed in embarrassment but the gleam in Eirik's eyes told her he didn't think her ridiculous at all. Even better, she had the impression he had never received a compliment that had pleased him more. Had he even kissed anyone? It wouldn't surprise her if he hadn't, in the circumstances, and he had looked awed by the experience. What had he thought? He'd mentioned the softness of her lips, but did she taste, smell, feel as good as he had hoped?

She took a step back, intimidated all of a sudden. He was so strong, he was looking at her with such intensity... What could she say?

The words were out before she could think. "Thank you."

Was she thanking him for the pendant? For the kiss? For wanting to pleasure her the other day? For the calm way with which he had welcomed the shocking news she had imparted to him the previous week? She had no idea.

But he nodded, as if he understood anyway. "You're welcome."

THE FOLLOWING MORNING, Freyja finally found the courage to ask Eirik what she had meant to ask him for days.

"Would you show me how you make your pottery?"

He stilled, as if unsure he'd heard her correctly—or as if he didn't want to show her how he created the pieces. "Why would you want to see that?"

She felt herself flush. "I don't know. I guess I have no idea how you do it and I'm curious."

"You mean that you want to learn how to make pottery?"

No. That was not what she meant. But she couldn't tell him the truth, that she wanted to watch him handling the delicate clay and shaping it into something unique, wanted an excuse to look at him while he worked, wanted to discover yet another fascinating side of him. He would refuse if she said that.

"No. I don't think I would be good at it anyway."

"You don't know until you try."

She smiled. He was always so encouraging. "For today, I would like to see you. You will at least agree I have to know what to do if I decide to try."

He returned her smile, eyes glinting with mischief. Oh, how had she ever thought that man gruff? No one smiled like him, with such unfettered joy. "I will agree to that. Very well," he said, rolling his sleeves to his elbow. "You can watch me. Sit down."

Even better. She would definitely watch.

While she settled herself at the table Eirik scooped a handful of clay from the pot on the floor next to the door. She guessed this was where he'd deposited the mud he'd collected in his basket the other day.

He rolled and twisted it in his hands a moment. Once it was the consistency he wanted, he started kneading it slowly on the table in front of her. Lovingly. As odd as it was, that was the word that came to Freyja's mind. He was not beating the stiff dough into submission, pummeling it, or even handling it roughly—quite the opposite. He was caressing it. It was fascinating, soothing to watch.

And, well... also very arousing. Surely she was not the only one thinking that this was a lot more sensual and intimate than it had the right to be? Eirik's every gesture sent ripples of delight along her spine, burrowing under her skin and reaching deep to the core of her womanhood. She couldn't detach her gaze from him. Fortunately, he was too focused on his task to notice.

Freyja was thinking that it couldn't get any worse when it

did just that. Straightening back up, Eirik pressed his thumb into the middle of the ball he'd shaped, creating a deep depression which he widened slowly by repeating the gesture many times, while turning the clay in his palm. The muscles on his forearm twisted and corded as he did, pulsing in rhythm with the movement. Freyja thought she was going to pass out from desire. Everything within her was hot and tingling.

She must have let out a moan because Eirik glanced at her, brow arched. Then his expression changed.

Heat instantly seared her insides, moving like a wave, rushing from her skull down to her toes. She knew what he was thinking. The same as what she was thinking. That this was reminiscent of a woman's sheath—and his caresses very evocative. Here he was, nudging, brushing, stroking, creating an opening in the clay that yielded to his touch, like she had that day in the tub.

By the gods, it was the most erotic moment of her life and she was utterly entranced. No wonder the man was so skilled at pleasuring women. No wonder he had coaxed responses out of her body that were unprecedented. He had total mastery over his fingers, using them without thinking, applying just the right amount of pressure where it was needed, allowing him to do what he wanted.

"See?"

Oh, yes, she could most definitely see.

"I..." She couldn't breathe or say more.

Tilting his head at her response, he went back to the bowl that had appeared in his hands as if conjured up by magic. He smoothed the sides, flattened the bottom by tapping it gently on the table then cut the top flat with a knife. Freyja watched on, her throat dry. It was obvious he had done this a hundred times and could have made a perfect bowl in his sleep. He made it look so easy. And yet everything was perfect. The smoothness, the proportions, the thinness.

"Here, all finished," he said, plunging his hands into the basin of water next to him.

And once again, she could do nothing but watch, as he scrubbed his elegant fingers clean one by one, getting rid of the mud.

"Have you ever decorated bowls with scratchings or a pattern of holes along the rim for example?" she asked, desperate to make it appear as if she was thinking of pottery instead of what else he could do—to her—with those nimble fingers.

Eirik frowned. "Do you know, I've never thought to do anything like that. I always leave them plain." He crossed his arms over his chest, considering. "It could work but I'm not sure I would be very good at it. That's a different skill altogether. My friend Torsten would do a good job, he's very skilled at carving shapes into wood and bone. I could ask him. Or even better, I could ask you."

"M-me?"

"You said you were good at embroidery. This will not be very different, I guess. Take something sharp and puncture little dots into the clay while it's wet enough. Try."

As soon as he had mentioned the possibility Freyja was seized with the need to do just that, decorate this beautiful bowl, leave her mark on something he had made. And it would be more than a line of holes.

"Do you have a needle?"

"No, sorry." He rubbed the back of his head, as if embarrassed by the admission. "When I need to mend my clothes, I usually borrow one from my sister. Not that I'm great at it, mind you, I just do my best not to damage the garment further. Do you want me to go over there and ask?"

She shook her head. "No. Let me go get a feather from the

chicken enclosure. The tip will be hard enough for our purpose, I should think. Even a thin piece of straw would do." Now that she had made her mind up she would not be deterred or delayed.

"Yes," Eirik agreed, following her outside. "Then it will be my turn to watch you."

Freyja almost tripped at the announcement. It would seem she had not thought this through. How would she fare working under his heated gaze? Was this a good idea? As if to ensure she would indeed have to decorate the bowl in front of Eirik, they found a couple of sturdy feathers as soon as they opened the gate to the chicken run. One was a shimmering copper, the other black with greenish ripples. Beautiful. They brought them back inside, to the bowl waiting in the middle of the table.

"Use this one," Eirik instructed, handing her the red feather.

"Why?" She frowned and tested the tip of the one she had already selected, the black one. Did he think this one too soft? It wasn't, even if it was slightly thinner, which was why she had chosen it. She wanted the details to be as delicate as possible.

"The color is almost identical to your hair."

With this, he took a lock of her hair and twisted it around his forefinger. All the air left Freyja's lungs. What was the man doing to her? That simple gesture had wreaked havoc through her. Was he trying to seduce her, or was it all in her mind? Either way, she could not give in. The kiss they had exchanged the other day proved it. She desired him too much. If they touched, there would be no stopping her. She would push him down onto the pallet and make him give her what he had sworn never to give any woman.

With a trembling hand, she took the feather he was handing her. "I suppose I'd better start before the clay dries too much," she said, her voice hoarse.

Though what she would achieve she wasn't sure. With her

mind in turmoil and her body quivering with desire, she might well ruin Eirik's beautiful bowl.

"Do you know what you're going to do?"

"No." She hadn't the faintest idea. "All I know is I don't want to spoil what you made."

He gave a snort. "Don't worry. If you do, I'll just roll it back into a ball and start again. This is what is good about pottery. Mistakes can be erased."

Yes. If only it were the same in life. But in life, it was the opposite. Every decision had a consequence, one that had to be taken into account from that point on. There was no going back, only adapting.

Freyja sat back down. What could she draw? Her gaze flicked to Eirik's right bicep, where the outline of his arm ring could be seen under the thin linen of his shirt. And suddenly she knew. She would use flowing, intricate lines like the ones adorning his arm ring, and make them into apple tree branches, her favorite tree. That way the drawing would be a bit of him and her intertwined together in a way they could never be in real life.

Decision made, she took the bowl in hand. It felt heavy and wet, unlike what she had imagined, almost alive. She started by tracing wavy lines running around the rim then added clusters of flowers representing the snowy blossoms appearing on the trees at the arrival of spring. At first, as predicted, she was very aware of Eirik's gaze on her, but she soon forgot it and lost herself to the task. It was nothing like embroidery, in truth, but she was able to apply her skills to distribute the blooms in a pleasing pattern. Lastly, she scattered a few petals here and there and pricked tiny holes at the center of the flowers to represent the stamen.

It was finished. And the result wasn't bad at all. Eirik, at least, seemed very impressed.

"If you can do something like that with a hen feather and

some clay on your first try, I'm curious to see what you can do with a needle and thread."

She shrugged. "I've been embroidering since I could hold a needle so I suppose there is no merit in me being skilled, as you said. And most women embroider, whereas you create something truly unique." Even if other people made pottery, they didn't produce such unusual or delicate objects. "Thank you for showing me how you did it. It was most enlightening."

Sitting as she was, he towered over her and she had to lift her head to meet his gaze. He held out his hand to her and helped her stand up.

"It was my pleasure to show you, Freyja. Now I will have to cook the bowl. When it's ready it will be yours."

"Thank you."

She would cherish the gift, a souvenir of the most desire-charged moment in her life. Together they had created something beautiful and unique. Tears started to sting her eyes. She brushed them away with an angry hand, but there seemed to be no stopping them and despite her efforts, a couple fell on her cheeks. No! She couldn't cry now. She had promised herself she would not. But weeks after having made the most shocking discovery of her life and pretending nothing was happening inside her body, she couldn't help it.

It *was* happening, she was having this baby.

Alone.

"Why are you crying?" Eirik asked softly, wiping the tears from her cheek.

He hadn't expected Freyja to cry now. They had spent a very enjoyable moment making the bowl together, and now... What had upset her? Was it something he'd said? He didn't think so. And it had seemed to him that she had liked watching him make the bowl. In fact, if he didn't know better, he would have thought she'd been aroused, as much as he had been. Never would he have thought that making pottery would be something to rouse his senses, but then again, never had he done it in front of a woman before, a woman who was looking at him as if she wanted to eat him whole.

But now she was sobbing, the sound piercing a hole through his heart.

"After the—" She stopped, as if about to mention something she would rather keep secret and swallowed. "After leaving Denmark I d-didn't think I would ever feel joy in my life. Everything had been destroyed. I didn't think I would know the simple satisfaction of creating something n-new," she stammered, struggling to breathe between sobs. She placed both her hands over her midriff, fingers splayed, cheeks streaked with tears. "But now…I am most definitely creating something new."

"You are." He was so moved he could hardly talk himself but he had to. He had to reassure her. "A baby, the most beautiful thing in this world."

"But I don't know if I'm capable of having this baby," she said, the words exploding out of her with unwonted ferocity. It seemed to him that she had struggled with the notion for weeks and was finally allowing herself to acknowledge the harsh reality, say out loud what she thought deep down. "Don't you see? I'm scared, more scared than I've ever been in my life."

"Of course, you're capable of having this child." Eirik understood her fears, which he shared, even if he tried not to dwell on it. Giving birth could be a dangerous time for a woman, and Freyja was so small she would be a fool not to worry about it. "I know it is your first child, but Cwenthryth and Helga will be here to help and—"

"I don't mean that I'm worried about delivering the babe, even if I am. I mean I'm scared of—" She stopped and skewered him with the most intense, pain-filled stare he had ever received in his life, one that sliced at his guts. "What if I cannot love it?

My own child? What if I look at it and all I see is his father, as he labored over me? How will I bear it? It wasn't supposed to happen like that. A mother is not supposed to resent her child! I wasn't supposed to be alone to welcome it into the world!"

It was too much. Her pain was too much, his own suffering was too much. Sharing it would help them both.

Eirik swept Freyja into his arms, cradling her tight against his chest while she wept. He let her cry, did not try to soothe her in any other way than by holding her. She had held on to her fears and doubts for too long. For weeks he had watched her go on as if nothing had changed. Something had to give.

"It will be fine," he said eventually, feeling her going limp against him. "You love Asta like a daughter, even though you didn't carry her. That alone should tell you that you will have no problem loving a child of your loins. I know it. You can trust all will be fine."

He did trust her.

And for the second time in his life, this time while holding a trembling woman in his arms, Eirik made a secret oath.

Whatever happened, Freyja wouldn't be alone to raise her child.

11

———

After Freyja's outburst, as could have been expected, Eirik spent an agitated night. He couldn't stop thinking of the look on her face at the idea of what was to come. He would have liked nothing more than to lie with her in his arms again, but with Asta in the hut, this time it was not possible. The memory of the night they had spent together after he had coaxed pleasure out of her was torturing him, making it impossible to fall asleep. Lying on his left side made no difference, he simply could not relax enough to even close his eyes. To add to his dismay, he heard Freyja stir long into the night as well. Imagining her in bed wearing only her shift, twisting and writhing, only caused his loins to heat up. And everyone, even him, knew men could not go to sleep while hard as nails.

At dawn, he went out for a swim, his usual way of putting order in his thoughts. Usually, he took it slowly, taking the time to admire the sky as he floated on his back. This time, he kept his head down and only stopped when his lungs begged for a respite, because today it was not so much his thoughts that bothered him as much as the tingling in his groin. He would exhaust his body into surrender and hope the water would help cool his blood.

When he entered the village again, Arne was cutting wood outside his hut, one of the few people out and about at this hour.

"Eirik," he called out when he saw him walk past, "do you have a moment?"

"Of course."

"I was wondering if you could make a batch of mead for me. No one does it quite like you do. I will give you a silver coin for it."

Eirik snorted. The man was not known for his generosity. This offer was unprecedented. "What happened? Have you sold your father's sword to a pedlar?" He would not be above doing such a treacherous thing.

Arne laughed. "Not yet, though I'm thinking of it. The rusty old thing is of no use to me, is it? I'm no warrior, like he was. No, I only did my friend a favor in town and he paid me in coin, would you believe it."

It was best not to ask what that favor had been. Knowing his friend, it was bound to be something Eirik had rather not hear about.

"You do know you'll have to wait for the mead to be ready?" It was not as if he could speed up the fermentation process to please anyone, even if he had been offered a king's ransom. "I do have a batch I started about two weeks ago, though, so you can have this one. It'll be faster."

For a silver coin, he could afford to be magnanimous. And the boon had come at the right time. He had already decided to go into town during the week to buy a bolt of cloth for Freyja. With her stomach expanding, she would need to make herself a new dress soon. He had already seen she only had one extra dress in her bag, and it was the same cut as the one she was currently wearing—in other words, soon to be too small.

"Thanks. I am not a patient man, as you know, but I can wait, when it's for a good cause." Arne slapped him on the back and winked. "Anyway, how is the Danish girl Wolf entrusted to you? We haven't seen much of her, have we? It's almost as if you were keeping her to yourself."

Eirik's smile disappeared from his face. "She's well, thank you," he said, his voice suddenly icy. What was it to the man how Freyja was?

Arne didn't let the change in mood deter him. "Have you bedded her yet?"

"No. Not that it's any of your business."

Only his brothers—and now Freyja—knew about the oath he had made on his sixteenth birthday. Because he had pleasured many a woman, everyone assumed he had a normal love life, even if people had come to the conclusion that he would probably never marry.

"What are you waiting for? She's beautiful."

Yes, she was, but Eirik hated to hear another man say it. Not that he was jealous, he told himself sternly, but it grated on him to see that her appearance, which she owed to her parents, was the one thing Arne had chosen to praise about her.

She was beautiful, stunning in fact—he would remember forever how she had stood, naked, in the tub the other day—but there were so many other things to admire about her.

He loved the way she spoke, with an accent stronger than anyone else in the village. He loved her courage. Traveling alone across seas to come settle in another country was no mean feat. He loved her generosity. What she was doing for Asta was beautiful and selfless. He loved her ability to get on with everyone. In just a few short weeks she had become close friends with Aife, Cwenthryth, and Eahlswith. He loved her resilience. Many women would have collapsed upon being told they were to bear their attacker's child, understandably so, but she was bearing it with dignity and courage. He loved—

It was when he stopped himself from finishing that sentence that Eirik knew he was in deep trouble.

He'd made it almost twenty years without falling for a woman.

It seemed he would not make another week. It was already too late.

"*Faðir,* can I have a word with you?"

Sigurd raised his head at the question. Apparently, it was obvious that the conversation would be a serious one, because he dropped the willow branches he'd just taken out of the soaking tank and led Eirik to the bench by the side of the hut. The weaving of a new basket would have to wait. This could not.

"Of course, Son."

Son.

Eirik swallowed hard. The whole reason he was here was summed up in that one word. This man, who had not sired him, considered him as his son, making no difference between him and his other two boys, though only Moon was of his loins.

"Did you have something to ask me?" Sigurd asked when silence stretched between them.

Yes. That was one way of putting it. Taking a deep inhale, Eirik finally spoke.

"How on earth did you deal with the terrible knowledge that the babe your wife was carrying had been forced upon her? How did you make the decision to raise me as your own? How did you manage to love such a child? To love...me, all the while knowing what I represented?"

There was another long pause, during which he stared at his

feet. Then Sigurd forced him to look up and meet his gaze before he answered.

"I dealt with that terrible knowledge because there was no other choice." His blue eyes bore into him. "If I had not, if I had bolted like a coward when your mother told me she was with child, I would have left her to deal with what was a nightmare on her own. And *that*, I could never have done. I knew from the moment I saw her that she was the only woman for me. The least I could do was offer my support, and thank the gods she accepted it. I never really made the decision to raise you as my own, because I felt you were mine from the moment I found out the woman I loved was carrying you. Meeting you only confirmed it. You were mine—I knew it as soon as I set eyes on you, lying on your mother's body, so beautiful and innocent. Loving you was the easiest thing I have ever done. You were the best boy any father could have. You're now a man I am proud to have raised, and I will call you my own until the day I die."

Eirik fell into his father's arms, too moved to answer. He'd always known he was an integral part of the family, but hearing it repeated so unequivocally said was beyond humbling.

"What's brought this on?" Sigurd asked when they drew back. He sounded worried, as if he feared being told Eirik wanted to deny his family and leave the village. But that would never happen.

"Freyja is with child. Just over two months, by her estimation."

He could tell his father was confused, and no wonder. It sounded as if he was telling him he had gotten her with child, despite the fact that she had only been here for about a month. But of course Eirik was not the father of the babe, could not be. They had never lain together, even if people probably assumed they had.

"How is that—"

"She was raped in Denmark." Though she had not told him as much, he guessed that was the reason why she had fled the country, to get away from her attacker and the memories associated with him—and perhaps the danger he represented. Had there only been one assault? For the first time, he wondered if that was the case. Shortly after his wedding, his friend Steinar had confided to him the fact that his wife had been the victim of a man posing as her half-brother for months. Had Freyja known the same fate? It didn't bear thinking about.

"Raped?" His father's face became a mask of fury. It was not hard to guess what he was thinking about. His own wife, raped and left to carry her attacker's babe as a result. "I hope Rune gave the bastard what he deserved," he said through gritted teeth.

Yes, Eirik had thought the same thing. All he knew about the man who'd been called Devil by the local Saxons pointed to him making his daughter's attacker pay for what he'd done. And rightly so. Eirik wished he could spend a moment with the bastard, make him suffer for what he'd done and ensure he didn't hurt anyone else ever again.

"I know not what happened to the man. Freyja refuses to talk about it." He shook his head, knowing he would not have the strength to press her for more details if she didn't want to share them with him. "She only told me she was with child because I walked in on her retching one morning."

He wasn't sure she would have said anything had he not seen the irrefutable proof himself, though how she had hoped to hide her increasing stomach from him was anyone's guess. But perhaps she hadn't worried about that because she had imagined she would leave the village before it started to show.

The thought that she could be gone before the end of the year, or rather the pain that it caused him to imagine himself without her, proved that he was in even deeper than he had ever thought possible, and that this conversation with his father was crucial.

"This is why I'm here," he said softly. "I want to do for her and her innocent babe what you did for my mother and me. I want to offer Freyja a chance at a happy life but I don't know if I can." It could be dangerous. Would it not bring to the surface the demons he had tried so hard to bury? "I don't know if I'm strong enough."

His father didn't even hesitate. "The simple fact that you want to do it means that you're strong enough."

Eirik wasn't sure he quite agreed but he didn't comment. This proof of trust meant everything to him. And perhaps he would be strong enough. It was like his father had said. It was not as if he had a choice anyway. He could not let Freyja face this alone.

"In any case, I cannot think of anyone more suited to the task." There was another silence then his father spoke again. "You love her, I take it?"

Yes, he must do, Eirik realized, to constantly be thinking about her, to want to protect her, to want to offer her and her child a chance.

By an odd twist of fate, if he married her, he would find himself in exactly the same position as his father had been. Married to a woman carrying a baby forced on her, and the two of them parents to a child that didn't share their blood. He, of all people, knew that such a family could work.

"I think I do. I think that what I feel for her is love," he said slowly. "But how can it be? She's only been here for a few weeks."

And I had sworn to live my life alone.

His father gave a rueful smile. "That doesn't mean a thing. It took me just a few days to fall in love with your mother. Hell, I often wonder if I didn't fall for her the moment she appeared in the village, looking like all my impossible dreams had come true." For a moment he appeared lost in reminiscing, then he shook his head. "In any case, this isn't about me. I'm just saying that it is possible to know in a heartbeat."

"Yes, perhaps."

"Definitely. So go speak to her."

Eirik didn't go straight to see Freyja. He needed time to absorb all his father had told him and accept the fact that he was going to break a twenty-year-old oath for a woman he had known for less than a month—and that he didn't even mind.

Instead he went for another swim in the lake, the place where he took refuge in times of need.

And never had he needed it more than now, when his life was about to change.

"I WILL MARRY YOU, if you will have me."

Thunder fell at Freyja's feet. Eirik had come back to the hut a moment ago, his wet hair indicating that he had been to the lake for a wash or a swim—or both. She had forced herself not to dwell on how mouth-watering it made him look, without much success.

As she was putting her embroidery away, he'd made his shocking announcement. And now here she was, blinking at him in disbelief, trying to make sense of what she'd just heard.

"I b-beg your pardon?"

Had he really said he would marry her?

Eirik placed himself in front of her. "You needed a place to stay and protection when you arrived in the village. It was my honor to provide that place and that protection. Now this inno-cent babe needs a father. I will be that father."

Tentatively, as if he feared her reaction, he placed a hand

over her stomach. It was hard and unyielding, unmistakingly rounded. His fingers slid lovingly over the curve. Something fluttered in her stomach. Not the babe? It was too early to feel it, surely? No, it had to be the emotion provoked within her by Eirik's words and his touch, because her eyes were also burning.

He wanted to be here for her, help her through this nightmare. And she wanted him to be here for her, for this babe she was not ready for and had no idea how to welcome on her own.

But she could not let him do what he intended to do. How cruel.

"I'm sorry, Eirik," she said on a sob. "We cannot marry."

His hand on her stomach stilled. "If you're referring to the oath I took when I became a man, then it—"

"No," she cut him off before he started to think that this was his fault. It wasn't. It was hers. "I'm referring to the one I took thirteen years ago."

She could tell he was confused, and no wonder. This was a secret she'd kept from everyone, even Wolf. It was time to finally tell Eirik what the situation was.

Freyja swallowed hard. Could she do it? Would he not hate her for not being honest from the start, for letting him believe they could be together? Would she find the strength to tell her story?

With the desperation of someone throwing themselves off a cliff, knowing certain death was awaiting them, she said, "I'm already married. My husband, Arvid, is in Denmark. That is why I'm here. I left him."

It was Eirik's turn to feel thunder fall at his feet. At least, he looked as if he'd been turned into stone. For a long moment, she waited. This was the moment he would fly into a rage and tell her she should have told him before.

But when he spoke, what he said took her by surprise.

"You are married. And that man didn't kill the bastard who

raped you? He just allowed you to leave instead? Where is he? Why did he not set off after you?"

She closed her eyes. Trust him to immediately think of her protection. But the situation was not what he imagined.

"You don't understand. That man who raped me... He was my husband."

12

———

er *husband* was the man who'd raped Freyja.

Fucking hell, that meant it might well be as he'd thought earlier, that she'd had to endure abuse for months, if not years since the moment she got married.

Eirik closed his eyes and flexed his bicep, the one with the arm ring, the left one. It had become a reflex. Every time he needed to be reminded of his oath, he did this. The tightness around his muscle was like the very physical manifestation of the constraint he'd placed around his life, and he always drew strength from it.

Even after all these years, he could still remember the day his father had placed the arm ring on his bicep. The coolness of the metal had been like a branding of sorts. As he'd looked at the beautiful object that signified his acceptance into a family that should never have been his, determination had solidified in his heart.

He would become a man, as that could not be helped. But he would be a good man. He would never, *ever* hurt a woman, like the bastard who had raped his mother. He would never allow his masculine urges to rule him.

He opened his eyes again, brought back to the present by a whimper. Freyja seemed to have collapsed over herself. Pale as death, she was awaiting his comment to her revelation, possibly even reliving the dreadful assault. He could not bear it. Forget what he was thinking, forget his disillusion, in that moment, she needed him.

Without thinking he scooped her into his arms and sat down on the stool behind him, settling her on his lap. The difference in size between them had always pleased him, and never had he had more reason to appreciate it than now, when she needed the comfort of his embrace.

"How many times?"

With her face in the crook of his neck, he felt her swallow. She had understood what he was referring to, then.

"Once."

He wasn't sure if that answer made him feel much better. Once was once too many. "Tell me everything when you're ready."

Eirik clenched his jaw. He'd heard about her parents many times. Based on what he'd been told, he couldn't believe that Rune and Eowyn would have forced any of their daughters to marry a man she didn't love, or even want. So if Freyja had been married to a man she had chosen for herself, how come that man had raped her? He trusted her instinct, she would never have married a bastard of her own free will.

Something here wasn't right, and he couldn't wait to hear what it was.

"I married Arvid the year I turned twenty," she started, keeping her face hidden in the crook of his neck. "He was a farmer and very good with predicting the weather, so our crops were always the most abundant around. He could also tell a good horse from a nag at a glance, which ensured we always sold our animals at a good price. He was meticulous where his tools were concerned, but he was easily distracted, and not the best at keeping his clothes clean."

There she was again, giving him what could be seen as inconsequential details, but they helped him create an image of the man in his mind.

"I see," Eirik said.

And he did see. Arvid was a rough character, with shorter hair than most, a square jaw and a flat nose. An eye for selecting the right animals, but a propensity to take his wife for granted. A carelessness that gave her twice as much work as he should. Or maybe this unflattering image was influenced by his knowledge of what had happened two months ago. But how could he help it?

There was no excuse for rape. Ever.

"To say it was love at first sight would be an exaggeration, but there was an undeniable attraction between us from the moment he came to live in our village," Freyja continued. "After a few months, it did turn into love. Another few months and we got married. Everything was perfect."

Yes. Perfect. Until it wasn't. Or even before that.

She had made it sound as if everything had been perfect *on the surface*. But Eirik knew that wasn't always the case. Steinar had apparently had the perfect marriage to his first wife, Astrid. But then, at her death, things had started to come to light. The "perfect marriage" was anything but. He, himself, appeared like a man happy to go from woman to woman. No one knew he never actually bedded them, or why.

He asked Freyja, his voice soft. "What was the issue that no one saw in this perfect marriage?"

She stilled, as if shocked he should have understood that all had not been right. Then she whispered. "In thirteen years of marriage, my womb didn't quicken once. We wanted a family so this was hard to bear, as you can imagine. People started to talk, wonder if Arvid had scattered bastards all around the place, spurning his wife's bed because she could not give him children."

She put a hand over her swollen stomach and he heard her whimper again. The reason for her anguish was not hard to guess. In more than a decade she had not borne her beloved husband a child, at a time when the three of them would have been a family. And now that she had left him after a dreadful assault, she was going to have to give birth to a babe who would have no father.

The cruel irony would be hard to swallow. In fact, it was enough to make him murderous.

Tightening his hold over her, he waited.

"In the winter, Arvid had an accident," she carried on. "The weather had turned icy overnight, but heedless of the change, we went to the nearest waterfall, a place that had held special meaning for his family for as far back as he could remember. Anyway, the track back down the hill was treacherous, as you can imagine. He slid on a patch of ice and fell." She paused, evidently reliving the whole scene. "He went rolling down and his head hit a rock at the bottom of the slope. There was nothing I could do but watch in horror. I ran for help and some neighbors came with me, and then brought him back home as best as they could. For a while, we feared he wouldn't make it. He just lay on his bed, unaware of what was going on around him."

This was awful but Eirik still didn't see how that could have led to the man raping his wife. If anything, he should have been grateful for her care of him in this difficult time, and appreciated his time with her more.

"After a few days, he seemed to recover. He left the bed without any help, talked normally and ate as if nothing had happened. There was only one problem." A huge problem, if the bleakness in her voice was any indication. Eirik braced himself for the revelation. "He didn't remember me. At all. I was a stranger to him. It was as if the past thirteen years had been erased from his mind."

When Freyja delivered the blow and finally dared to look at him, her eyes were veiled with pain. The depth of her despair was impossible to fathom, the direness of her situation unimaginable. Having her beloved husband look at her as he would at a stranger would have been beyond painful.

Had the man been putting on an act or had his confusion been genuine? Eirik couldn't help but wonder. Had it only been a ploy to rid himself of a wife he no longer wanted and to replace her with someone he'd just met? Such a thing as forgetting the woman you'd married seemed too incredible to be believed, impossibly convenient. And this was Freyja they were talking about. Eirik felt as if he would never forget her as long as he drew breath, and they had known one another for only a little over a month. But in that time she had carved her way into his bones, remodeling his being in the same way he shaped raw clay into whatever he wanted when he made pottery.

"The village healer had heard one such case when she was a young woman, one of her uncles," Freyja said, as if she'd heard his musings. "He had sustained the same kind of injury, a blow to the front of the head. It was rare but not unheard of, she told me. There was nothing to do but wait. If Arvid didn't remember who I was on his own, then nothing or no one would make him remember."

"So you waited, not knowing whether he would finally recognize you." The agony she must have gone through was barely conceivable.

"Yes. In vain. People tried to tell him we were indeed married, but I could see in his eyes he truly had no idea who I was." She took in a deep inhale. "About a week after he woke up, he asked me my name. It was the last blow. I had assumed that he would at least remember this, but he did not. That day I had to accept that the man I had married was no more. In his place was a stranger who refused to accept that I still loved him, who talked to me as if I were a nuisance asking for something he could not give me. Unable to stay with him in those conditions, devastated to see that I meant nothing to him, I went to stay with a friend in the village."

"Of course," Eirik murmured. It would have been unbearable.

"One night, after a few weeks had gone past, Arvid came to find me. He told me he was sorry for the pain he was causing me. He said he wanted to try and bed me, to see if it helped jolt his memory." She paused. "I agreed. At this point I was desperate. If there was a chance it would work, then it was worth a try. And after all, *I* remembered him—he was still the man I had married, the man I had loved, even if weeks of solitude had made me see that nothing would ever be the same between us. But perhaps, I could make him fall in love with me again? Or even if I could not, perhaps having me in his arms would indeed jolt his memory? Despite the healer's words, I found myself hoping a night together would bring back the man I loved, even if only for a moment. I was so miserable without him."

She bit her bottom lip, as if she hoped he wouldn't think less of her for agreeing to go to the man. He did not. What she was saying made sense, and he defied anyone to have acted differently than she had. Of course, she would have wanted to try anything to save her marriage, to make the man she loved see her as he had once seen her.

But still, everything within Eirik coiled, because now he understood where this was going.

Things had not gone the way she had hoped.

"I followed Arvid to our house and to our bed, but as soon as he touched me, I knew it had been a mistake to agree to his proposition. It would never work. It was nothing like it had been before. He was...different. Cold. There was this light in his eyes that frightened me. He kept saying that if I insisted we were married, I might as well prove it by doing my duty by him. It quickly became obvious that he didn't intend to use our joining as a way to get us close again, only to satisfy his lust. He didn't care about my feelings, only that, as his wife, I 'owed' him this. That's what he said." Freyja closed her eyes and seemed to collapse over herself. "I began to struggle, to tell him I didn't want him if physical release was all he was after, but he..."

But he had ignored her, too lost to his masculine needs. Eirik clenched his jaw. This was exactly what had happened with the bastard who had fathered him, what he had feared would happen to him if he ever found himself in bed with a woman, the whole reason behind his oath.

"You didn't manage to fight him off," he said, his voice grim. How could she have? Not only was she a wisp of a woman, but she would have been too distraught to see that the man she had loved had been reduced to this monster, and likely not as forceful as she would have been with another man.

"No. He was too strong. When he left the pallet, he laughed and said that perhaps he could make his peace with having a wife in his home and in his bed, considering the advantages it brought him. I was welcome to stay, as long as I opened my legs to him whenever he wanted. That night while he slept, I fled, went back to my parents in the next village."

Eirik braced himself to hear what had happened to Arvid. It made no doubt that Rune had torn the man from limb to limb, like any man of sense would have, for hurting his daughter so. "What did your father do to him?"

"Nothing." She lowered her gaze. "I didn't tell my parents

why I was there, I only said that I had finally accepted I could not save my marriage and wanted to leave Denmark. I was too ashamed."

"Why were you ashamed? You did nothing wrong!"

She shook her head. "But don't you see? I followed Arvid to our hut, I agreed to bed him, at least at first... I felt so foolish for having believed he wanted anything else than physical release. I couldn't tell them the truth anyway, because if he'd known, my father would have killed him."

"So?" Eirik couldn't help but growl. "It would have been no more than he deserved for taking advantage of your love for him, for using you so cruelly."

"Perhaps. But it would have solved nothing."

Eirik stared at her.

How could women be so reasonable? He remembered thinking the same thing the day his mother had confided what had happened to her. She had been happy to accept Wolf's punishment of Olaf, arguing that killing him would not erase what he had done or change what she had gone through. His father, however, even after all those years, had had murder in his eyes. It was obvious that if Olaf ever dared to show his face in the village again, he would not make it out alive.

Yes. Women were really different to men.

"Anyway, what I don't understand is why, after thirteen unfruitful years, this coupling I didn't want, managed to make me with child," Freyja said.

"Yes, that is odd."

Had the accident unlocked something inside Arvid? But the blow had been to his head, not his groin. How could something happening to the upper part of his body have had an effect on his potency as a man? Perhaps he should speak to Helga and Cwenthryth. As women used to dealing with everything to do with childbirth, they might have an explanation for what had happened.

Poor Freyja had endured unimaginable suffering, physical and mental. The husband she had once loved had taken advantage of her feelings for him. The man she had welcomed in her bed willingly time and time again had been unable to make her with child, but her attacker had forced her to carry a babe who would never know its father. She was now alone, away from home and the people she loved, and she had a little girl to take care of, one who was in danger of being abducted by her scheming uncle.

No wonder it was a mess in her head.

"I'm so sorry."

Feeling the unfairness of the situation but unable to do anything about it, he just held her, hoping to transmit some of his sympathy to her, hoping it would help. But it did not. Because he, too, felt the cruel sting of irony.

He had finally put his doubts aside and decided to offer Freyja marriage. For the first time in his life, he had considered breaking his oath, and it had to be with a woman who couldn't be his, at least not in the eyes of the world.

"Do you want Asta and me to leave?" she asked in a small voice. "I would understand if you preferred—"

"Well, *I* wouldn't understand." In fact, he would be offended to see that she thought him so heartless as to send her away now. "And no, of course I don't want you to leave. I hope you consider this your home."

She stilled and looked at him straight in the eye. "You want me to stay with you even knowing I cannot marry you?"

It was a valid question. But he didn't even hesitate. "Yes. Just tell me this." Perhaps he was a fool to insist, but he had to know. "Would you have accepted my offer had you been free to do so?"

She went red to the roots of her hair, which gave him the

answer he'd been hoping for. Nevertheless, he had the pleasure of hearing her say the words out loud.

"I think you know I would."

His heart expanded. She wanted him too, that was the important part. They didn't need to be married to live together. They already did. For all intents and purposes, he, she, and Asta already were a family, whether they wanted it or not. He didn't need to be Freyja's husband to be the father of her children, all he had to do was love and support them, which he intended to do.

And so he kissed her.

It seemed the natural thing to do. The thing he wanted to do. And she didn't push him away, instead melting into him. It was a sweet kiss, nothing like the fiery one they had shared before, more like a proof of his commitment to her and his determination to help.

"Let's just carry on as we are for now, shall we?" he said when they drew back, slightly breathless.

"Yes."

She appeared as relieved as he was to see that their painful discussion had not caused the end of their arrangement. It was admittedly an odd one. But it was theirs, it suited them, and it made him happier than he had ever been.

13

Freyja had almost finished grinding her flour with the quern-stone when a knock on the door made her lift her head. She went to open it and found a smiling man holding a parcel in his hands.

"Good morning, Freyja. I'm Elwyn."

Yes. She had already recognized Eirik's brother, whom she'd glimpsed a couple of times around the village. She smiled back, wiping her hands on her apron. "Good morning. I'm afraid Eirik is not here at the moment. He went to see Moon just after breaking his fast. Perhaps you could—"

"Not a problem, I don't actually need to see him, I just wanted to drop this off. Would you give it to him when he comes back?"

"Yes, of course."

Once the door had closed again, she couldn't resist peeking inside the leather bag, which she'd recognized as one belonging to Eirik. It had been sitting empty under the shelf only the other day. Why was his brother returning it full now? Inside, she had the surprise of seeing a bolt of fabric of an exquisite blue hue she had not thought possible to get from dyeing. What would Eirik want to do with that? He only wore subdued colors, and anyway, delicate as it was, it seemed more appropriate for a woman.

A woman.

Freyja stilled, her hand in the bag. Had he been any other man she might have wondered if he'd bought the fabric for the woman sharing his bed, but she knew he didn't share anyone's bed—and why. So what was this? A present for his mother? Was that why Elwyn had been the one procuring it? It was possible.

And she was being indiscreet.

She closed the bag and placed it on the table, ready for Eirik to find when he came back later. It had nothing to do with her and she should have respected his privacy.

As she exited the hut to feed the chickens a moment later, Freyja had another surprise. At the pigpen, the spider web was back.

Chest swelling with joy, she moved closer to inspect it. Just below where the original one had been, was a new, bigger, even more intricate one. The spider had worked well, and was now busy putting the final touches to her creation, getting ready to trap unsuspecting creatures into the thin strands.

Order had been restored. Freyja smiled and stroked her stomach pensively. If the web was indeed to be seen as an omen, then it was a good one, one meant to show her that everything was possible. She could make a home here, if she persisted despite the obstacles in her way, just like the spider had. The small, unassuming animal could have found another spot, but she had decided that this was where she wanted to be and she had not let anything deter her.

Feeling more positive than she had in days, Freyja went back to the hut. The flour she had just ground would be made into flat cakes for when Eirik and Asta came back.

Her family.

"AH, Elwyn, well met. I was on my way to see you." Eirik gave his eldest brother a slap on the back. "Did you have the chance to go into town yesterday?"

"Yes, and I found what you wanted. I just left the bag with Freyja at the hut. I think you'll be pleased. The weaver had some excellent choices this time."

"Perfect. Thank you."

After Arne had paid him for the mead in coin the day before, Eirik had gone to see Elwyn to ask a favor. Would he go into town and get a bolt of fabric for him to give to Freyja? He could have gone himself, of course, instead of bothering his brother, but he had promised he would not leave the village while Harald was lurking around, and he meant to keep his word. It would not do for her to worry, not after they had agreed he would look after her and Asta.

Elwyn wouldn't mind going to the weaver in his stead. He had excellent taste for such things, as his wife Bee kept telling everyone, and he often had business in town anyway, so he was the perfect man for the mission.

Eirik only hoped Freyja would be pleased with his idea.

"I think it was high time she had something to use," Elwyn added, crossing his arms over his chest. "She is showing, more than I expected."

"Yes," Eirik agreed.

Unable to deal with the shock of being told that Freyja was carrying a child, the child of a man who had raped her, he had told his family about it. She had agreed they had the right to know, as they would inevitably see her stomach swell in the weeks to come and ask themselves questions, even if they understood that he could not be the father. The time frame didn't correspond, and of course, they were aware of the oath he had taken, an oath that precluded him ever fathering children.

"If I may, Brother…"

Eirik tensed. He could sense he would not like what he was about to hear. "What is it?"

"I cannot help but feel that Freyja being put under your protection might be the opportunity you had been waiting all your life. You've never looked better, or happier."

No surprises there, he had never *felt* better, or happier. As to this being the opportunity he'd been waiting for without even knowing it, he had already reached the same conclusion.

"I agree. I will do my best not to let it pass."

There might not be another. And even if there were, it would not be with her.

"All right, time for me to go," Elwyn said. "It's late. Bee and the children will be waiting for me."

Eirik nodded, realizing that the joy he felt inside was the realization that he, too, had someone waiting for him at home.

When he entered the hut and was welcomed by a smiling Freyja and the delicious scent of warm flat cakes, he knew for sure that this was the life he was meant to have. The life he'd secretly wanted all this time and that had been forced on him.

He closed the door, feeling truly at home for the first time since he had moved into the hut.

"Your brother, Elwyn, came by earlier and left a parcel for you," Freyja informed him, nodding toward the table where the leather bag was.

"No, this isn't for me. What's inside is for you."

Her eyebrows shot to the roots of her hair. Oh, how he loved her spontaneous reactions! "For me?"

"Yes. Open it."

Slowly, her gaze never leaving his, she tugged at the laces holding the bag shut. When it was open, she peered inside. Her cheeks seemed to catch ablaze when she saw what the bag held. "But... I don't understand..."

Warmth spread through his chest in turn. How wonderful it was to surprise and please someone, much better than getting a gift oneself.

"You will need to make yourself a new dress soon, to accommodate for the babe," he explained. "I could have bought one ready-made, of course, but I thought you might prefer to make one to your liking, and maybe plan to let it out again in another few months' time. But if you want me to—"

"No," she cut in, clutching the bolt of fabric to her chest as if afraid he would take it from her. Then the expression in her face changed. Her lip started to wobble. "I love this. 'Tis the most amazing color I have ever seen, fit for a queen."

Eirik was bemused. If that were the case, then why did she look on the verge of tears? "Why are you crying if you like the cloth?"

"Because I've been wondering how to get what I needed for days, but I kept putting it off. I had no idea where to go, or even if I would find the courage to start on a new dress," she whispered, sounding ashamed by the admission. "So I don't know how to thank you for this. You making it look as if none of this was any issue helps more than you can ever know. But I will repay you. I have coin in my—"

He took her wrist before she could move, his long fingers keeping her captive. "No. No payment required. You have done more than enough for me already."

"I've done nothing."

"You've done more than you think."

They stared into each other's eyes. Was he about to kiss her again, Eirik wondered? Was the need to put his lips on hers what was torturing him? It could well be. Worse, he seemed to see the same urge in her eyes. Could he lean in and—

"I'm famished! What is there to eat?" Asta asked, bursting into the hut.

They sprang apart, like two naughty children caught red-handed.

There would be no kissing now, the moment had passed. Eirik forced himself to think that it was for the best.

Freyja decided to go to the lake.

Eirik had gone after their meal, as he did most days, and she was curious to see what he did there.

Swim as if he were chased by the giant sea serpent *Jǫrmungandr* itself was the answer. She watched, awed at his strength as he went from one end of the lake to the other, his arms hitting the water in powerful strokes. Finally, when she was sure anyone else would have dropped from exhaustion, he stopped and made his way back to the shore on his back, his pace a lot slower, as if he were looking at the sky above. Then he stood up. Water cascaded down the most powerfully muscled back she had ever seen, gathering in rivulets along his spine, before ending on the place just above his buttocks, where two dimples drew the eye. Oh. The man was magnificent.

Unable to resist, she walked forward.

At the sound of her footsteps, Eirik turned around. "Freyja."

His face betrayed no surprise. He seemed to have expected her to come see him one of these days.

Freyja drank in the sight. His body was submerged almost up to the navel, which was the reason she had dared make her presence known. Was he naked? She hadn't been able to see while he swam, but he might well be. Her throat went dry at the thought.

"You are an incredible swimmer," she breathed, forcing herself to look him in the eye.

Not that it surprised her to see his skill. And now she knew why he had such broad shoulders and a chiseled chest. If he swam like this every day, then of course his body would develop accordingly.

He shrugged, as if there was nothing extraordinary in that fact. "My father taught us from a young age. His family drowned when he was only a boy, and it was important for him to ensure that his wife and children could swim."

"Oh. Of course. I'm sorry." She'd known what had happened to Sigurd. Her father, who had grown up in the same village as the little orphan everyone called "Beast," had told her about his tragedy. How had she not thought?

"Don't be sorry, you haven't done anything wrong." The corner of Eirik's mouth lifted. "My sister Aife is probably an even better swimmer than I am. You should see her go. She's tireless and fearless, the best of all of us. Can you swim?" he asked, tilting his head.

"Not as well as you can, but yes." She was grateful he was not dwelling on her blunder but allowing her to recover.

"Come join me then. The temperature of the water is very pleasant today," he said, dropping gracefully to his knees to hide his body from view again. "I promise I will rein in my strength and not humiliate you."

How could she resist an invitation from a teasing Eirik? And she wasn't sure she wanted him to rein in his strength. It was one of the things she liked best about him.

"I don't have a change of clothes," Freyja forced herself to say. Shouldn't she be reasonable? She hadn't meant to actually go into the water.

"Neither have I." He nodded to the pile of clothes on the shore some distance away from her. Her question was answered. He *was* naked under the water. Just like that, her decision was made.

"Very well. I will come join you."

14

They swam for what felt like hours, going back to the middle of the lake to feel at one with nature. Though, as expected, she was nowhere near as strong and elegant as Eirik in the water, Freyja was pleased to see that she could follow him without too much difficulty.

After a while, however, she had to slow down. She was not as used to the exercise as he was and it was starting to show. When her movements became less fluid, Eirik never said a word, he simply led her back closer to the shore, to a place where they could get their footing once more. This thoughtfulness moved her all the more so that she could tell it was not a conscious decision on his part. Being caring was just second nature to him.

"How did you like that?" Eirik asked. Even though he had been swimming strenuously before she'd joined him, he still showed no signs of fatigue.

"Very much. I hadn't been swimming for a while." Not since the summer before Arvid's accident in fact. And she'd enjoyed herself immensely. It had done her body and her spirit good to be in water, especially that, though refreshing, the lake was a lot warmer than the one she was used to. "It did me good."

"I'm glad. Just tell me when you want to go out."

"Another moment."

Now that they were treading water and she'd gotten her breath back, she was in no hurry to leave. Eirik smiled at her. He was keeping his shoulders submerged under the surface of the water, just like she was, which meant he was probably crouching down, since he was so much taller than her.

"You might get a taste for swimming, you know."

"Yes," she agreed slowly. She might well get a taste for everything she could do with him naked.

Just then, they spotted a man boarding a boat in the distance. Freyja had seen the half-dozen skiffs moored by the shore when she'd arrived, but rather stupidly, she had not thought anyone would come disturb their peace. Soon the boat started to veer toward them. It was obvious the move was deliberate. Eirik muttered a curse under his breath.

"Who's that?" Freyja asked, worried by his reaction. Did he think the man meant trouble? She had not recognized him, all she knew was that it was not Harald.

"Arne, one of my neighbors."

"Do you not like him?"

"I don't hate him but he's not always the most subtle of fellows."

Mmmm. Definitely not the best person to meet right now then.

"I'm naked," she whispered unnecessarily. She hadn't minded Eirik seeing what he had already seen—and stroked—but another man was another matter entirely. They were too far out to get back to the shore though, and it was clear that the man was aiming straight for them, blocking their way.

"I know." He sounded even more worried by the idea than she was. "Stay behind me with the water up to your chin," he instructed, standing straight with his back to her. "I'm big enough to hide you, I should think."

Yes, that, at least, was not in doubt. Two women her size would be able to hide behind his bulk. From where she was, she had a splendid view of the small of his back, his smooth skin and those tempting dimples. It was enough to make her mouth dry, even though she was surrounded by water.

It wasn't long before the boat drew near enough for Arne to call out to his friend. "Eirik!" He gave a broad smile, looking delighted at this meeting he had provoked.

"Arne."

"I see that you have finally allowed your beautiful guest to leave your hut," the wretched man said, making it sound as if Eirik had kept her in bed all this time for his pleasure. Oh, if only...

"I do not allow or forbid anyone anything," was the curt answer. Freyja could easily guess Arne had no idea of the reason why she kept close to hut. He'd not been one of the men instructed to look after her. "And Freyja does as she pleases."

"So I see. Or at least, I *would* see if you weren't blocking the view with your big, ugly body. I would rather have—"

"Fuck off, Arne." Eirik's snarl sent shivers all the way down Freyja's core. No, she definitely did not mind his swearing, now less than ever. He sounded so protective it warmed something inside of her.

The man laughed, as if aware he had nothing to fear from the big Norseman, who might rant but would never actually hurt him. "Yes, I think I had better do just that. Oh, just before I go, I hope you put the coin I gave you to good use and did not squander it on whores who would—"

"I seem to remember I told you to fuck off. I meant it."

"No need to bite my head off, my friend! I will leave you to go back to your seducing of your beautiful guest. Good luck. With those gruff manners of yours, I'm not sure what you will achieve."

She could tell the man's comments had been in jest, but Freyja was glad when he started to row away from them. Eirik had been right, he was not the most subtle person she had met in the village, nothing like his likeable brothers.

"Are you all right?" Eirik asked, turning back to face her. "Don't worry about Arne. He can be rather coarse but he would never hurt you."

No. This she didn't doubt. He was like too many men she had met, brash but ultimately harmless. It took real inner strength to inspire respect without loud actions or words.

Strength such as men like Eirik possessed.

"You're getting cold," he declared, looking at her mouth. Freyja touched it with a light finger. Had her lips turned blue? It was not impossible, as she was getting a bit chilled now that she was no longer swimming. "Come, let's get out, while there's no one around."

Eirik turned and started to make for the shore.

"Wait," she called out. She was not so cold that she couldn't do what she had been thinking about since the moment she had entered the water.

Eirik did come to a halt but he kept his back to her. She came to stand right behind him and wrapped her arms about his trim waist. He was so tall that her nose was buried between his shoulder blades. He felt as cool as the water wrapping around her body and though he was wet, she could still smell his intoxicating wood scent.

"Please let me touch you," she begged. The other day in his hut he had gifted her with his caresses. Today it would be her turn to give him what he needed. "You deserve to feel pleasure too, to know you are desired."

She was so small compared to him, she could have felt

ridiculous with her face pressed against his impossibly broad back, but she only felt powerful. Placed where she was, he would be able to feel her breasts pressed against him, feel her nipples poking at him, and her rounded stomach nudging at his buttocks.

She hoped he found the intimacy arousing, because she would not bear to be rejected now.

"This, just like pleasuring women, will not cause you to break your oath," she whispered. "No harm can come from letting a willing woman give you what you have given to so many."

"Freyja..." He sounded agonized.

"I know. And I will not do anything you don't want me to." Remembering how it had hurt her to see Arvid ignore her protests, she would never have forced him, or indeed anyone, into anything. But she was certain he wanted her, only he thought he didn't deserve to have what other men allowed themselves without scruples. "But perhaps you can accept this gift I'm giving freely."

After what felt like an eternity, Eirik took her hand in his and placed it on his shaft, forcing her fingers to close around it. It was thick and hard, and also beautiful, she imagined, just like he was. If only she could see it.

"Touch me, Freyja," he rasped. "Please. I need this. I need you. I'm burning for your touch."

A sigh of pure longing escaped her lips. He was accepting her offer, he was allowing her to do what no other woman had done. How long had he been hard? From the moment she had entered the water?

The notion that he had been aroused all the while, hidden from view, send a bolt of heat between her legs and a burst of joy through her chest. Just above her breasts the little baby bean had become scorching hot with the metal in contact with her feverish skin. It would forever be close to her heart because Eirik had ensured she never lost it again. This reminder of the kind of man he was only increased her arousal further.

While her right hand kept her hold on his iron-hard shaft, her left hand started to caress the smooth flesh of his buttocks. Mmmm. The man was really made of stone. She could have stroked him all over, licked his deliciously wet skin, and nibbled at his flesh. But for now, there was a place she wanted to lavish her attention on.

She pleasured him in long, slow strokes, moaning all the while, keeping herself pressed against him so he could feel the heat of her body and the coldness of her pebbled nipples. Then, little by little, she increased the speed and started to nip at his shoulder in teasing little bites. His breathing soon became labored.

"Freyja, stop! I'm—"

He was about to come, that was what he meant. And it scared him because he had only ever done that in private.

"I know. Let yourself go. You're safe with me." Deciding to be wicked, she repeated the words he had told her the other day in the hut, when he had pleasured her. "I will not stop until you have drenched my hand."

The words seemed enough to push him over the edge, and soon she felt his shaft pulse convulsively, as it released his seed. Her whole body went up in flames at the sensation and the knowledge that she was the first woman to allow him to experience this release.

"Fuck," Eirik said, lifting his head up to the skies, air coming in and out of his lungs in big, ragged breaths.

Freyja smiled, knowing he always swore when emotions ran high. It would seem she had well and truly unmanned him.

Still panting, he disappeared under the surface, sliding from between her arms as easily as if he'd been made of water itself.

For a long moment, so long that she actually started to worry, he stayed under water. Surely he had not passed out? Should she go after him? Before she could panic, he resurfaced, taking her with him, lifting her into his arms to give her a kiss like no other she had ever experienced.

It tasted of fresh water, lust, tenderness and pure male satisfaction.

"Thank you," he said, placing his forehead against hers.

"There's no need to thank me." She couldn't tell him the truth, that she would have liked to do much more. That she wished he'd reached his release into the warmth of her mouth instead of the coolness of the water. "It was perfect."

"It was."

With her still in his arms he walked over to his right and placed a leg on what she assumed was a piece of rock at the bottom of the lake. Lowering her slightly, he slid a muscular thigh between her parted legs, making her sit on him. Then with that thigh, he started to rub her in her most intimate place. Freyja moaned. How had he known she desperately needed the friction? Pleasuring him had sent arousal spiraling through her body, and she needed release.

"You need this," he said, his mouth at her ear, his voice dark as sin.

"Yes."

"Take it. Use me. Get what you need. Forgive me, but right now I can't give you what—"

"I know."

She understood what he had not said. He didn't want to risk pleasuring her, as it might push him over the edge and make him do what he had sworn never to do—take her, right here where they stood.

Shamelessly, she ground her core against the leg he was offering, knowing in the state she was, it would not take her long to reach her release. Stroking him had inflamed her body and her imagination. Eirik was holding her, both hands at her waist, supporting her, helping her increase the pressure on the place she needed it the most.

Pleasure rushed over her when he bent his head to capture her pebbled nipple between his lips. The searing heat of his tongue, after the coldness of the water, shot straight down to her folds. She whimpered and arched her back, forcing herself deeper into his mouth. His hands moved lower, started to knead her buttocks and it was too much.

Her heated core started pulsating, this release unlike any she had ever felt, more subdued, not as sharp as usual but intensely satisfying, as warm and comforting as the best of hugs.

For a while she stayed limp in Eirik's arms, perched on his thigh, her arms around his neck, her face against his chest, where she could hear his heart pumping.

"When we first met I thought you were gruff. I have no idea why," she whispered. This was the truth, though why she was telling him this now, she had no idea.

"You thought me gruff because I *was* gruff," he answered in a growl worthy of the wildest beast. "I couldn't help it. I knew from that first moment that you were going to be like no other woman I had ever met and it frightened me."

Oh. And he had been right to be frightened, because she had just made him break his oath. Would he not hate her for what she'd done? "I'm sorry I—"

"Don't be sorry. Having you and Asta here with me is the best thing that could have happened to me. I was lonely and I didn't even know it. I would not change a thing. If in exchange for the gift you have given me I have to allow you to stroke me to the best release of my life, then so be it." He gave her a kiss, the chasteness of it odd after the wicked acts they had just committed. "Worry not, I'll live."

"Yes," she said, unable to stop a smile. "I certainly hope so."

"Come now, it's getting late, and you will be cold."

He strode out of the water with her still clinging to his neck. He carried her as easily as if she had been a babe, and she gladly allowed his strength and warmth to wrap over her. She had missed this! A man who took care of her, who made her feel feminine and beautiful. Arvid had once been strong and loving, and it had been wonderful.

Eirik was just as wonderful.

They got dressed without rushing, each watching the other with a smile on their face. There was no embarrassment, no awkwardness. The silence was one bred of trust, the smiles ones lit by understanding. Then they walked back to the hut, their hands brushing with every step, their breathing in unison. There was no need for more after the moment they had shared. The sun's last rays were making the leaves around them glow. It was a perfect summer evening, suspended out of time. For a moment, Freyja could fool herself that everything was going to be all right.

Hurried footsteps interrupted her reverie.

Rothgar shot out of the woods. His face was red from running and his eyes were wild with panic.

"Ah! *Faðir* said I would find you here."

"What is it?" Freyja asked, panic invading her in turn. Why had the boy wanted to find her? Why did he look so worried?

"It's Asta. She's gone."

15

Gone. Freyja stared at Eirik, her chest hollow, her legs reduced to warm gruel.

Harald. He had found his niece and abducted her. Without having any proof, she knew that was the case. The little girl wouldn't have fled. She wouldn't have left the village where she had found peace, a dear friend, and the beginnings of a family.

"How do you know she's gone?" she heard Eirik ask. He had knelt in front of the boy and was looking at him straight in the eye. She was grateful to him for taking over because her mind had stopped functioning. "Tell us what happened."

"We were decorating the tree house together and she said she would go to your hut to get some pheasant feathers," Rothgar started, his speech altered by worry. "I waited, and waited. But she didn't come back so I went to your hut, thinking she might have stopped to play with the cats. She wasn't there. And then when I went to *Faðir* to ask him if he'd seen her, I saw this lying on the ground. I know it's hers, and I know she wouldn't have left without it. And she will miss it tonight when she goes to bed."

With those words, he produced a long piece of brown and white fabric. Freyja immediately recognized the belt that had been woven using tablets, the one that had once belonged to Asta's mother. The boy was right. Even in the unlikely event that Asta had fled of her own accord, she would never have left behind the only thing she had from her parents. It was too precious. More than likely it had been lost while she fought off an attacker—her own uncle.

Her fist clenched around the belt, Freyja started to run, followed by Rothgar, but she had to stop when her belly, unusually taut and heavy, forced her to slow down. Eirik was already at her side, offering support.

"What the fuck do you think you're doing, running like that in your condition?" he snarled in her ear. "You'll hurt yourself."

What was she doing? Getting her daughter back, that was what. Now that Asta had been taken away from her, Freyja understood that she had indeed come to love the little girl as her own. She would not let anyone take her away, much less hurt her.

"Don't you see? Asta didn't flee. This is Harald's doing," she panted. How had Eirik not realized it? "And it is my fault. I should have warned her that her uncle was after her, I should have told her that he wanted her back. She would have—"

"This is not your fault. Harald is the only one to blame. No one forced him to be such a wily bastard."

Perhaps not. But they were wasting precious time arguing. "Let me pass, I have to go to him, and—"

He cut her with unusual fierceness. "Out of the question. If someone goes to him, it will be me."

Yes. Freyja didn't doubt he could accomplish anything. But this was her battle, *her* daughter. This man had not asked to be saddled with her, or Asta. She had to do this. She had to at least try.

"Do you really think I will remain here, while she's in danger?" she asked, barely resisting the urge to hit at his chest. Who did he take her for? "Is that the kind of mother you think I am?"

"No," he sighed. "Of course not. Forgive me." He nudged at her, and they started to walk again. Much faster than her, Rothgar had long since disappeared, probably to see if his father had any news.

"Do you know the quickest way to the harbor?" she asked Eirik.

Time was of the essence and she couldn't quite remember how she had gotten to the village all those weeks ago. It had been dark and she had been too busy checking that no one was after them to pay much attention to her surroundings. She had just gone south, doing her best to remain hidden. But Eirik knew the area well, so he would get her to Harald as fast as possible.

He sighed again. "I do, but 'tis too late to go anywhere tonight. Night is already falling. I will go speak to my father and Wolf, see what we can do on the morrow. This cannot be improvised."

Freyja didn't answer. Yes, ideally they should mount an expedition, give themselves every chance, but in reality there was no time to lose. It was a little girl's safety they were talking about.

"Why do you think Harald waited for so long before acting? It's been weeks since he came and Ketill told him where to find Asta." She had her idea, but she wanted to see if Eirik agreed with her.

"I'm not sure. I didn't dare hope he had given up, but so long a delay is odd."

Yes, it was odd. Unless...

Unless he had waited until the last moment before boarding a ship back to Denmark so that no one could come after him. He would have guessed that she, and the Norsemen harboring her, would not simply let him take the little girl away. So, had he bided his time while concluding his business here, made them relax their guard, then taken the little girl at the last moment, certain he could disappear with her before anyone could get her back?

It would make sense, and meant that she was right. There wasn't a moment to lose. But Eirik didn't seem to share her sense of urgency. For the first time since she had arrived, she couldn't agree with him.

They had to act now.

"Here," he said as they reached his hut. "Wait for me, I won't be long. I need to go see Wolf."

Freyja nodded and watched him go, already knowing she would be gone by the time he came back. Say what he might, she could not afford to wait. As soon as she was on her own, she turned and headed to the field where the village horses were kept.

She didn't have a mount, but she would borrow Doe from Eahlswith. She'd heard Eirik say the mare Sven had given his wife after their wedding was gentle. Such an animal would carry her to her destination safely. As to what that destination might be, Freyja wasn't sure. The harbor seemed the safest bet, though. If the merchants were indeed preparing to leave, this was where they would be. If they were not going yet, there would be people there who would know where Harald was.

Light was fading fast. Fortunately, Freyja didn't need help to saddle the mare because she knew no one would let her leave the village on her own, much less at this late hour. Not everyone knew whom she was hiding from, and why she needed protection, but Sven and Eahlswith definitely did. Had she gone to them for help, they would have refused and warned Eirik instead.

Feeling guilty for not asking her new friend for permission before borrowing her mare, she saddled Doe and mounted. A moment later, she was underway.

It was folly, of course. She should have waited for Eirik, gone to find him at Wolf's hut, but she feared if she didn't go now, she would let the men persuade her that it was better to wait until morning. This, she could not afford. As scared as she was, Asta would be a hundred times more frightened. She had to get to her.

Luck was on her side. The moon was so bright she could almost see as if it were daylight, and the North star helped her stay on course in the unfamiliar surroundings. Still, it took longer than she would have liked to reach the harbor.

As soon as she drew near, the smell, a foul concoction of rotting fish guts, stagnant water, and unwashed bodies, hit her like a blow. Unfortunately, being with child had made her already sensitive nose twice as sensitive. A wave of nausea invaded her. Freyja swallowed it back. No, she couldn't falter now, Asta was relying on her. She pushed on, Doe weaving her way through wooden sheds and coils of ropes.

There wasn't a woman in sight, which only added to her unease. What if these men away from home decided they might as well pass the time in a woman's arms? She had heard their bawdy jests during the crossing from Denmark—it was clear that they intended to make the most of the local women while they were away from home. She would have to be careful if she didn't want to be one of them.

Dismounting, she made her way to a group of men mending fishnets while sitting on wooden barrels. At least these looked like local Saxon fishermen, ending their night of hard work, not Dane visitors. They might be too busy and weary to think about bothering her.

"I'm here to see Harald the Tall, a Danish merchant arrived

back in the summer," she told them, making sure to keep her gaze lowered and not to smile. "With lank hair and a beard streaked with white?"

"That's not much help, is it?" the one nearer to her snorted. "Norsemen all look like that, don't they? Tall with long hair and a beard?"

Well, no, they didn't. Most kept their hair clean and not all boasted such a distinctive mark in their beards.

His friends laughed, evidently agreeing with this assessment. "You might want to ask one of the merchants over there. It'll be easier, for we don't know any of them."

Going to the Norsemen was precisely what Freyja had tried to avoid. But there was no other choice. Nodding her thanks, she walked over to another group of men playing dice, Danes, as was evidenced by their looks.

"I'm here to see Harald the Tall," she said again, in Norse this time.

"What business have you with him?" a man whose face was deeply scarred asked, straightening up. He didn't seem too pleased by the request.

"What do you think?" one of his friends said, elbowing him in the chest. "She must be the tenth whore asking after him since we arrived. The man is spending all his coin on cunt, it would seem, and why not? I'd do the same if I could. Alas, I am not as rich."

Freyja winced at the appalling crudeness. But perhaps it was not all bad. If they took her for a whore, they would not ask what business she had with their friend, or suspect she was here for Asta. No doubt after abducting his niece, Harald had warned everyone that some local Norsemen might come after him. The men would be on the lookout but they wouldn't be suspicious of a woman on her own, especially if they thought her here to pleasure their friend.

"Well, do you know where he is?" she carried on, doing her best to appear natural. "He won't thank me for being late and I've wasted enough time already trying to locate him." This at least was true.

"He's over there, sleeping under the pile of cloth, already on his back. You know what to do, I take it?"

More laughs. Freyja thanked him and turned in that direction without further ado. She did indeed know what to do with Harald.

"Hey," the scarred Dane called after her, "once you're finished with him, come back for me. I, too, happen to have coin to spare. I'm Leif Thick Rod. I'll let you see why if you're a good girl."

Ignoring the laughs following his declaration, Freyja hastened away from the men.

Under the pile of filthy cloth she did find the person she was looking for. He was snoring, like a man with no worries. Asta was nowhere to be seen, which worried her. Had she gotten it wrong? Had the little girl fled instead of being abducted? If so, where had she gone?

Unable to resist, Freyja kicked Harald in the ribs. The look of bewilderment on his face when he recognized her was deeply satisfying.

"What the—"

"Where is Asta?" she snarled.

In this moment, she felt as strong, as menacing, as dangerous as Eirik himself would have been. Because she had right on her side. And Harald had better answer her.

He sat up, rubbing at where she had kicked him. "No need to attack me, she's not here anymore. She's with her future husband. I brought her last evening."

Last evening! He meant that the girl had spent the whole night with the man who wanted to marry—and no doubt *bed* her? Freyja feared she might vomit. This was exactly what she had feared.

"You bastard!"

"I'm not the bastard here. This is all your fault," the man had the gall to say, standing up at last.

"How is it my fault?" Freyja cried out. How dare he blame her for this?

Harald straightened to his full, impressive height and smirked. "I had intended to wait a year to bring her to him, as you know. But when you abducted her in the middle of the night, you made me see that I had better act before I lost her altogether. I decided to hand her over while I had her. A year makes little difference in the end, anyway. And that way, Garulf will be indebted to *me*, no one else. Little Asla will not—"

"Her name is Asta!"

"If you say so."

The nausea Freyja had succeeded to suppress since she'd arrived at the harbor, threatened again. She clenched her jaw, unable to speak or open her mouth for fear she would indeed be sick. This was a hundred times worse than she had imagined. Harald cared so little for his niece that he didn't even know her name.

"In any case, why do you worry about her?" Crossing his arms over his chest, he nodded at her stomach. "I can see you're about to have your own child soon. Isn't that enough for you?"

What was he talking about? As if the two could be compared! She bunched her fists. In a few weeks, Asta had become as dear to her as a real daughter and she would do anything to save her.

"Take me to your Saxon friend," she said, the words exploding out of her mouth. There wasn't a moment to lose, why were they even arguing? "He wanted to marry a Norsewoman so he can have me instead. I will make a far better wife than Asta.

I'm a grown woman already, I speak his language, I can cook, I can—"

Harald guffawed. "I doubt he wants someone who *cooks* for him."

No, he probably didn't, and that was the whole problem. Freyja swallowed. They had to go, leave this place, for she wouldn't be able to stop her stomach from roiling for much longer.

"Well, I can give him what he wants better than a girl who has no idea what a man's body looks like and what to do with it."

"Mmmm. You might have a point there, and he did seem disappointed by the girl's appearance. Not the most sensual creature in the world, is she, my niece?"

No, because she's ten summers, you foul bastard! Freyja wanted to shout. *No wonder she has the body of a child!*

"Well, I have all the curves he wants." Thanks to the babe she was carrying, she appeared plumper than she had ever done. "And I will submit to his will."

She would do what needed to be done to get the girl out of there, bed the Saxon if need be. As to actually marrying him... It was only an offer she had made to sway Harald. She had no intention of actually staying with the vile man, she only needed to get to Asta, get her out of his clutches. The rest could be managed. She was no powerless ten-year-old girl.

"There's only one problem." He nodded at her stomach again. "He might not like that. Not many men like having to deal with another man's spawn."

"Or he might see this baby as proof that I am fertile and can bear him healthy sons in time." Now that she was here, Freyja would not be so easily deterred. She had to talk her way into this, lie if need be, be as brazen and shameless as she could be. "In any case, I do not want the child. If your friend wants me to give it up when it's born, then I will."

It was when she had to say out loud that she didn't want her child that Freyja realized the opposite was actually true. Somehow in the last few weeks, with Eirik's support and trust in her ability, she had come to accept that she was carrying her estranged husband's child, she had come to love it and look forward to meeting it. She placed a hand over her stomach, addressing a silent apology to her baby. Denying it had hurt, but she had to do what it took to convince Harald to take her to his friend.

"So you really intend to offer yourself up?"

"Yes." Anything rather than leave her daughter with this Garulf. She would find a way out of his house, but she had to get there first. As if to strengthen her resolve, she tightened her fist around the belt she had put around her waist. Asta would not lose another mother. "It is time I settled anyway, and found a husband to provide for me. One man is as good as the next."

Harald made a face indicating he hadn't liked that comment, even if she suspected he thought the same of women. "I have no idea why you would sacrifice yourself for a girl you hardly know."

Freyja didn't answer. What could she say that would find an echo within him? If he had sold his ten-year-old niece for his selfish benefit, he was clearly past all human decency.

"Well. It cannot hurt to try. If I bring you to him, Garulf will see that I am making good on my word, at least, and doing my best to offer him a woman more to his tastes." He reached to seize a lock of her hair between his thumb and forefinger. Freyja forced herself not to move. At any other time she would have spat in his face, but she had just promised that she would submit willingly. She had to prove that was not a lie. "You do look like a real Norsewoman, the likes of which he will not have seen often, if ever. He might like that. And even if he doesn't, or if he objects to the brat you're carrying, I will have lost nothing."

Yes. So let's just go! she wanted to scream.

They had to leave before Eirik and his friends thundered into the harbor, searching for her. This was a very real danger, because he would have guessed where she was as soon as he saw she was not in the hut, and he would not let her face Harald alone. It was already a miracle that he'd not caught up with her on the road. Perhaps his discussion with Wolf had gone on long into the night. Whatever the reason for the respite, she had to make the most of it.

She started to move, leading Harald to where she had left Doe.

"You have a horse then?" he asked, following her at last.

"Yes. Let's go."

EIRIK SHOVED the axe into his belt and ran to Fenrir, murder on his mind.

He was not a violent man but he would get Asta and Freyja back, even if he had to kill a man—or two—for that. What had possessed her to go alone, in the dark? And how had he been so stupid as to leave her in the hut while he decided the best thing to do? Couldn't he have guessed she would not remain idle while Asta was in her foul uncle's clutches? She had told him as much.

Do you really think I will remain here, while she is in danger?

And yet he'd gone to Wolf. How stupid could he be? Freyja and Asta needed him. If either or both of them were hurt, it would be his fault. He'd spent all his life ensuring he didn't hurt any woman, it was not to let another man do it. Keeping his oath had cost him enough. He would not let guilt ruin what was left of his life.

Fenrir flew over fields and ditches, as strong as his

monstrous wolf namesake once he'd been freed from the chain holding him captive. The moon was watching over them, shedding her silver light around, aiding the enterprise.

"Good boy," Eirik repeated incessantly to his horse, "take me to her."

Was it folly to set off alone? Earlier, Wolf and his father had agreed they should wait until the morning, as he'd suggested. But then he had gone back home and seen that Freyja was gone. The silence in the hut had been deafening, and before he knew what he was doing he'd run back out, an axe on his belt.

It seemed he was just as rash as Freyja, because here he was, galloping through fields in hot pursuit. After a while, though, he slowed back down to a light trot. By going too fast he might miss her. He scoured the horizon, in the hope of seeing her familiar figure in the distance. He saw nothing.

Finally he reached the harbor, which was bustling with activity despite the early hour. Eirik let out a grunt. How would he find anyone in this hive, much less a small woman and a little girl?

"Harald!" he bellowed, confident his voice would be heard over the din. "Harald the Tall. Come out here if you dare!"

No one moved and nowhere did he see the greasy-haired man who'd come to the village the other day.

"He's busy with a whore," someone eventually said, a man with a heavily scarred face and a tunic that was both filthy and too big for him. "I doubt he will see you right now."

A few laughs followed this answer.

"Oh, he will see me," Eirik growled. Whore or no whore, the Dane would tell him what he wanted to know. "Just tell me where he is."

"Don't listen to Leif," someone else said. "That woman was no whore. Didn't you notice she spoke Norse as well as you and me, you louts? And she was far too beautiful to go with the likes of us."

Grunts answered him, but Eirik was not interested in the comments. That beautiful woman who spoke Norse had to be Freyja. And the scarred man thought she was a whore. What did that mean? Had he seen her in the merchant's arms? Had Harald attacked her? His blood ran cold at the thought.

By the gods, he had to find her. Now.

"Where. Is. Harald?" he repeated, feeling on the verge of an outburst. The men would speak, whether they wanted to or not. They seemed to understand the danger they were in because one of them called out.

"You won't find him here. He's gone to see a friend."

A friend.

The Saxon who wanted a Norse bride, regardless of her age, no doubt. Eirik spat on the ground. "Where is this 'friend' then?"

The men looked at one another. Evidently they knew they were signing their leader's death warrant by pointing him in the right direction, and they didn't care for that responsibility. Eirik didn't feel any guilt at the idea of killing Harald. The man should have thought of the consequences before abducting his niece. He glared at the men.

"We can't tell you," one of them eventually said.

There would be nothing more to be gained from this sorry lot of cowards. Eirik turned his back on them and ran back to his horse. If they didn't want to help him, he would not stand here, wasting time. The man had said Harald had not been gone long. If he left now, he might find someone along the road who had seen him and could point him in the right direction.

"Wait."

Eirik turned to see a blond man about a decade younger than him standing next to a crumbling shed. He recognized him as one of the merchants who'd been avoiding his gaze a moment ago. Had he come to stop him from going to Harald? Not giving the Dane time to pounce, Eirik pounced first, pinning him to the wooden wall behind him, which shook as if caught in the eye of a storm.

"If you think you can stop me from going to your friend, then know this," he warned. "You can't. So go back from whence you came and leave me alone."

"I'm not here to stop you," the man managed to say. Eirik relaxed his grip marginally. He needed to hear this.

"Then why are you here?"

"Because I know where your daughter and wife are."

16

"Why should I believe you? Why should I even listen to you?"

Eirik released his choking hold on the man, took a step back and glared at him. How did the man know he was looking for Freyja or Asta, whom he clearly assumed to be his wife and daughter? He had not mentioned anyone earlier, merely saying that he wanted to see Harald.

Something wasn't right here, so he had to hear him out.

"You will listen to me because you have no better choice." The man coughed, looking relieved to be able to explain himself. "At the moment you have no idea where to go to get them, but I know where Harald left the little girl. I was with him when he took her to his friend last night."

Eirik's heart started to beat louder. Could it be that simple? The man knew where the Saxon was and wanted to help?

"How do I know this is not a trap?"

"You don't." The Dane shrugged, as if trusting him to see reason for himself. "But at the moment you have no idea where to go, you're only wasting time. Even if I lead you to the wrong place, you will have lost nothing. But this I can guarantee, without me you will never find the place, or at least not in time."

Yes. That was the worry. That he would be too late to prevent a rape.

"Why do you want to help me?" He had not spoken out earlier. "Are you not afraid of retribution from your friend, like the others?"

"Harald is not my friend!" The man shook his head. "And 'tis wrong what he's done. I have a sister back at home the same age as his niece and I would never— Just imagining what she might — And then your woman offering herself in her condition— 'Tis all wrong. I was there, hidden under the cloth, when she came this morning. I heard everything and yet I said nothing. It was all wrong. I wish I had been as brave as she was. I'm ashamed. But here is my chance to redeem myself."

Eirik didn't need to hear more to be convinced. The man was sincere, that was not in doubt. He sounded too concerned, too dejected at his own weakness, too horrified at Harald's actions to be anything other than honest. Besides, as he'd said, he was his only chance. If Asta had really been taken to the Saxon, and Freyja had really offered herself in exchange, then there was no time to lose. Trying to guess where they were would lead nowhere. He had no idea where that could be.

"Do you have a horse?"

"Yes. Over there."

"Then lead the way."

As they rode through fields, his heart pounding in rhythm with the horses' hooves, Eirik's mind was whirring. What if this was a trap, as he'd first suspected? What if it wasn't but he was too late anyway? He tried very hard not to think of what he would feel if he was told that the little girl he considered as his daughter was hurt or the woman he'd come to love had been raped a second time.

It would be his worst nightmare come true.

He would have failed to stop what he had tried all his life to prevent from happening.

"Here," the Dane said eventually, bringing his horse back down to a trot and veering off the main road.

A moment later the two of them skidded to a halt in front of an isolated farm. Thank the gods the Dane had come to him because for some reason Eirik had assumed the Saxon lived in town. He would never have thought to search for him in such a place.

If that was the right place, of course. He still wasn't completely sure.

But then, he saw a small figure slip through the window before falling to the ground in one graceless heap. Asta. His heart leaped in his throat. Thank the gods, he was indeed in the right place.

He started to run, followed by the Dane who had jumped down from his saddle at the same time as him.

"Oh, Eirik!" the little girl cried out, falling into his arms.

"Sweetheart, are you all right?"

"Yes, but you have to go to *Moðir*." She shook her head. "I didn't understand anything of what the old man said to me or to her, but he will hurt her, I'm sure of it. I escaped through the window when she told me to. I didn't want to leave her alone with him, but she—"

"You did well to obey her. I will be the one helping her. You just stay safe."

He looked around in desperation. He had to get to Freyja, but he didn't want to leave Asta alone, at the mercy of any passerby, nor could he take her with him. He didn't want her to see what was happening in that farm.

The Dane cleared his throat, evidently thinking the same thing. Whatever was going on in there, whatever was going to happen when Eirik got his hands on the man, was not suitable for a child to see.

"Go. I'll stay here with the girl." He nodded and handed him the only weapon he seemed to carry, a long knife with a curved blade. "I will not harm her, I swear."

No. Suddenly Eirik was certain of it. The man had brought him to the right place and he looked sick at the thought of what he had allowed to happen. He would keep the little girl safe.

"Stay here with my friend," he instructed Asta before turning to the main building.

FREYJA WAS careful not to betray any relief when she saw Asta slip through the window in the corner of her eye. At last the little girl was safe and out of the way, now she would only have herself to worry about. She placed a hand on the shard of pottery hidden in her sleeve to reassure herself.

Would she actually have to use it? She dearly hoped not.

From the moment they had reached the farm, nothing had happened the way she had imagined—or rather dreaded—it would.

Harald had jumped down from his horse and signaled to her that she should do the same. The two men accompanying them were ordered to stay behind and look after the horses.

"Here. Before we go anywhere, let us make sure you are unarmed," he said, taking the eating knife from the sheath at Freyja's belt. It was the only thing she had that could be used as a weapon, and it was clear he didn't trust her not to use it on his friend. He was right to be suspicious, because at the first opportunity, she would.

Once he was satisfied, he led her to a low stone building whose size and state indicated the occupant was a man of some means. Who was he, that the Dane wanted to please him so desperately? Freyja pushed the question out of her mind. It mattered not who Garulf was, or what hold he had on Harald, only that at the moment, he had Asta in his possession and he meant to make her his wife.

One knock was enough to bring the Saxon to the door. As soon as he saw who was visiting, his face underwent a drastic change. It went from calm to annoyed.

"Harald. There you are. I have a bone to pick with you! What the hell were you thinking by bringing this wisp of a girl to me? I asked for a bride, not a child. She can't even speak my tongue or understand what I'm saying. What good is she to me? This is not what I asked of you."

Freyja could barely breathe for relief. Against all odds, the Saxon agreed with her that Asta was not suitable to be his bride. At least he was not quite the lecher she had taken him for. Dare she hope that her daughter had not been hurt last night? It seemed too good to be true.

Seeing that no one was taking any notice of her she rushed to Asta, who was huddled in one corner of the room, looking scared but unharmed.

While the two men started arguing, she hugged the little girl. In her arms she felt so fragile. "Sweetheart, are you all right? The man didn't hurt you?"

"No. When we were alone, he asked me all sorts of questions, but I could not answer so I just stared at him. Eventually he grew tired of it and just went to sleep. Oh, *Moðir*, I'm so relieved to see you."

"Me too." She tightened her hold around Asta and placed a kiss on the top of her head, grateful beyond belief that the worse had been avoided. "Now let me listen to what they are talking about."

"Calm yourself," Harald was saying, "I saw that you weren't

pleased with my first choice and in truth I knew I had been a bit hasty. So today I brought you a second choice, one I know will satisfy you. Just look at the woman."

The man turned to face her and his eyebrow arched, indicating his interest. Evidently he liked her better than the child he'd been offered. Good, that had been part of the plan.

Freyja stood up and walked over to the men, diverting the attention away from the little girl who remained seated in the corner. At the earliest opportunity she would order her to flee.

"Good morning. I'm Freyja," she told Garulf.

He was not overly tall, stocky, perhaps a decade older than she was, with short brown hair. There was no cruel streak in his eyes, but she did not let that fool her. People didn't have to be cruel to act cruelly. He might not mean to hurt the woman he intended to marry, but he was not above asking a near stranger to find him a wife, and though he had not been satisfied with Harald's choice, he had not sent him on his way with a curse either. It would have taken him less than a heartbeat to see that Asta was just a child. That she didn't speak his language was of no importance.

So it was better to stay on her guard.

"Freyja," the Saxon said, looking pleased. "That is a beautiful Norse name."

"It is, for I am a true Dane." She kept to herself the fact that her mother was a Saxon. For some reason, he seemed intent on marrying a Norsewoman, so she would make sure to be that Norsewoman. Fortunately, she looked too much like her father for anyone to doubt her identity. She decided to make her accent stronger than it naturally was. "I only arrived here in the summer but I am determined to stay. Your country is beautiful."

"It certainly is." The flattery had worked. "Much better than a frozen wasteland, I should imagine."

Frozen wasteland? Was that how he imagined Denmark? She bit her tongue. "Much better."

"You know why Harald brought you here. Are you happy to become my wife?"

Happy. Would anyone be happy to be chosen by a man to be offered to one of his friends? Was he really that deluded? But there was only one answer to that question.

"Yes," she said with as much calm as she could muster. "It is time I found a good husband. You seem an ideal choice. I think you are a man of some means and you appeal to me. I think this will be a good match."

Whatever it took to get Asta out of here. By now Eirik would have noticed her absence. He would have alerted everyone. The Norsemen would be coming after her. Whatever ordeal she would endure here would not last long. In the meantime, she could lie if need be.

"I will be a good wife to you. I speak your language, And I am fertile, as you can see. In time, I will give you sons."

She stroked a hand down her swollen stomach, emphasizing its curve. Her heart was beating loudly in her ears. Would the Saxon protest he didn't want a woman heavy with someone else's child? That was her only fear. He tilted his head, considering, and she did the only thing she could think of to sway him.

She licked her lips in a manner she hoped was suggestive enough to provoke his desire. Apparently it was, because his attitude instantly changed.

"Yes. You are fertile and willing. That's good."

He mouthed something Freyja couldn't quite catch. But she knew she'd won. Relief mingled with dread swept through her. She had not expected him to be quite that excited by her gesture.

"Harald, leave us."

The Dane smiled, not having missed his friend's satisfaction. "Shall I take the girl back with—"

"No," Freyja and Garulf said at the same time, though she wasn't sure it was for the same reasons. They looked at one another and she nodded, indicating that he should speak for them. He was pleased by her reaction, the perfect one coming from a submissive spouse.

"It pleases me to keep the girl here for now," he declared, showcasing what he wanted her to see as generosity. "She will be able to help my wife with various tasks."

He would use her as a slave, that was what he meant. But as it suited Freyja to see Harald leave alone, she nodded again. "Thank you."

Leaving the two women inside, Garulf walked his friend back to his horse.

Quick as a flash, Freyja seized the earthenware jug she'd spotted on the table earlier and smashed it against the wall. A dozen shards fell at her feet. The one in the middle was long and sharp, shaped like a dog's tooth, and big enough to inflict damage if need be. Perfect, just what she had been hoping for. She picked it up and hid it in her sleeve. Then she pushed the rest of the pieces nearer the wall and covered them with a sack of flour.

There. No traces of her deed remained.

"Asta. Listen to me," she told the little girl next, resisting the urge to go to her. She had to make the man forget she was in the room when he came back. "As soon as I tell you, go out of the window." Fortunately, she'd already seen that it was low enough for the girl to reach. "I will tell you to go in Norse, so that the man doesn't understand what I tell you. It won't even look as if I was talking to you. As soon as I see that he's forgotten about you, I will tell you. Once you're out, run and hide. Understood?"

"Yes."

There was no time to say more. Just then the Saxon came back in, looking mightily glad with the events of the day. Freyja forced herself not to panic when he closed the door behind him. For better or for worse, she was now at his mercy. At least Harald was gone, and in her mind he had been the greater threat.

"You speak my language then?"

"Yes."

"That's good. It's going to make things easier."

So he really intended to make her his wife, rather than simply take advantage of her? The tension in Freyja's shoulders relaxed marginally. Perhaps he did want someone to cook for him after all. And perhaps he would not force her to share his bed, at least not until they were married. If she could keep him at arms' length for a day or two, then Eirik would come and he would rescue her.

Yes... *If* he found out where she was, of course. There was no way he would find the farm without someone leading him to it. It was well hidden. Well, she couldn't worry about that now— she had Garulf to deal with. He was looking at her stomach.

"Who is the father of your babe?" he asked with a frown. "Will he not want to know where you—"

"No. My husband is dead."

It was only half a lie, as she saw it. The lover she had married was dead to her, even if the man who was legally bound to her still lived in Denmark. But Arvid was of no consequence now. He wouldn't come after this babe he didn't even know he had fathered or likely wanted.

Though she was curious, she didn't ask Garulf why he was so set on marrying a Norsewoman. She didn't need to worry about that either, in a few days she would be gone, never to see him again.

The Saxon nodded, satisfied. "Good. Obviously, when it is born, we will have to get rid of the child. I am not raising another man's spawn." He made a face, as if the thought was repugnant to him. "But as you said, it proves you are not barren. That is good, as it means you will be able to bear the many children I mean to plant in your womb. I am not getting any younger and have no time to lose. This is why the puny girl Harald brought me was really not a good idea. It will be years before she can bear anyone sons, whereas by next summer you will be ready for my seed to take root."

The tension in Freyja's shoulders was back. Who was this man talking so casually of "getting rid" of her child? Of "planting his many children in her womb?" She was glad to have ensured herself access to a weapon, small as it may be, glad that Asta could not understand what was being said.

"It will be as you say."

She forced the words through clenched teeth and managed to keep an impassive face by remembering she didn't mean any of it. She was only playing a role until Eirik came to the rescue.

And she didn't doubt for a moment that he would, even if it took longer than she wanted.

It was not just wishful thinking destined to help keep panic at bay. The story of his life would ensure he came to the rescue of a woman in danger of being raped. Nothing was guaranteed to make him react more.

"You really are ready to submit to my will, I see. I'm glad. A girl of ten summers with no knowledge of lovemaking and no womanly appeal is not my idea of a bed partner. I really don't know what Harald was thinking, bringing the waif before she was ripe." He gave a lecherous grin. "If you must know, I find your rounded shape very pleasing. And I have heard that women with child were insatiable. I can't wait to see what you're capable of."

Oh, he would see.

Loath as she would normally be to hurt someone, she would

plunge the pottery shard in his neck, in his groin, wherever she could access, as soon as he touched her. She was not going to let him do any of the things he planned to do to her. Having already been raped once, she had no intention of going through it again. Harald had made the mistake of leaving, so she would fight tooth and nail. One to one, and armed with a weapon, she might have a chance.

The first thing to do was to make sure there were no witnesses to the unpleasant scene about to unfold.

She took a step to her right, bringing her hip in contact with the corner of the table. Pain exploded in her hip. *Sorðinn*, in her desperation, she had been more forceful than she'd intended.

"Ouch! Now, Asta," she said, careful not to look at the little girl, making it sound as if she was just talking to herself, cursing her clumsiness, "quietly, the window. Run."

17

———

The plan had worked. Asta was safely out of harm's way. Now assured that the little girl would not see anything she wasn't meant to see, Freyja turned her attention back to the man facing her. She was free to act as she wanted and do what needed to be done.

"Are you all right?" he asked, taking a step toward her. "Careful there, you don't want to hurt yourself."

This solicitude was odd in the light of what he intended to do. She decided to use it. Perhaps if she asked, he would agree to wait until they were married to possess her? She decided to give him a chance to prove he was not as bad a man as the arrangement he had concluded with Harald had led her to suppose.

"Could we do this properly, and wait until we are married to sleep together? I think it would—"

"Nay. Before we do get married, I need to see that you are indeed a lusty woman capable of satisfying a man." There would be no swaying him, she could tell. One glance at his groin told her that he was already hard. "Being able to bear children is one thing, but I have needs and I will not shackle myself to anyone who does not satisfy them."

With those words, he reached to his braies and started to free his swollen member. Freyja swallowed. This was it. She had to take control now. If he bent her over the table her weapon would be useless. If he lay over her, he would see her reach to the sleeve and stop her before she could strike. She had to make sure he didn't see the shard before it was too late. There was only one solution.

She dropped to her knees.

"Mm. Even better," the man said, grabbing her hair none too gently. "Show me what you can do with that pretty mouth of yours. Get me nice and ready."

Swiftly, Freyja seized the pottery shard hidden in her sleeve. Steeling herself, she grabbed the man's shaft with one hand and sliced the jagged shard straight across it with the other.

The howl of pain resounding through the house was one she would never forget. She had no idea how deep she had managed to cut him but she instantly knew she had done enough damage to save herself from rape and give her and Asta time to escape. That was all that mattered. She stood up while Garulf fell to the floor in one heap, blood already soaking the earthen floor.

Trembling, Freyja stared at the mess. She should flee, not remain here, rooted to the spot. But suddenly she seemed incapable of moving.

Just then the door burst open.

Anyone would have been welcome in that moment, but the man standing in the door frame, eyes ablaze with fury, was the one she would have chosen to see.

"Eirik," she said, with what little breath was left in her lungs.

"Freyja." He ran to her.

The feel of his arms wrapping around her caused her legs to buckle. No, she chided herself, not yet. They were not quite safe yet.

"Asta?" she asked, clutching at his tunic. Had he seen the

little girl? She had left the hut only a short time ago. Had she had time to hide before Eirik arrived?

"She's outside, with a friend. Safe."

Her whole body finally relaxed. "Thank the gods."

Eirik tightened his hold around Freyja when her legs wavered, offering support. It had been so close. Too close.

"Are you all right?" he asked, a hand settling on her stomach. She seemed to be, but he had to be sure. If she had been hurt in anyway, the man writhing on the floor in a pool of blood would wish his death would come sooner.

"Yes, I'll be fine. We need to go."

Not quite what he wanted to hear, but he would have to be satisfied with it. What exactly had happened between her and the Saxon wasn't clear, but one thing was certain, he'd been punished for it, at least in Freyja's mind. Eirik thought back to his mother, who had not wanted her husband to kill her attacker once Wolf had beaten him to a pulp. To know that the deed had been avenged in some way had been enough for her. No doubt Freyja would feel the same. What she had told him about Arvid seemed to indicate that she did not believe in revenge.

He wasn't sure he agreed, but he could not butcher a man in front of her, so he didn't do what he was itching to do and plunge his dagger into the Saxon's chest to extract his still beating heart.

"Will he live?" he asked, staring at the mess between the man's legs. Perhaps this horrid injury was the best punishment, after all.

"I know not," she told him honestly. "And I'm not sure I care."

"No. Neither do I."

The man could go rot in his Saxon hell, for though Eirik could not know for certain what had happened, he could all too easily guess what had been intended. The man's braies had not fallen to his ankles by accident. He'd gotten nothing less than what he deserved for wanting to take his pleasure with an unwilling Freyja.

He tightened his hold around her, a good way to stop himself from reaching out to the bastard and finishing what she had started.

"Come," he said. "Let's go to Asta. She'll be anxious to see you."

Eirik's heart exploded when he saw the little girl run to her new mother and Freyja fall to her knees to wrap her in a hug. In that moment, he knew. This was his family. No matter what happened, he would ensure that these four people who had been brought together by chance would stay together for as long as they lived.

"Are you all right, *Moðir*?" Asta asked, looking Freyja over.

"Yes, I'm all right. You were so brave, doing exactly what I asked you to do. I'm so proud of you." They hugged some more in silence, then after a while, Freyja stood back up and wiped at her eyes. "Here you go, sweetheart," she said, unfastening the woven belt at her waist. "This is yours."

"Yes, oh, thank you!"

"You're welcome. Now, come this way," she said, leading everyone to the back of the farm. "We need to leave before someone comes."

They did, so Eirik followed her without a word. Next to a row of stables was a tethered horse he recognized. The chestnut mare was none other than the one Sven had gifted Eahlswith on their wedding day.

"Is that Doe?" he asked, understanding dawning. This was why he had not overtaken Freyja before reaching the harbor! Because she had been on horseback as well. Fool that he was, he'd assumed she had gone on foot, so he'd kept slowing down and retracing his steps to make sure he didn't miss her. But she had been brave enough to actually ride. Of course she had, he should have known.

Freyja blushed a furious shade of crimson, like a thief caught red-handed. "Yes. I know I never asked for the permission to borrow her but—"

"It's all right. I understand you had no time to lose. And she doesn't appear hurt." He untied the mare, then turned to the Dane, who had followed them and was standing to the side, waiting. "I'm Eirik. What's your name?"

"Halfdan."

Eirik snorted. "That's my brother's name." It seemed significant, somehow, a further proof that the man could be trusted. "What are your plans now?"

"I don't know. I'm not sure I can go back to the harbor after what I did," Halfdan answered, echoing his thoughts. If they had been seen leaving together, if Harald got wind of what he had done, the man might find himself in a hard situation. "I'm not sure I want to, to be honest."

"Come back with us to the village. You might find that you'd like to settle there. Do you have a trade?"

"I'm a blacksmith's son but I never had the opportunity to do much, what with having to come here every summer with the merchants."

Eirik didn't ask why he had been forced to come. In truth, he cared not, and they had to leave as quickly as possible.

"You being a blacksmith is just perfect. I know our smithy, Magnus, is looking for someone to help at the forge. He will be delighted to have you, show you how to best use the skills you do have."

The man's eyes lit up. "You truly think I could live there?"

"Yes. We seem to have made a speciality of welcoming people in need."

He turned to Freyja, who nodded her approval, tears in her eyes.

"Come to the village," she told Halfdan. "You will be welcomed there, as I was, and happy, I daresay."

The Dane beamed at her. "Very well, I will."

Instead of smiling back at him, Freyja made a grimace. Something was clearly still bothering her. "Are you saying that you cannot go back to the harbor with the merchants because you betrayed Harald by telling Eirik where to find Asta and me? I'm sorry if that is the case."

"It was no betrayal, for I never owed him anything," Halfdan growled, all mirth gone from his face. "But, yes, I told Eirik where the farm was when he came looking for you. I was one of the two men accompanying Harald last night so when your husband asked after you, I knew where to take him."

"Eirik is not Freyja's husband," piped little Asta, shaking her head.

Eirik gave a taut smile, because he had the impression that, had the girl not spoken, Freyja wouldn't have corrected the mistake and let him believe they were husband and wife, which suited him fine.

Halfdan's face registered intense surprise, but before he could say anything, Freyja took him by the hand. "I thank you. It was very brave of you. Without you, I—"

"Please," he said when her voice broke. "It was the least I could do."

He flushed and Eirik wondered if the man was not smitten. Well, too bad. Freyja might not be married to him, but she was his anyway. If the young Dane liked red-haired beauties, he would simply have to find one in the village. He cleared his throat, a tame way of putting an end to the moment when he was fighting the urge to rip the man's hand from Freyja's. He had enough presence of mind left to accept that she would not appreciate this gesture of possessiveness.

"Do you want to travel with your daughter or will you entrust her to me?" he asked her.

She smiled at the use of the word "daughter." Then, before she could answer, Asta spoke—as could have been predicted. Eirik was glad to see her spirit unbroken by what she had gone through.

"I want to ride with *Moðir.*"

"Very well."

Once Freyja was settled on Doe, he lifted the little girl up to her.

"Follow us," he told Halfdan, who had already vaulted on top of a tired-looking gelding. They would have to ask Wolf if he had a horse to spare, and give the poor beast the rest he had clearly earned in his long life.

Eirik climbed on Fenrir and finally, *finally*, took his two girls home.

As soon as they arrived at the village, Merewen and Frigyth rushed over to them, worry etched over their faces. While Eirik lifted the half-asleep Asta off the saddle, Freyja jumped to the ground. But she was so tired after a tension-filled, sleepless night that she stumbled and almost twisted her ankle.

"Dear God, Freyja, look at you" Eirik's mother exclaimed, steadying her. "You're exhausted. Wolf told us what happened. Are you all right?"

"Yes. I'm fine."

As she said the words, her eyes started to burn. No, she didn't want to start crying now! But the relief of being back to the safety of the village, of knowing that she had succeeded in saving Asta, of seeing the women worry about her, everything made it impossible for her not to collapse.

Eirik's arm wrapped around her before she even realized she needed the support. Merewen nodded her approval at the gesture.

"When Wolf and the men came to collect Eirik at the hut this morning and didn't find either of you, they set off for the harbor," she informed them. "What happened? Did you meet with them on the way back?" she asked, turning to Eirik.

"No, we weren't at the harbor. When I arrived, Harald had already taken Asta and Freyja to a different location. I went there, with the help of a friend." He nodded toward Halfdan, who was waiting by his horse. "We will have to send someone to get the men and inform them of what happened."

"Yes." The Icelander's wife smiled. "They might well have done some damage to this Harald by then."

"Good. It is nothing less than the bastard deserves for what he did. I trust Wolf and *Faðir* to make sure he understands we never want to hear from him again." Eirik's hold around Freyja tightened at the same time as his voice hardened. She sighed, relishing his fierceness. "Now, let me get the girls home. They didn't sleep last night and need a rest. Will you take care of Half-dan, see that he has something to eat and drink? He'll want to speak to Wolf when the men come back."

"Yes. Of course. Tell us if we can do anything else," his mother said, giving him a smile.

Freyja took Asta's hand and followed Eirik to the hut. Her knees almost buckled when the familiar smell of smoke and cooked meat hit her nostrils. She was home.

She was safe.

Eirik made them sit while he poured them both a glass of milk and placed bread and cheese on the table.

"You two stay here while I go see Knut and Thorfinn," he

instructed once they had emptied their drinks. "The black-smith's sons will go to the harbor, make sure Wolf and his men know what happened."

Freyja nodded. Lying down would be good. Feeling Asta safe in her arms would be good. In any case, she wouldn't have the strength to do more. "Thank you."

Eirik brushed a tender finger over her cheek. "Sleep, Freyja, my mother's right. You look about to collapse."

She was, but she wasn't the only one. "You didn't sleep last night either, you—"

"Don't worry about me. I'm not the one who had to deal with a vile Dane merchant and a lecherous Saxon, I'm not the one with child." His worried gaze landed on her stomach. "Just take Asta to bed and rest."

She did, as soon as he'd walked out of the door.

And the next thing she knew she was falling into oblivion with the little girl by her side.

18

Freyja only woke up when the sun had passed over the zenith. Nestled between her and the wall, Asta was still asleep, her belt held in a closed fist, as usual. Eirik was in the hut, sitting on his stool, watching over them. She stretched, her body heavy but her mind at peace. The nightmare was truly over.

"Have you slept?" she asked Eirik.

He gave a curt nod, as if it was not important if he had or not. "A little. Here, have something to eat. You didn't have much earlier."

No. She'd been too tired, the priority had been to rest. But now she realized she was indeed famished. No wonder. She hadn't had much to drink or eat since the previous afternoon. Grateful for Eirik's thoughtfulness, Freyja stood up. First she emptied a cup of ale, then she accepted the slice of bread smothered with fresh goat's cheese he was handing her. He had sprinkled roasted seeds and honey over the creamy base.

"Here. This was my mother's special treat for us when we were children. I hope you like it."

Freyja moaned when she took the first bite. It was delicious, just what she needed. "I do. A treat indeed."

He smiled, pleased. "Will you come sit outside? The day is still warm."

"Yes, it will do me good, help me clear my head from sleep."

Eirik took a bowl filled with cracked nuts, the rest of the bread, and the pot of honey, which he placed between them on the bench.

"Please tell me. What happened in that farm before I arrived?" he asked, once she had finished eating.

Freyja had been expecting the question, but she knew she would find it hard to answer honestly. It had been so frightening. Her gaze flickered to the window. Asta was not too far, probably within hearing range. Had she woken up? Eirik usually spoke to her in Norse, so that the girl wouldn't feel excluded, but this time he had asked his question in their mothers' language. Like her, he didn't want to risk Asta hearing anything disturbing.

"Halfdan said you had offered yourself to Harald, or rather, to his friend, in exchange for Asta," he said when she remained silent. "Is that true?"

"Yes. What else could I do? I knew you and the men would come to our rescue, so I had to buy time," she started, keeping her gaze averted. He would be angry at the risks she had taken, but there hadn't been any other choice. "I had hoped that Garulf, the Saxon, would not want to touch me, at least not straight away, but I was mistaken."

"No surprises there." Eirik gave a growl, as if he hadn't expected any different. And in truth, she had been rather naïve to believe she might avoid being bedded. "So you had to defend yourself as well as protect Asta."

"Yes."

But how could she explain what she had done? Wouldn't he be shocked?

Freyja stood up and began pacing around. Eirik stood up in turn and waited, arms crossed, for her to start her explanation.

"When we arrived at the farm, Harald took away my eating knife, the only thing I had that could pass as a weapon, so I had to find something else to defend myself. It was you who gave me the idea, actually." Swallowing, she walked closer to him and placed her forehead against his chest, needing the comfort of his embrace more than ever.

If he shielded her from the world and if she didn't have to meet his gaze, she might find the courage to explain what she had done.

When he closed his arms around her, she carried on. "Since you showed me how you make pottery, I have started to look for it everywhere I go. So I noticed what was on the table as soon as Harald brought me inside the house. A pitcher. At some point, they left Asta and me on our own, so I took it and broke it against the wall, hoping I would get a shard I could use as a knife of sorts. I was lucky and I did find myself in possession of a perfect jagged piece, which I hid in my sleeve."

"Such a clever idea. I'm impressed, though not surprised by your cunning." A hand draped over her nape in unmistakable approval.

"Garulf said... Well, it soon became clear that he wanted to bed me so..."

Freyja swallowed. Would Eirik not be repulsed by what she had pretended to do? As someone who'd led a chaste life, or as near as, would he even know about such an act? Before their tryst in the lake, he had never had a woman use her hands to pleasure him, so he might not be aware they could use their mouths.

But she had to tell him.

"I could not let him take control, at the risk of not being able to use the weapon I'd created, or have him turn it on me. And the mere idea of feeling his hands or his lips on me was unthinkable." She shivered. "So instead of waiting for him to throw me to the ground or bend me over the table, I—"

"You knelt at his feet," Eirik supplied when she stopped. "You grabbed his cock and you slashed at it, before he understood what you'd planned."

"Yes." She was very relieved he hadn't condemned her. Rather he'd made it sound as if that had been the obvious, easiest solution, as if he would have done the same thing in her place. Evidently, he did know about the act.

Eyes aglow, Eirik cradled her cheek in his palm. "Listen to me, Freyja. You don't need to be ashamed of what you did. It was very brave of you. And being hurt was no less than what the man deserved."

"Thank you. And thank you for coming after me. I know I should have waited for you to come back from Wolf's but—"

"You did what you had to do for your daughter, and you succeeded. You can be proud of yourself. I have asked Halfdan to go back to the farm and see what has become of that Garulf. I'll let you know what he tells me."

"Thank you."

They stayed locked in each other's embrace for a moment, sharing the warmth and comfort. Then a tentative voice called out from behind them.

"*Moðir?*"

Feeling self-conscious, Freyja drew away from Eirik. It was the first time, as far as she knew, that the little girl had seen her in his arms. Only that morning she had told Halfdan that they were not married, but after witnessing the embrace, she might start wondering whether there was something between her new mother and the man giving them shelter.

Well, so what if she did?

There *was* something, something as undeniable as it was wonderful.

"Have you had a good sleep, sweetheart?" she asked, opening her arms to her.

"Yes. And now I'm hungry."

"No surprises there," Eirik said, already heading to the hut. "Come. We have everything you need inside."

LATER THAT NIGHT, as she lay on her pallet with Asta in her arms again, Freyja made a decision. She, the little girl who'd been entrusted to her, the innocent baby she was carrying, and Eirik would be a family of sorts. Just like the strands on his arm ring, the four of them were now inextricably linked. She might never be able to marry Eirik, but that didn't mean she couldn't be with him and let him raise her children.

They wouldn't be the first people to do such a thing as living together without having their union officially recognized, and she doubted anyone would dare or even bother to say anything.

In the morning, when Asta left, as she usually did, to go see her friends, Freyja decided today would be the day she started her seduction of Eirik. She would see if there was at least some hope he could accept an arrangement between them.

After the ordeal of the day before, and him coming to her rescue, she felt that now was the right time. She hadn't missed the thunder in his eyes when he had irrupted into the farm. His oath and her inability to marry another man while she was still Arvid's wife notwithstanding, there was something between them, something that should be nurtured.

Yes, she would see if, as she hoped, they could allow what was between them to blossom.

Eirik came back a moment later, wood in his arms, and set

about rekindling the fire. It seemed as good an opportunity as any.

Feeling bolder than she had ever felt, Freyja bolted the door while his back was turned. She didn't want him to feel trapped, but she didn't want anyone else to come in and interrupt, if by some miracle she managed to do what she intended to do. In preparation for this moment, she had not gotten dressed and was wearing only her shift.

She stood by the door and waited for Eirik to turn around and notice her.

Once the fire was roaring again, Eirik sat on the stool and helped himself to a cup of ale. When he lowered the cup, he stilled. Freyja was standing by the door—and she hadn't dressed yet. Her hair was flowing over her shoulders in a cascade of copper, and her eyes were aglow with intent. The part of him he was always trying to suppress reared its ugly head.

Mine, it roared. *Now*.

Through her linen shirt he could see her nipples, dark and provoking, taut and ready for a man's attention. His mouth watered at the idea of suckling them, first through the thin material, then while she was naked and warm in his arms. He already knew the taste of the delicious buds of flesh, he had already suckled her once, at the lake, and even allowed her to do what no other woman had done, and now he wanted to do it all over again.

No.

The word exploded in his mind as reality crashed over him. That was a lie. He didn't want to do it all over again, he wanted to do what he had denied himself that day and every day of his adult life.

For the first time since he'd taken an interest in women, he wanted more than the solitary releases he'd had to contend with. He wanted to feel shared pleasure with a woman, *inside* a hot woman who wanted him. Could he do it? Could he allow himself that forbidden delight with Freyja, the woman he knew more intimately than any he had ever met? Perhaps. There was no fear he would be overcome and lose all control, as she meant more to him than life itself, and he would rather cut his own throat than hurt her.

Unable to bear the tension between them or to make such a momentous decision, he prepared to stand up. She stopped him with a raised hand.

"Don't move."

Her voice was hoarse with need, as frayed as his nerves felt. And he couldn't have moved, even if he'd wanted to. He was rooted to the chair by desire and indecision.

As he watched, rendered powerless by her beauty and boldness, she lifted her shift over her head and dropped it to the floor at her feet. Naked in the morning light, she was gloriously rounded and feminine. Perfect. The fire between her legs burned like a beacon, calling out to him. His cock twitched in demand.

"What are you doing?" he asked, his voice getting stuck in his throat.

"What do you think? I want you, Eirik," she said simply, coming within touching distance of him. "I've wanted you from the moment we met, when I didn't know you for the generous, amazing man you are, and I'm tired of fighting my need. We've already given one another pleasure. It was glorious, unlike anything I could have dreamed. Now I want that pleasure to be shared between us. And I think you want that too."

As if to illustrate what she was saying, she took his hand and placed it on her breast. He groaned, because he had not often allowed himself the indulgence of touching a woman's naked breast before, and hers was unbelievably soft, just the perfect size for his hand.

"You want me?" he asked through clenched teeth.

No other woman had been so explicit before, and it sent a jolt of pure longing through his veins. He had sensed the other women's desire, he had seen and smelled it, but they had never pressed him for more once he had decided to pleasure them, they'd been happy to take what he offered and leave it at that. Freyja was the first to insist she wanted to return the favor, the first to admit to her need for him out loud, and the first he actually considered surrendering to.

She covered his hand with hers and made him squeeze her lightly. "I do want you. I want to feel you inside me."

Inside. The very thing he had promised himself he would never do. He should remind her of what he had sworn all those years ago. But his throat was incapable of producing any sound. It was then that it hit him. When he had taken his oath, he had forgotten to take one thing into account. That he would fall in love and the need for that woman would be impossible to ignore. It was easy not to listen to his bodily urges with lovers who meant little to him.

But with Freyja?

With the woman who was everything he had never known he needed... How was he supposed to resist? Did he even want to? He wasn't sure.

"I'm with child."

"Yes," he managed to rasp. What did that have to do with anything? Or had he been so lost in lewd musings that he had missed a part of the conversation? It was not impossible. His groin was on fire, meaning that his mind was not functioning as well as it should have. "You are."

Did she think it made her less desirable? It did not, quite the contrary. She had lost the gaunt look she'd had when she'd first arrived, and the new, rounded contours suited her.

"So I cannot fall with child from this joining."

Oh. Yes. Now he saw where she was going with this. She meant that he need not worry he would leave an unfortunate woman to deal alone with the consequences of his actions, like so many men did, like that Olaf had done. Because there would be no consequences. With her he could let himself go.

She really was the answer to all the prayers he had never dared formulate.

"The door is barred."

Was it? He stole a glance behind her and saw that she had indeed taken every precaution. The minx! This had all been carefully planned. Knowing that it was not a whim only sent his arousal spiking further. For once, he was not in charge, for once, he might allow himself to relinquish control. For once, he might be able to experience what a normal man could.

"I—"

"And I'm willing," she carried on, taking his other hand and placing it over her other breast. By the gods. She would be the death of him. Could she sense his resolve weakening even as another part of him stiffened? Probably. He wanted her so much his face must be a picture of hunger. And of course the staff between his thighs was so hard he was surprised it had not come out of his braies yet. "More than willing. I'm desperate."

"Yes." He could see that.

She leaned in toward him like the temptress she was. "So, if you take me, you won't have to worry about forcing your attention on a woman. You won't have to worry about being seen or having to face anyone else's comments afterward—this will be for us only. You won't have to worry about fathering a child who will grow up without a loving father. If you take me, you will not be breaking any oath. You will only be doing what we both want. What we both need."

No sooner had she finished the sentence than he leaned forward and took her right nipple in his mouth. Enough was enough. She was right, he needed this. They both did. He had no idea why he was fighting it anymore.

"Yes!"

Holding his head between her hands, Freyja forced him to suckle her harder. But there was no need to hold him in place. He was right where he wanted to be, filling his mouth with the most tantalising bit of woman he had ever tasted.

Above him, Freyja was panting hard, and her legs had gone unsteady. With his hands at her waist, he could feel her wavering. Could he bring her to completion like this he wondered, just by licking her? Was that even possible?

"Eirik, please," she rasped, "do to me what you have not done to another woman. Allow me to show you what you've been denying yourself all this time."

"Are you doing this for me then?" he growled. Somehow that didn't seem satisfactory.

"No, I'm doing it for me also," she said on a sob. "Please, I need you. I need you to make me feel whole again, loved again, I need you to prove to me that someone on this earth still wants me, and for the right reasons."

It was too much. He might be able to fight the desire raging inside him, but he would not deny her. Arvid would *not* be the last man to have touched her, she would not be allowed to feel soiled and unwanted.

Releasing her nipple from his mouth, Eirik drew her to him until she was sitting on his lap, straddling him. Then he kissed her with all the strength of his desperation—and doubt. Would he be able to do this?

"I do want you, Freyja. I do want to show you that someone wants you, because I do, more than my next breath," he said against her lips. "But I-I don't know how to do this. You know I've never done it."

How much the admission cost him! He felt ridiculous. What

he wouldn't have done in this instant to be as experienced as his friend Sven, or as self-assured as his brother Moon. He was a man of seven-and-thirty summers, damn it all, not a green lad, he should know how to make love to a woman, he should be confident in his ability to bring her the pleasure she needed.

"You do know how to make love to a woman," Freyja answered, her eyes gleaming. "If you don't remember how you touched me the day you watched me bathe, I certainly do. And a man who can make a woman feel so much pleasure with just a few caresses is certain to give his lover satisfaction when he takes her."

She lifted herself off him and tugged at the laces of his braies, causing desire to ignite in his loins. There was not the least doubt in her eyes. She trusted him to do what other men did, what they both wanted. Finally free from his constraints, his member strained upward, begging for attention.

"Hold me," she breathed. "I'm not strong enough on my own, but if you hold me, I will be able to ride you...if you agree."

"Yes." That was the best solution. She knew what she was doing, she would make sure to use his body in the way that gave her the most satisfaction. If she was in charge, she would get her pleasure. All he had to do was hold her in place and stay hard for her, an easy enough task. Suddenly he did not feel so useless. "Take me."

Freyja rewarded him with a radiant smile. Slowly, she lowered herself onto his waiting member, stopping only when he was fully seated inside her. Then, closing her eyes, she threw her head back and gave a deep sigh.

Eirik's whole body burst into flames. Never had anything felt so good, and he instantly knew he was not going to last. The heat of her sheath was like nothing he had ever experienced, or even imagined. The softness was unbelievable. And then she started to move. The feeling was so exquisite, he almost came there and then. Fuck, perhaps staying hard long enough for her to reach her release would not be as easy as he'd first thought.

"Freyja. Please."

"Yes. I'm here. Now you take me."

"Yes," he whispered, burying his face in the crook of her neck. Suddenly he knew just what to do.

Holding her firmly, he started pumping his hips. He couldn't help it, his masculine instinct had taken over, showing him what to do and how. Somehow his untrained body knew how to move to get what it needed, to get more of Freyja's sweetness, now, before it was too late.

"Eirik, yes, more," she rasped, echoing his thoughts.

Was it the arching of her spine that brought him to the edge, or the insanely lewd moan she gave when he pinched her nipple? He didn't know. Either way, he knew he was going to erupt like never before.

"Stay with me," he pleaded, suddenly afraid.

"Always. Come for me."

White heat flashed behind his eyelids, and his body exploded in a rush of pure joy.

He heard Freyja give a keening cry, as if the feel of his seed shooting inside her had provoked her release. Could it be? Was that what he was feeling around his cock? Her pleasure? He had felt those spasms on his fingers countless times, and he thought that it might well be.

But he couldn't think right now. He could only feel.

"That was—"

"Just a start. We are not finished yet," he rasped.

Well, *he* was, but this lovemaking had been too fast for her to find satisfaction. She needed more. Hell, *he* needed more, needed to know that she would remember this first time together as earth-shattering. Because he was determined that she would stay with him forever. That they couldn't marry didn't mean a thing, he had to make her see that.

Eirik waited to make sure he'd recovered some of his strength, then, still embedded within her, he stood up and carried Freyja over to the pallet. Once she lay under him, like the most precious offering, he withdrew and straightened back up, looking his fill. That he was still fully clothed and she naked only added to the thrill of the moment.

"You are so fucking beautiful." Like living flames that had burned his resolutions to cinders. "But what's this?" His finger brushed against a small bruise at her hip he hadn't noticed before, too entranced by her nakedness. His blood, so hot a moment ago, ran cold. "You didn't tell me that bastard had hit you?"

"No, and he didn't. This is nothing," she said, reaching out to draw him closer. "I bumped myself against the table at the farm, that's all. Please, ignore it... Just look at me like you did before."

"I will do more than look at you."

He would touch her. He would devour her.

First he gave her breasts the attention they deserved, then he began his slow descent, intent on feasting on the whole of her. Freyja squeaked when he swirled his tongue around her navel and then lifted her head in shock when he went lower still.

"Eirik! Wait!" She tugged at his hair to try and stop him but he didn't relent. "Eirik!" she repeated, sounding almost panicked. "You can't do that. You... We've just..."

With his mouth on her he couldn't answer but even if he had been able to, he would have ordered her to let him do this, let him love her the way he needed to. He wouldn't be denied, not now. He had waited too long for this, for *her*. She tasted of him and her combined, both new tastes to him. A revelation.

He couldn't get enough of it.

"Yes...ah..." She was no longer protesting. "More, yes!"

Triumph surged through Eirik. Like a starved man, he lapped at her softness, suckling, exploring, melting from the inside. He groaned. This new delight would be something he indulged in as often as possible.

His finger slid into impossible, slick softness. Only a moment ago he had been inside this woman, giving her what they both needed. She had taken him inside her body, the most wonderful gift anyone had given him. The thought was dizzying. For a moment they had been one, in a way he had not been with anyone else in his life. It had been wonderful, and he already knew he would not be able to leave it at that.

Already he could feel desire blooming in his veins, stirring him anew. When Freyja finally erupted on his tongue, Eirik's whole body sizzled.

As soon as she had recovered from this release, he would take her again, slowly, until they both forgot there had ever been a time when they had not been joined as one.

19

When he woke up sometime later, Eirik wondered what was happening. What was he doing on his pallet, fully dressed, in the middle of the day? He opened his eyes and it all came back to him. He was not quite fully dressed, and he was not alone. Freyja was lying in his arms, her gorgeous hair draped all over his chest. There was an excellent reason for him to be on his pallet, asleep, in the middle of the day.

For the first time in his life, he had made love to a woman. And it had been nothing like what he had dreaded, or even like what he had imagined it might be. It had been beyond wonderful. Freyja had showered him with the best possible gifts. Physical pleasure that had sent him straight into oblivion, and the realization that he could be trusted in a woman's arms.

How could he express his gratitude?

The answer came to him in a flash.

He remembered her telling him a few weeks ago that she would like to learn more about the place where her mother had spent her childhood. She'd told him it was less than a day's walk from here, in a farm along the south road, by a river with a watermill. He had never heard of such a place, but his parents might know where it was. They had been here longer than him, and Eowyn might have mentioned the farm to his mother, who'd been a close friend.

So, leaving Freyja asleep on the pallet, he put some order to his clothes and went to find them.

His father was outside the hut, sawing a huge tree trunk into equally huge logs. He stopped and wiped his brow when he saw him. It seemed that a pause would be welcome. "Son. What brings you here?"

"A question."

"Yes, I know the place you mean," his father told him, once Eirik had explained what he wanted. "Take the road south, walk to the other side of the woods, leave the small Saxon village behind you, and then turn right when you see a boulder in the shape of an ox. The last time I went there the watermill was still in good working order, but the farm was falling apart. That was almost a decade ago, so I'm not sure what you'll find."

"It doesn't matter." That the place had changed quite a bit was to be expected. "Thank you."

He made to turn around, impatient to tell Freyja that he knew where to take her now. They could go on the morrow, if the weather held.

"Wait," his father called out before he could walk away. "How is Freyja?"

The question brought back her ordeal of the previous day. Remembering the bruise on her hip and what she'd had to do to defend herself, Eirik's mood instantly darkened. "As well as she could be. She is very brave. She wants nothing more than to forget what happened and move on with her life. I'm not sure I would be quite as forgiving in her stead."

"Tell me about it." The look of thunder on his father's face likely matched his own. "I'm afraid we men are not cut of the same cloth."

"No, apparently not."

"How are things progressing between you?"

For the first time in his life Eirik wondered if he had not gone as pink as a maiden. "It's...fine," he said, not trusting himself not to betray his unease if he spoke more than two words.

Things are more than fine. I can still taste her on my tongue, and my whole body feels different for having finally been allowed to do what it was born to do. She made me feel things I could never have imagined. She gave me no choice but to find out what it means to be a man, and I'm grateful.

"Good. I like her," his father added. It looked as if he had heard his thoughts as clearly as if he'd spoken them out loud.

"So do I."

With those words, Eirik walked over to the forge, where he hoped to find Halfdan. He had promised Freyja he would tell her what had happened to Garulf, and the Dane would be back from the Saxon's farm now, with news.

"Eirik, there you are. Forgive me, I wanted to come and see you this morning but Magnus needed me to—"

"'Tis no issue," he assured him quickly.

Quite the contrary. Had he come knocking at the door earlier, Halfdan might have interrupted the best moment of his life.

"I'm afraid I don't have much to tell you, though. When I arrived at the farm, I saw no one. There was a pool of blood on the floor in the main room, right where you told me, but no trace of Garulf. Whether he managed to recover enough to go get help or died of his wounds and was taken away to be buried, I know not."

Eirik nodded. Perhaps this uncertainty was best. If he was

told for certain that the man was still alive, the temptation to go finish what Freyja had merely started might prove impossible to resist. It was like his father had said. Men and women were not cut from the same cloth.

"Thank you. If you don't mind, go see Wolf and ask him if he thinks he can find out the man's whereabouts." He paused. "It's better if you do. If I go, I will only ask Wolf to bring me the bastard's head on a platter."

"Aye. I'm not surprised. I would do the same if it were my wife."

"Asta told you that Freyja is not my wife."

"I know, but I'm only saying... I mean, I truly I thought you two were... From the way you—"

"Yes. I can guess what you thought," Eirik growled. "But we are not married."

More's the pity, he almost added.

"Anyway. I hope you've been made welcome in the village?" he asked, changing the subject.

Halfdan beamed. "Yes. It's just as you said, Magnus is delighted to have help at the forge."

"I know. His two sons have trades of their own and are not interested in taking over. I assume he offered to house you in the room at the back of the forge for now?" Halfdan nodded. "Excellent. Now if you'll excuse me, I have to go."

Back to Freyja.

He found her up and fully dressed this time, not half-naked and ready to seduce him.

More's the pity, he thought for the second time that day.

She flushed when she saw him, but she didn't avert her gaze. That was good, as it meant that she didn't regret what had happened earlier. Relief washed through him.

"Are you well?" he asked, cursing himself for the stupid

question. Why wouldn't she be? He had not hurt her, had he? Quite the opposite.

"I'm well," she said, coming to nestle into his arms. The pleasure that simple gesture gave him was indecent. "Thank you, Eirik, for the gift you gave me today."

"I think I should be the one to thank *you*." She had been the one introducing him to new delights, showing him what men and women were supposed to share, trusting him with her body.

"It was my pleasure." She gave a delightful—and rather naughty—chuckle against his chest. "I told you not to worry about your ability to please a woman. You acquitted yourself of the task more than well, and I think you know it."

He didn't think she was saying that to ease his fears. He knew she had felt pleasure in their joining. As he'd promised himself while he was licking her, he had taken her a second time, slowly, making sure to enjoy each thrust and each withdrawal. And that time, he had not wondered what the spasming around his cock was. Her pleasure, unmistakably. It had precipitated his own.

Yes, despite his inexperience, he had managed to bring her satisfaction. What had seemed inconceivable with every other woman had been natural with her. He pressed the tip of his nose to hers, more thankful than ever for her understanding and patience. If only he could find a way to express himself adequately.

This reminded him of what he had planned to do in the morning. For a moment, lost in the pleasure of her embrace and heated memories of their lovemaking, he'd quite forgotten.

"There's something I'd like to do tomorrow."

Her cheeks went such a violent red color that he guessed she thought he was talking about something they could do in bed. His groin tightened, signifying its agreement to the scheme. Whatever she was imagining, his body would agree to it.

"No, I don't mean it like that," he whispered in her ear, though of course, now that the idea had crossed his mind, he could think of many things he'd like them to do together in bed. Freyja bit her bottom lip, looking chastened. He took her mouth, not wanting her to feel bad about having misunderstood. "But with the right woman, I suppose I could be persuaded," he added, his lips against hers. There were many things he had yet to discover.

"What is this thing then?" she asked, once he'd released her.

"I have found out the location of the farm where your mother grew up. I can take you there tomorrow if you want."

Her face lit up in delight. "You would do that?"

He snorted at the question. A few weeks ago he had offered to marry her, look after her unborn child. That day at the lake he had surrendered to her entreaties and allowed her to give him the pleasure he'd refused everyone else. Last night he had ridden to her and Asta's rescue without help, and only that morning he had broken his vow for her, making love to her twice despite his resolve never to possess a woman. Didn't she know by now that there was nothing he wouldn't do for her?

Taking her for a stroll to the other side of the woods didn't even register.

"Freyja. I would do much more for you, and I think you know it."

One day, he hoped she would allow him to prove it.

Freyja sat on the riverbank, hugging her knees, listening to the babbling of the stream, allowing her thoughts to flow as freely as the rapid waters at her feet. Right in front of her, the watermill was turning in an endless, timeless rotation. That massive wheel had once been unclogged by Freodheric, the young Saxon who had been her mother's first love.

This story was the reason she was here right now. She had wanted to come pay her respects to the man she had heard about many times, and who had meant so much to Eowyn.

As she and Eirik had walked in the sunshine, she had explained to him what had happened decades ago.

"When my mother was about ten, her grandmother, who had raised her from birth, died." Though he had not once asked the reason behind this expedition, she thought she owed it to him. "As she lay on her deathbed, the old woman told her to go to the farm, that the people would look after her there."

She'd thought, as had everyone around, that the farmers were good people, who welcomed orphaned and undesired children under their roof. In reality, as the young Eowyn had soon discovered, they treated the poor little souls like slaves, safe in the knowledge that no one cared enough about them to complain. Still, there had been no other choice but to stay. All her family was dead. Who else would welcome a young girl who had nothing to offer?

Freyja's chest constricted when she thought that this fate had almost befallen Asta, who was much the same age now. Had she not been on that boat, the little girl would have ended up as Garulf's slave, if not his wife.

She shook her head, pushing the thought away. She *had* been on the boat, and Asta was safe. She would be loved and have a normal life.

"But the farmer was a cruel woman who worked her hard, as she did all the children and young people she was supposed to look after," she continued. "It was a difficult life, but despite her misery, my mother found love with Freodheric, a Saxon who had been brought to the farm like her, at a young age." Freyja gave a rueful smile. It was hard, impossible even, to imagine her mother in love with someone other than the fiery Dane she had eventually married. "When the two of them grew old enough to look after themselves, they agreed that they would flee together and get married but they..."

"What happened?" Eirik asked when her voice failed her. The look in his eyes was black as thunder.

"Freodheric died before they could escape." It was such a tragic, tragic story. "One day the farmer's son came back to live at the farm. He took an immediate dislike to Freodheric and made sure to give him the worst, most dangerous jobs. Shortly after his arrival, he sent him to unclog the watermill wheel. It was winter, and the poor boy was already weak from exhaustion. He did what he was supposed to do, but could not escape in time when the wheel started going again. His mangled body was brought back to the farm without comment. My mother didn't dare show her grief, for fear of becoming the man's next victim. A few days later, she found the strength to leave the place where she had been so unhappy."

"I'm sorry. That's a terrible story."

"Yes." A pause. "I don't know why I wanted to come, really. I expect the old farmer has long been dead, and her son also, but I feel as if I needed to—"

The end of Freyja's sentence was lost in a gasp, as at that moment they turned a sharp corner and happened upon the farm. Or rather, what little was left of it.

She and Eirik came to an abrupt halt as they took in the scene of devastation in front of them.

The farm had been utterly destroyed. All around what appeared to have been the main building, the grass had been burned to the ground, and was only now showing timid signs of new growth. To one side, the remains of a hay loft did their best not to collapse. Just behind them the stables were little more than gaping holes. At the center of it all, charred pieces of wood that may once have been roof beams lay haphazardly atop a pile of crumbled stones. There were too few to have constituted a house the size of the building her mother had described, indicating that, following the disaster, the local people had come and helped themselves to what they could salvage to build their own homes. No one had done anything to build the place again.

Freyja stared at the scene in disbelief.

Had the fire been deliberate or accidental? She couldn't help but think that someone, possibly one of the unfortunate children who had been mistreated there, once grown and strong enough to put their plan to execution, had wanted to destroy the place where they had been so unhappy, and prevent others from suffering as they had suffered.

"My father told me he hadn't come here in nearly a decade, and wasn't sure in what state I would find the place," Eirik said in a shocked whisper. "He made it sound as if it had already started to show signs of neglect. But I'm sure he didn't expect this."

No, how could he? Judging from the way the vegetation had not yet started to reclaim the pile of rubble, the fire had been quite recent. How could the Dane have predicted it? Well, there wasn't much to be gained from staring at the place, so Freyja turned her back on it and started heading toward the river they had spotted earlier. Following it downstream, it did not take them long to find the watermill.

As she saw the place she had imagined in her mind many a time, she felt the inexplicable urge to cry. The baby she was carrying must have made her more emotional than usual, she decided, because, in truth, sad as it was, Freodheric's demise meant little to her.

Not trying to fight the emotions welling inside her, she sat down on the grassy bank. Eirik remained by the tree, leaving her to her thoughts. They quickly turned to the poor Saxon boy who had lost his life that winter day. What had he looked like? How had he spoken to her mother? Had he made her melt when he'd touched her? That last question brought heat to her cheeks. What was she doing, wondering about such things? She had never once imagined her parents as people with bodily urges and desires. The memory of her lovemaking with Eirik had to be responsible for this.

But there *was* something she had thought of time and time again.

"I remember as a young woman I used to wonder how my mother could have loved two men in her life," she said out loud, watching the waterwheel's soothing movement. It had seemed, not like a betrayal of her father, exactly, since the two of them had met years afterward, but still, it had seemed odd to the girl she had once been to think that her husband was not the only man with a place in her mother's heart.

"And now you don't wonder?"

Eirik's deep rumble, coming from closer than she had expected, caused a shiver to go down her spine. She hadn't heard him move. How? He was not exactly a frail youth. She twisted her body to lift her head to him. Her breath caught in her chest when she saw him, so fierce and strong, standing right behind her. From this angle, he was truly awe-inspiring.

"No, I don't wonder."

Because now she knew it was possible to love two men sincerely. Having met Sigurd's most tortured son had made that clear.

She had once been in love with Arvid, the Dane who had wooed her, she was now in love with Eirik, the half-Saxon who had protected her. The feelings inside her were very different, admittedly, because the circumstances and the men themselves were very different, but the result was the same. In the same way she had once not borne being parted from Arvid, she could not imagine being without Eirik.

Could she confess to it?

Could she tell him she had fallen in love with him when they both knew she wasn't free to act on that love? Would he accept a situation that was unsatisfactory at best, insulting at worst? He had once offered to marry her, which showed he was ready for a life-long commitment. The day before, he had accepted the desire burning between them and acted on it, which showed trust and feelings deeper than she could have hoped. Considering all this, would he agree to settle for anything less than a proper marriage, to compromise his integrity for someone who could not be his wife in truth?

She couldn't be sure and she was not brave enough to ask.

How cruel life could be. What had she done to deserve being forsaken by her first husband? To not be able to be with the only other man who, against all odds, wanted to be with her and offer her unborn child and adopted daughter a chance at happiness?

She hadn't done anything to deserve this. But that was not how life worked, of course. Sometimes it just wasn't fair.

Freyja looked at the mill again. Her mother had suffered when she'd seen that her beloved Freodheric had died. But him dying, as hard to deal with as it had been, had meant that she had been free to be with another man when she'd later met someone who could make her life complete. Eowyn had been able to marry Rune and bear his legitimate children. Freyja didn't have that luxury.

The man she had once loved was no more, but he was not dead. He'd been replaced by a complete stranger who didn't want her, only the pleasure her body could give him, even if he had to take it by force.

It was worse, in so many ways.

Of course, some people would argue that she could just

ignore the fact that she had a husband in another country, and pretend she was able to marry. After all, Arvid himself didn't feel as if they owed anything to one another, and no one in the village, save Eirik, knew she was married. But the two of them did know the truth. She *was* married. When she had made that commitment, she had meant to honor it. She refused to soil Eirik and make a mockery of him by marrying him while she was still bound to another man. He was an honorable man, he deserved to be able to lead an honest life, not one built on a lie.

Eirik sighed and threw a stone into the fast-flowing river.

How odd life could be. Against all odds, after two decades on his own, battling doubts and self-disgust, he had finally met a woman with whom he could have built a normal life and let go of his demons—only to find out that they couldn't be together because she was already married.

Many people would no doubt tell him that her marriage to a man who was in another country, who did not even consider her his wife and would never get to hear about it, was no impediment to a union between them, but he would never force Freyja to live a lie or break the vows she had once taken in good faith. He loved her for her honesty and he agreed with her, however much it galled him, that they had to do this right or not at all. Besides, he didn't need to be married to be with her.

As long as she lived with him, he could wait for the rest.

Perhaps one day they would be allowed to be together. Perhaps when his hair had turned gray and his body gone frail, he would finally be able to call this woman his own. In the meantime, he would get what he could of her. He would protect her and her children, and he would love them.

He already did.

It was like his father had said. The decision to look after and love a child who was not of his loins was not a decision at all. It was an inevitability, because this innocent baby might not be his but it was Freyja's. And Freyja was the woman he loved. He could not let her face this alone or be without her.

Another stone disappeared under the surface of the water.

Should he tell Freyja he had fallen in love with her? Was it even worth it? Didn't she know it already? Now that they had made love, he thought they both knew where they stood. But the words had not yet been spoken. Perhaps tonight, once Asta was asleep, he would take her to the bench and tell her. Yes, that was the best way. He would not be able to remain silent for much longer.

A third stone was thrown in the river, then a fourth.

"By the way," he told Freyja, once the beating of his heart had slowed down. "I went to see Halfdan yesterday. He told me that he had not found any trace of Garulf at the farm. We don't know where he is, whether he is alive and hidden somewhere, or if he died and was taken away to be buried. He's going to tell Wolf, who will investigate."

She nodded, looking thoroughly uninterested. "Where he is doesn't matter. Let Wolf decide what to do, if he finds him. As long as I don't have to see him ever again, I care not."

Mmmm. This was exactly the answer his mother had given his father all those years ago, when she'd confided in what had happened to her. And his reaction to it was the same. In love with a woman carrying a child imposed on her during a rape, who had adopted an older child, and who was forgiving toward the people who'd hurt her, it seemed he was really reliving the same life as his father. With one exception. He would not be able to marry the woman his heart had chosen.

He was about to tell Freyja Garulf had better hope he never crossed paths with him when he heard a voice behind him.

"Excuse me?"

Lost to his musings, he had not noticed they were no longer alone, but when he turned around there was a woman by the oak, looking unsure whether she should talk to them or not. She appeared to be about Freyja's age, and Saxon.

"Can we help?" he asked, doing his best to sound reassuring.

"I hope so. I'm looking for a farm I was told was in the area." She took another step forward when she saw Freyja raise her head in recognition. "One that offers refuge to orphans?"

"Yes. We know the one you mean," Freyja answered, nodding to the ruin in the distance. They could just about make out the pile of rubble behind the trees. "It was over there, but as you can see there isn't much left of it."

The woman stared at the heaps of stones and charred wood in horror, her eyes wide as cart wheels. The hope that had flashed on her face only a moment ago had been utterly wiped out. "But... but... It—"

"Did you want anything?" Eirik asked, coming closer. It might not be long before he needed to assist her. She looked unsteady on her feet, about to collapse.

"I was hoping to have news of my daughter. To get her back, in fact. My daughter, the daughter I had to— But if the place has been destroyed then— I'm too late. Too late."

She fell to her knees and started crying, the sound heartbreaking.

Freyja, who had picked herself up, knelt by the woman's side and placed a hand over her arm. "You left your daughter there, with the farmers, for them to take care of?" she clarified.

Eirik understood her confusion. The farm had been meant for orphans, but clearly the little girl had had a mother. A loving mother, by the sound of things. Why had she left the girl there?

"I-I didn't have any choice. I was forced to remarry, and my new husband didn't want the girl I'd had with my first husband. He had heard of the farm, as the couple who ran it had taken in some of his acquaintances' children in the past, and he made me take her there. And so I did. Do you hear? I did!" She was getting agitated and her next words barely made sense. "For a whole year I cried myself to sleep every night— Then I fell with another child. But I lost the babe and my husband was not— I couldn't b-bear any of it..."

The words quickly became unintelligible as the woman dissolved into a fresh burst of tears.

"It's all right," Freyja soothed, drawing the woman into her arms as naturally as if they had been friends all their lives. "Of course, you couldn't bear it a moment longer. And you did well to leave your husband. Only a cruel man would force you to give your child up, and unfortunately, there is no arguing with cruel men. None of this is your fault. But it will be all right now."

Eirik was stunned. He didn't know what to tell the woman, how to comfort her, but Freyja seemed to find it easy to find the right words. And how had she guessed that the Saxon had left her husband? Perhaps her own experience of having left Arvid helped.

The woman's sobs seemed to subside after a while. Above her head, Freyja threw him a meaningful glance. Somehow, he understood all the silent questions she was asking him. Did he think the farmers who had run the farm at the time Eowyn had lived there had passed on their vile methods to their children and grandchildren? Had the little girl been mistreated? The sobbing woman didn't seem aware that this was the fate that had befallen the children on the farm, at one time at least. There was no need telling her, she was distraught enough as it was.

And anyway, mistreated or not, because of the fire, the little girl had disappeared.

This was where he could help. Words of reassurance he'd left to Freyja, but practical advice he could offer. It was his turn to speak.

"Come back to our village. My friend, Wolf, might be able to help. He knows everyone in the area, Norse and Saxons alike."

There was no guarantee a discussion with the Icelander would yield any results, of course, but a spark lit up in the woman's eyes, so he carried on. There was no other choice. They couldn't just leave her behind with her dashed hopes and no one to turn to. "With the help of his friend, the reeve in town, Wolf might be able to find some answers for you, find out what happened here."

He didn't dare to suggest that they would find the little girl safe and well but the woman nodded.

"Oh, if only."

He held out his hand to her, then helped Freyja up in turn. The Saxon tried to give him a smile in thanks and only managed to squeeze more tears from her eyes.

"Come. I'm sure Wolf will help you. He helped me not so long ago." Freyja offered her arm, which the woman gladly accepted. "If anyone can sort out this mess, it is him."

"Thank you. I'm Matilda, by the way. You and your husband are very kind."

Eirik exchanged a look with Freyja. Neither of them rectified the woman's mistake. It seemed that people were destined to believe the two of them were a couple. Let them.

They were anyway, in all the ways that mattered.

20

"Will you be all right alone in the hut while I take Matilda to Wolf?" Eirik asked Freyja as they reached the village sometime later. It would not be long before sunlight started to fade away and the temperature dropped. He wanted her home and warm when it did. Tonight would be a cold night.

"Of course."

He gave her hand a squeeze before leaving her. He could tell she had been shaken by the poor woman's story, and little wonder. It was horrific, and would remind her of her own ordeal, even if mercifully she had never been forced to abandon a daughter. If he could be affected by Matilda's distress, he did not imagine what a woman with child would feel. He had not missed how the babe seemed to make her more emotional than usual, a common enough occurrence, or so he remembered from what his brothers had told him at the time their wives had been with child.

"Come," he told Matilda, leading the way to Wolf's hut at the other end of the village. She followed him without a word.

The door opened on Merewen, who took one look at them

and nodded to the back of the hut, where her husband sat on a massive chair, sharpening his eating knife. Evidently, she was too used to people coming for help to mistake their purpose. As soon as he saw them, Wolf dropped what he was doing and stood up.

He, too, had guessed that his advice would be required.

"Wolf, this is Matilda," Eirik started, nudging her forward. "I'm hoping you can help her. Freyja and I met her today by the watermill on the other side of the forest."

The Icelander nodded. "Of course. Just tell me what the matter is."

Eirik turned to Matilda. "I will leave you to explain your situation to my friend in private. Meanwhile, I'll go see my sister's friend, Inga. She will give you a place to sleep for a few days, while we see what we can do about your daughter."

The Saxon thanked him with a watery smile that tugged at his heart. "Thank you, really. I don't know what I would have done without—"

"No need to thank me. I'm only doing what anyone would do."

One last nod at Wolf and he was gone.

As he knocked on Inga's door a moment later, Eirik smiled to himself. What would have happened if Wolf had agreed to his suggestion that Freyja should stay with the woman upon her arrival a few months ago? Seeing her only in passing in the village, he would never have gotten to know her for the wonderful, generous, brave soul she was. He would not have fallen in love with her. And he would still be alone.

His smile widened.

Yes, no matter how galling it was that they could not get married, his life had taken a turn for the best when Freyja and Asta had arrived, and he shouldn't complain. Hadn't he decided as a young man that he would never marry anyway? It was nothing less than he'd come to expect.

Inga opened the door on the second knock.

"Eirik." She arched a brow when she saw the smile floating on his lips. He could not blame her, as he was not a man known for grinning for no reason. "Can I help you?"

He sobered at the question. This was no laughing matter. Poor Matilda might never get to see her daughter again. "Yes. Or, at least, there is someone you can help."

She invited him in and he explained the situation as succinctly as possible.

"Of course, I can have her here. Bring her when she's ready."

He couldn't help another smile. Those where the exact same words he'd told Wolf when he'd been told about the situation Freyja was facing. Inga would now do for Matilda what he had done for her. Would she also fall in love with her guest? The idea amused him. Well, only time would tell.

"Thank you. I will."

When Eirik finally reached his hut, night had fallen. He found Freyja sitting outside on the bench. That fact alone was enough to give him pause. What was she doing here, in the cold, when he'd imagined her safe in the warmth of the hut?

When he drew nearer, she lifted her head up. Even in the moonlight, he saw that she'd been crying. His heart almost failed him.

Not again! The time he had pleasured her in the tub, he had found her outside the following morning, crying because she had found out she was with child. Now, the day after they had made love and all but declared their love to one another, he found her on the same bench, crying again.

What had happened this time?

"What is it?" he asked, sitting next to her. "Are you worried about Matilda? I'm sure Wolf will do everything he can to help her, and my friend Inga agreed to have her in her house. I went to see her just now."

"Thank you. But it's not that." She took his hand in hers. "A man came to see me while you were with Wolf."

A man! Eirik's whole body tensed. Not that bastard Harald, surely? Or Garulf, recovered from his injuries, looking for revenge? Why, oh why had he not put an end to their miserable lives when he could? At least he would now be sure Freyja was safe from harm.

"Who was it?" he growled. "Not Harald?"

She shook her head and placed a hand on his cheek, as if realizing only now that he would have been worried. "No. A Dane from a village not far from mine back home. I'm glad we asked Halfdan to tell a few trustworthy men at the harbor where I was, in case someone did try to find me, because, well, someone just did."

Yes. That had been a good idea. Which went to show a good deed was never lost. But he still needed to hear that all was well.

"What did the man want?"

"He was carrying a message from my parents, who'd asked him to seek me out as soon as he could upon landing. They knew I would find refuge in the Norsemen village, at least at first."

By the gods, why did that sound so ominous? "Not bad news?" he asked, heart in his throat.

Had her brother's wife died in childbirth? Was one of her parents unwell? Did it mean she would leave, go back to Denmark to be with them? Please no. Hadn't they faced enough obstacles already?

"I don't know." She looked at him, eyes brimming with fresh tears. "Arvid is dead."

Dead.

Eirik stilled and waited for the explanation that was sure to come.

"Apparently he argued with a neighbor who accused him of stealing one of his sheep, and he was killed in the fight that ensued." Freyja sounded stunned. "I would never have thought him capable of such treachery, but of course, he is no longer the man I married so I suppose everything is possible."

Yes. And shouldn't she know it? The man was now capable of every foul deed, including raping his wife.

Or at least *had been*. Now he was not capable of anything anymore. Eirik clenched his jaw, unable to feel any grief for the bastard who had hurt Freyja so badly, physically and emotionally. Arvid had found himself fighting against someone stronger and even more vile than him, and he had lost. Everything about that was pathetic, and it was hard to feel sorry for him.

"I don't know what to make of his death," Freyja whispered.

"No, you wouldn't," Eirik agreed in a conciliatory tone.

But as far as he was concerned, it was unequivocally good news. He understood it would be hard for her not to mourn the man she had once loved, even if she was probably indifferent to the fate of the man who had treated her so appallingly, but in his opinion, Arvid had gotten what he deserved for what he'd done. It might not have been his fault he had lost his memory, but that didn't mean he had to take advantage of the fact. He might genuinely not have remembered that she was his wife, but he had known the woman under him didn't want to be taken. He had heard her protests—and chosen to ignore them. That he had once been a good, loving man did not erase what he had done, assaulting Freyja, making a mockery of her feelings for him, forcing her to leave all she knew and loved, imposing his child on her.

And so, Eirik could not pretend to be devastated by the

Dane's demise, but wisely, he kept his opinion to himself. It had nothing to do with him.

Or...

After he'd allowed a moment for the news to sink in Freyja's mind, he took her hands in his. They were icy cold and he wrapped them in his much bigger ones.

"You know what this means, don't you?" He swallowed, knowing that after tonight his life would change forever. "You're now a free woman."

"Yes." She didn't seem to believe it was really happening. But it was. Thank the gods, it was.

"And that means we can marry at last."

She stared at him, emotion swirling in her eyes. "You still want to—"

He had lifted her onto his lap before she could finish the sentence, in a position that had become familiar to them. A position he was now assured to be able to enjoy until the day he died. Joy swelled within him.

"Freyja. Of course, I still want to marry you." How could she doubt it? "We were meant to be together, one way or the other. I am nothing without you and Asta. Before you arrived, I didn't even have a cat, for fuck's sake. Doesn't that tell you I was in a hopeless situation?"

"It does," she said, stifling a laugh. "But now you have two cats."

"Yes. Just what I needed. Now I need *you*." His chest was burning with the intensity of his need. What if she refused him? How would he bear it? "I offered you marriage a few weeks ago and I meant it. Then when I saw you were not free to accept my offer, I didn't let it stop me. I was prepared to have you and Asta in my life, knowing you would never be my wife. Yesterday I made love to you, even though it was the one thing I had sworn never to do."

"You broke your oath for me." Her eyes were full of awe.

"I wouldn't have broken it for anyone else. And now that I have met a woman I can trust myself with, I intend to make the most of it, discover all there is to discover between a man and a woman."

"Yes." She sounded breathless with anticipation, the same anticipation that was coursing through his veins. He would do with her all that he had denied himself for too long. "You're right, I am free. And so now I can tell you that I love you."

Oh, the vixen! She was throwing the most wonderful declaration he had ever heard in his face without so much as a warning. Didn't she know men were not as brave as women when it came to talking about their feelings?

"You love me?" He hadn't dared hope to hear as much today. In time, maybe, but now? It was such a gift.

"How could I not love you? You are thoughtful, generous and loving. You make my heart sing with joy and my body heat in desire. You make my daughter laugh. When we are together, I feel whole again, like the woman I once was." She tilted her head and looked at him pensively. "Now would be a good time to tell me you love me too, you know. Unless you... don't—"

He took her mouth in a fierce kiss, interrupting the outrageous declaration. He, not love her? It was as she had said. How could he *not* love her?

"I love you, Freyja."

The words that had strained to escape his mouth all day were finally allowed to come out. How wonderful it was to be allowed to express his feelings out loud. How wonderful it was to feel them in the first place.

He'd been right earlier. His life was about to change. For the better.

Feeling ten times lighter than usual, Eirik kissed her again, even more fiercely. "I love you. Now and forever. I love you. I will tell you so often that you will grow tired of hearing it."

Freyja sent her laugh to the skies. "I will *never* grow tired of hearing this. And I might well tell you just as many times."

"Good. So, will you marry me?" She still hadn't answered, and he needed to hear it, needed to hear she would be his at last. "Love me, give my life meaning, allow me to raise the two children you are generous enough to love, help me overcome the guilt and self-loathing I've been carrying since I became a man?"

Her laugh, so crystalline a moment ago, turned into a sob, a sound that tore his heart in two. Why was he such a boor?

"I cannot have you battling with self-loathing," she said, taking his head between her two palms. She had never looked fiercer than in this moment. "I will not let it happen. So yes, Eirik, I will marry you."

21

They were married less than a week later.

As he watched the woman he would soon call his wife walk up to him, Eirik struggled to contain the emotions swelling in his heart. This joy was something he had never thought to experience. How many weddings had he witnessed by the boulder standing behind him? Dozens. And now it was his own. Now, just like his friends, he would be able to lead a normal life. Now he, too, would have a wife and a family to love.

Now he would finally be allowed to be a man, without the shame it had brought for so long.

Freyja stopped next to him, and the smile on her lips had never been more radiant.

He took in every detail of his bride's appearance. She was perfection made woman, a beauty like none he had ever seen. Her fiery hair had been woven with late-blooming flowers matching the ones in the bunch she was holding. Her blue dress, cut from the cloth he had purchased for her the other week, had been embroidered at the hem and at the cuffs with apple blossom, the pattern an imitation of the one she had carved on the bowl he'd made for her, and the bean pendant over her bodice had been polished to a high shine.

It would have taken her long moments to get ready, and he could tell she was pleased with her and her friends' efforts. And yet, wretched man that he was, all he could think of was that he wanted to rip the finery off of her and get her naked and under him.

This woman was his. He could not believe his luck, might never believe it.

"*Ek ann þér*," he told her in Norse, before repeating that he loved her in their mothers' tongue. That double culture was something they shared and he wished he knew another thousand languages to tell her just how much she meant to him.

"I love you, Husband," she echoed.

And with that, the ceremony began.

As soon as they had pledged their troth to one another, Asta burst in from the crowd and threw herself between them, hugging both his right leg and Freyja's left leg.

"Will you be my *Faðir* now that you've married my new *Moðir*?" she asked, her eyes shiny with hope mingled with sorrow for the parents she had lost.

Eirik could not bear it. He bent down and scooped her up into his arms.

"Of course, Asta. I will be proud to call you daughter. And will you help us look after your little brother or sister when he or she comes? We will need you, you know, since you are part of the family."

"Yes! Of course, I will."

When he looked down, he saw that Freyja's cheeks were streaked with tears. He wiped them down gently with his thumb, smiling at her. There was a lump in his throat as well, and judging from the faces surrounding them, the two of them were not the only ones affected by the emotion of the moment.

His mother had hidden her face into his father's chest and it was obvious that she was crying.

Then Rothgar's voice, sharp as birdsong, sliced through the air, a welcome break in the tension.

"And then when you're bigger, Asta, I'll marry you."

THE BANQUET that followed the wedding ceremony was the most lavish Eirik could remember attending. Or perhaps it was the inner joy burning inside him that gave this impression. He usually felt too miserable at weddings to really enjoy the food and too dejected to take part in the merriment he thought he would never get to share.

Platters of smoked fish served with spiced whipped cream, heaps of sliced meat flavored with juniper, gruel sweetened with dried berries, pots of wild honey, wheels of yellow cheese, loaves of fragrant bread, piles of salted nuts, everything placed in front of him was mouthwatering. But the best offering of all was the woman sitting by his side, smiling at him every time he looked her way.

How could anyone be so happy? Feel so content?

After a while, he felt a hand settle on his shoulder. "Congratulations. This was a fine wedding."

"Wolf," Eirik said, nodding to the man towering over him. "I will never thank you enough for asking me to be the one to look after Freyja when she arrived in the village. You changed my life that day."

The Icelander's eyes gleamed. "I know I did."

What did that mean?

Eirik cocked his head. Had the man planned the whole thing? Surely not. Freyja had needed protection, and he *had* been the best person to provide it. All the other men were either too young or they had families to look after. His hut, by contrast, had been empty, and he was more than capable of defending himself. It had made perfect sense for Wolf to choose him. And yet... The Icelander had made it sound as if he'd had a purpose in mind when he'd brought the little Dane to him.

"Well, thank you," he repeated.

His intentions hardly mattered. Either way, on purpose or not, he had ensured he met the love of his life, the only woman who could have offered him a chance at fulfilment. It was all he needed to know.

A moment later, another hand landed on his shoulder, heavy, as if the owner meant to show off his strength, something Wolf would never want or need to do.

"I guess you *have* bedded her now, you swine," a voice whispered in his ear. "Or will very soon."

Arne.

Eirik let out an exasperated growl. The man was impossible, but as he knew he owed him the realization that he was in love with Freyja, at least in part, he was prepared to be forgiving. "I have, and I will thank you for never mentioning it ever again," he warned.

He would not have anyone, friend or not, imagining his wife naked and in bed. This delight was for him alone.

"Lucky bastard." Arne gave an exaggerated sigh. "I wonder if I will ever find a woman who wants me."

"You do, a different one every week. That's the problem, I'd say," Eirik replied roundly. "Now, bugger off and let me see to my wife's comfort. I think she needs another boiled egg. She cannot get enough of them."

By his side, Freyja giggled in acknowledgment of the private jest. "You should be nice to your friend," she chided, leaning in toward him when they were alone once more.

"I was. I wanted to send him sprawling to the ground for

daring to allude to you being naked, and I merely asked him to bugger off."

"Mmmm." She didn't sound convinced. "Mind you, I suppose Arne is used to your gruff side by now."

He scowled at her. "What on earth could give him the impression that I'm gruff, I wonder?"

She giggled again, which was exactly the reaction he'd been hoping for. His chest swelled. With her as his wife, there would be a lifetime of such giggling. "I don't know. Perhaps this fearsome scowl?"

"Well, that fearsome scowl, as you call it, is destined to disappear. Because now I'm happy with my life. Happy with my wife."

Her face softened. "Are you?"

"I am. I'm sure I will have forgotten how to scowl before this year is over. Come. I think it is time for us to dance," he said, leading her to the line of people weaving their way amongst the tables to the sound of the drums. "Unless you do want an egg first?"

"You know I don't, you wretched man!" She swatted at his chest, the gesture reminiscent of the one he'd seen his mother do every time his father said something she was not happy with. It seemed he really was reliving the life of the Danish "Beast." It suited him fine, as it was a particularly blessed life.

Everyone danced long into the night, then ate and drank some more.

It was only when he saw couples disappearing into the darkness, holding hands, that Eirik realized that this time, he wouldn't have to go back to an empty hut with an empty heart. This time he had something even better than a willing bed partner. He had a wife. Someone with whom he could be himself without fear. The thought was enough to make him stand up from his stool and swoop Freyja into his arms.

"Come, Wife," he said, nodding his thanks at Sven and

Eahlswith who had agreed to have Asta for the night so as to give them a wedding night they could remember.

At the pace he walked, it didn't take them long to reach his hut. Eirik deposited Freyja onto the floor, barred the door, removed his shirt and tunic in one fluid move and turned back to her.

The fire had been reduced to glowing embers, but he didn't have the will to rekindle it right now. It was not cold in the hut, and there was enough moonlight piercing through the window to allow him to see her. It would have to do, for he could not wait a moment longer to start his seduction of his wife.

"How do you feel?" he asked, drawing her into his arms once more. This was not her first wedding night, he'd suddenly remembered. Would she not start to think of Arvid, compare him to—

"I love you."

This was not precisely an answer to his question but it was all he needed to hear.

"I love you, too. Let me prove it to you."

Slowly, he unhooked the brooches holding her gown in place and let it drop at her feet. The temptation to get rid of the shift as well was strong, but he resisted it. He wanted to take his time or it would be over too soon. The thought of such a humiliation might have horrified another man, but Eirik only smiled to himself. Before Freyja, he hadn't trusted himself, fearing that his urges would make him do something he would regret. With Freyja, he knew that if he lost control, he would be the only one suffering from it. The only danger he was in was reaching his pleasure too quickly. But even if he unmanned himself, Freyja would not be hurt—and there were many things he could do to compensate for it.

"Can I?"

At her nod he started to unwind her hair, allowing the

flowers to scatter on the floor in a shower of petals. He took the last one between his thumb and forefinger and brought it to her nose, watching as she inhaled the sweet scent with a smile. This was going to be their first night as husband and wife, his second lovemaking ever, and he would make sure to enjoy every moment. He would remember every breath, every thrust, every moan.

He would touch her skin-to-skin this time.

Eirik feasted his eyes on his wife. Her body was tantalizingly close, yet still hidden from view. The only glimpse of it was the white column of her throat, the soft flesh begging to be kissed. He dipped his head to place his lips in the crook of her neck, and licked the vein he felt pulsing under his tongue. When she gasped, he brushed the nubs of flesh crowning her breasts, feeling them harden under his fingers. He circled them slowly, teasingly, then he kissed her temple. The scent of her hair jolted something deep inside him. This was the scent of his woman, the only woman he would ever possess. He cradled her cheek in his hand.

So soft...

"More," she moaned. "Don't stop."

Eirik cupped her breasts again, letting them rest in his palm a while, marveling at the perfect fit between them. Then he resumed his teasing strokes on her nipples. The feel of his thumbs brushing through the thin shift would be like a delicious torture. As waves of pleasure were unleashed in her body, Freyja arched her back in a silent plea for more, a plea he answered by squeezing the tender nubs.

His lips tingled with the urge to take her nipples into his mouth and suckle them, but he didn't allow himself that pleasure just yet. He would do it in a moment, in the comfort of their bed, when she was naked and desperate.

This time he would take the initiative, this time he would

behave like a man, a married man, a man in love, and choose what they did next.

"Take your clothes off," he heard her say.

The corner of his lips lifted despite himself. So much for taking the initiative... Not that he minded. The result would be the same. Mind-blowing pleasure.

"I will take them off if you take your shift off, too."

He should have known she would not hesitate. In this, she was the experienced one. At the same time as he kicked his braies away from him, she stepped out of her shift and stood in the middle of the room, naked as the day she was born, a goddess in full bloom.

"Look at you," Eirik breathed, allowing his gaze to wander over the beauty on display in front of him.

"I don't want you to *look* at me," she moaned. "Stop teasing me like this. Touch me again. I need more."

He was on her before he'd realized he'd moved. Her breasts, without the cloth barrier this time, settled in his hand as naturally as if they belonged there. He gave a low growl of approval. How had he gone so long without this? Without a woman to love? It seemed inconceivable now. He would not be able to wait much longer to possess her, not when she was so deliciously warm and tantalizing. Not when she was begging for it.

Closing his eyes, he knelt in front of her and drew one pert nub into his mouth.

Freyja might have died and gone to the place her mother called Heaven. What Eirik was doing to her breast was amazing, sending waves of pleasure all the way down to her toes, stoking the inferno burning in her loins. She dug her fingers into his hair, keeping him close, making him suckle her harder. The groans he gave only added to her level of arousal. He sounded as if he couldn't get enough of her.

"Enough," she rasped, head thrown back. "More! Now! Oh, please, wait. Yes, no, don't stop, do that again... Again!"

She didn't know what she was saying, only that she had gone mindless with need. Eirik stood back up, drew her to him, and grabbed her by the buttocks to make her feel the strength of his own arousal. He was so hard it was almost painful to feel him grind against her.

Almost.

How had this man succeeded in suppressing his masculine urges for more than twenty years? It seemed incredible. He was made to love women, and now she was the lucky one able to benefit from his generosity and skill.

"Tonight I will be the one making love to you, if you are prepared to be forgiving," he said in her ear, his tone urgent.

"There will be no need to forgive anything. You are going to make my body explode in pleasure time and time again. I just know it."

She had no fear whatsoever. He had almost sent her over the edge by suckling her. As soon as he took her, she would erupt.

"Lie down."

Obeying the curt order, Freyja stretched on her back, looking at Eirik with what she hoped was a heated look. Judging from the speed with which he took his place between her spread thighs, she had succeeded in provoking him.

"Am I not hurting you?" he rasped, careful to rest his weight on his elbows.

"No." Her stomach, though taut and rounded, was not yet big enough to pose an obstacle to their lovemaking. It might change in the months to come, but at the moment she felt more beautiful, more desirable than she had felt in a long, long while, perhaps ever. "Take me. Slowly. I want to feel every inch of you going in, I want to know you are right where you belong, with me, inside me. I need to know you're mine."

"I am yours, Wife, body and soul. Forever." His nostrils flared. "Are you sure you're ready? I should—"

"I have never been more ready in my life." Any more and she would be embarrassed. She could feel slickness running between her thighs, betraying a level of arousal she had never reached before. If he didn't take her now, she would die.

Eirik slid in, just as she had requested, excruciatingly slow, feeding her his steel-hard length inch by inch. She closed her eyes, relishing the moment. Once he was fully seated inside her, he stilled and gave her a kiss that melted all her bones one by one, until she could have sworn she was as liquid and as boundless as the sea that had brought her to this man. The feel of his tongue, velvety-soft, playing with hers, made her core contract in a series of pulses.

"What was that?" Eirik asked when he felt her tighten around him. "Do it again."

"That?" She smiled as she resumed her squeezing, loving that every sensation was new to him, that everything she did was a wonder. It made her feel as if this were the first time for her as well. She had feared she would draw comparisons with her first wedding night, but it was not so. This was all new and wonderful.

"Fuuuuck," he said between his teeth, the word little more than a long exhale. "Yes. Just like that."

"I love your swearing," Freyja said, breathless herself. She had once told his sister that she didn't mind him using coarse language, but that had been a lie. In reality, she loved it. "I love how you don't try to restrain yourself around me. I love how I make you lose control. I love...you."

"Fuck, fuck, *fuck*," he said, punctuating each word with a thrust of his hips, his mouth at her throat, his teeth sharp against her skin. "If you keep saying things like this, I'm really going to lose control. And this will be over before it has begun."

"So? What would be the problem with that?"

She hadn't forgotten how he had licked her after reaching his pleasure the first time they had made love. It had been the most wicked, delicious, pleasurable thing imaginable and she longed to feel it again.

"Ah, so you liked me licking you clean, Wife? You'd like me to do it tonight, is that it? You're hoping it will rekindle the fire burning inside me. You're hoping I will fuck you again once you've drenched my tongue?"

Yes. A thousand times, yes.

Freyja was thrashing her head left and right on the pillow, lost to the most wonderful sensations. Forget the swearing, the dirty talk was enough to make her fall in love with Eirik all over again.

"If you keep saying things like this, I too am going to lose control," she said, echoing his earlier words. "And this will be over before it has begun."

"So? I know for a fact that a woman's pleasure is as boundless as the sea. And I'm the best swimmer you know. I will be able to revel in it." Eirik lifted her right leg onto his shoulder and reared up, all masculine power. "Now. Give me your pleasure, Wife."

"Yes!" Freyja cried out, hurtled headlong into what would be the first in a long series of releases in this, her second wedding night.

It wasn't long before her husband followed her, and nothing had ever felt as good as the heat of his pleasure searing her insides.

She smiled and was asleep before he could withdraw.

22

───────

Eirik was going to die.

Freyja had been laboring for what seemed like days, and still the baby refused to be born. How much more of this would she have to bear? How much more would he have to endure? Nothing in his life had prepared him for this. How could it? It was pure torture, inhumane.

"You're doing really well," he heard Cwenthryth say, her tone encouraging, cheerful almost. "Not too long now."

He blinked in disbelief.

So this was normal? This agony, this endless suffering, was normal? He could barely breathe for anguish, and he was not the one doing the hard part. But Steinar's wife knew what she was doing and she didn't sound worried in the least, so he forced himself to calm. Maybe all was well. Freyja had asked if he could stay with her and he would not fail her. This was the first time she'd given birth, all this was new to her also. It was understandable that she should need reassurance and comfort. And he would provide it, whatever the cost to his sanity.

"One last time. Push."

Eirik closed his eyes, and willed his strength to pass on to

Freyja through the hand he was holding—his brave, his beloved wife. He might be about to collapse under the strain, but she would be able to do this. He trusted her.

There was a scream followed by a deafening silence. In the stillness, another cry was heard, more like a wail, really. Eirik opened his eyes, not quite daring to believe that it was over. But it was, finally. A baby was lying on Freyja's stomach. A perfect, healthy baby with the most bewitching set of eyes he had ever seen, of a blue as deep as the sea he imagined linked Denmark and here. How perfect.

Before he could think, he placed his hand over the little wet body—and his eyes started to burn. *Mine*, his heart roared, a visceral, uncontrollable reaction. His father had warned him this would happen but still it was a blow.

I knew it as soon as I set eyes on you, lying on your mother's body that you were mine.

Yes. This baby was his, because it was Freyja's.

"Congratulations. You have a beautiful daughter."

It was only when Cwenthryth beamed at them that he realized he had not even wondered whether the child was a boy or a girl. He had not cared. But another girl was perfect, more than he had ever hoped to have.

"Thank you, my love," he said, bowing his head toward Freyja. "I'm humbled by everything you've done. I love you, more than I ever thought possible."

It took him a moment to realize that she was crying. And even longer to understand that he was crying also. He could not remember the last time he had cried. Too long ago, probably, and for the wrong reasons.

This, by contrast, felt just right, because his heart was overflowing.

"Now. I need to go tell Asta," he said, placing a kiss on his wife's forehead. "She was very worried about you."

"Yes," Freyja agreed, lifting herself slightly onto her elbows. "Please, go tell her everything is well, while Cwenthryth helps me with the afterbirth."

The afterbirth? "You mean there's more coming? It isn't over?"

He shuddered and she placed a reassuring hand on his arm.

"I'll be fine. This is perfectly normal."

He had no choice but to trust in her, so he went to their eldest daughter, who threw herself into his arms as soon as he appeared on the path.

"*Moðir*?" she asked.

"All is well. And you have a sister."

"Oh!"

The hug she gave him threatened to start tears again. Eirik closed his eyes and let joy spread through him.

Sometime later, when he came back into the hut, he found Freyja sitting up with her back propped against the wall. The smile she threw him was radiant.

"Asta asked me to tell you that she is very proud of you and cannot wait to meet her baby sister."

"I imagine."

"I'll leave you to get acquainted with your daughter now."

With these words, Cwenthryth left the hut. Eirik didn't try to stop her. He was too stunned. It was only when he heard the door close that he realized he had not even thanked her for what she had done for his wife and child. He would have to remedy that as soon as he could.

He walked over to the pallet, feeling suddenly shy.

"Here." With a smile Freyja handed him the babe, who'd been cleaned and swaddled tightly. He saw that she had her mother's fiery hair, as well as her deep blue eyes. A true Norsewoman. A true beauty. "Meet Finna Eiriksdóttir."

He stilled, seized by the importance of the moment. "You named her after me?"

Finna, daughter of Eirik. He didn't know what to say.

"Of course, I did. Who else is going to be a father to her? Who else already loves her? Who else has given her a chance at a happy, fulfilled life? Who else is holding her as if she were the most precious thing he'd ever seen?"

Freyja was now crying freely. He couldn't stand it.

"Come here, my love."

He sat on the pallet next to her, using the arm that was not holding his daughter to draw her against his flank. Yes, the little girl was his, to love and protect until the day he died.

"Thank you," he said, placing a kiss on the top of his wife's head. "And perhaps one day I will give you a babe of my blood to add to our beautiful family." He placed a gentle hand over her stomach.

Freyja laughed through her tears. "I thought you were going to pass out during the birth. And now you want to witness another?"

He shook his head, stricken at his insensitivity. "Forgive me, I'm so happy I don't know what I'm saying. Of course, I don't mean you should have to go through another—"

"Eirik. I would like nothing more than to bear your children. At the very least, I would like nothing more than to let you try to father them."

Was she trying to kill him? He couldn't think of losing himself inside her heat right now.

"All in good time, my love. Sleep now." He looked at the baby in his arms and gave a low chuckle. "Look, Finna has already fallen asleep. So I will hold you both and keep you right where you belong."

∾

FREYJA TOOK in a deep inhale of the primrose-scented air. Spring was coming, along with the promise of a new beginning. She herself had participated in this outburst of life. It had been five days since she'd given birth to little Finna, and she had never felt better, even if her body had yet to recover fully.

She stilled, her attention on the scene in front of her. Eirik was walking back and forth along the vegetable patch with the little girl in his arms, his gaze locked with hers. A stream of words floated in the air around them, too low for her to hear, which was probably a good thing. She might well start to cry if she knew what her husband was telling their daughter. She had done her share of crying over the last few days, and she knew the lack of sleep was not the only reason for it. Happiness was.

Her heart was full.

A moment later, Frigyth came to sit next to her. There were tears in her lovely brown eyes.

"Is everything all right?" Freyja asked, worried. She liked her new mother-in-law, who was both loving and kind. She and her husband had welcomed her and Asta into the family with open arms, and she didn't like to see her upset.

"I've never been better, Freyja. I came here to thank you for what you did for my son."

"Please, I feel I should be the one thanking *you* for having raised such an amazing man." They were not that common, she should know.

"You know what I mean." Frigyth shook her head. "You finally helped him conquer his shame at being a man, for want of a better word, helped him unload the burden he'd been carrying for too long. I hope you will forgive me for being so honest, but as I know you are aware of the circumstances around his conception, there is no need for me to be coy. I..."

Emotion threatened to choke Freyja when her mother-in-law's voice died out. Even years after her ordeal, she had difficulty talking about Olaf's attack and no wonder. What had happened that day was a hundred times worse than what had happened with Arvid. Frigyth hadn't known her attacker, and she'd still been a virgin. She would have been in pain, possibly frightened for her life. And when she'd found out she was with child, she would have been devastated.

Thank the gods, by then she had already met Sigurd, who'd helped her heal.

"I do know what happened to you," she admitted in a low voice. "And I'm so sorry."

"I'm sorry for you too."

Feminine compassion passed through them. Freyja knew Eirik had told his father what had happened in Denmark when he was battling his feelings for her, and it was only natural that the Dane would have told his wife. She didn't mind them knowing.

"Anyway. His reaction when he found out what had happened made me regret confiding in him. We never thought it would make him fear his nature, w e only wanted to protect him from hurt. Wolf and Merewen would never have revealed what had happened to me, of course, but other people in the village know that Sigurd has not fathered him, so we thought that he should know the truth, so he could trust that we weren't trying to hide anything from him. One day someone might say something, either through malice, or even by accident. It would have devastated him to see that we had kept such a secret from him, understandably. So when he was old enough to understand, we felt there was no choice but to tell him."

It had been the right decision. If Eirik had to hear about the terrible truth, it was better that it came from his parents. They would be able to explain exactly what had happened and reassure him that it didn't change the place he occupied in their life and in their hearts, which they had done through the beautiful arm ring.

"I would have done the same in your place," Freyja admitted.

In fact, she would one day tell Finna she had been conceived by another man than the one she called father. Unlike Frigyth, however, because no one but the close family knew what had happened, she would be able to keep to herself the most sordid details of the story. All her daughter would be told was that her mother's late husband had sired her a few weeks before dying in an accident, and that Eirik had decided to take care of the babe when he had fallen in love with her.

"Yes," Frigyth said. "There was no other choice. But the price Eirik paid was even heavier than we had feared. Almost overnight, the carefree little boy we knew disappeared. He became a man, and at the same moment, he started to fear his nature. Had we known this would happen, I don't think we would have acted the way we did, or at least we..."

She shook her head as if unsure what could have been done differently. Freyja had no answer so she waited.

"I knew, of course, that having been raised by Sigurd, there was no risk of him ever doing anything contrary to honor, but he seemed to doubt himself. Aged sixteen, he condemned himself to a life of solitude, and yet now he has a beautiful, loving family. So you see, I have every reason to thank you. Now all my five children have found love and happiness. I could not have asked for a better gift."

The woman wiped at her eyes. Just then her husband walked over, as if warned by a mysterious force that she needed comfort.

"What's wrong, Birdie?" he asked, placing a hand on her shoulder.

Freyja loved the nickname the Dane had given his wife. It showed such affection. Maybe she should ask Eirik to find one for her, something only he would use.

"Nothing's wrong. I was telling Freyja how happy we are to have her in the family."

"Indeed we are." Her father-in-law looked at her with such intensity she was reminded he had once been called Beast. "My son couldn't have chosen a better wife."

My son.

There was such pride and such love in those two words that it brought a tear to Freyja's eyes. She hoped one day to thank Finna's husband for making her happy.

"We will leave you now." Frigyth stood up and took her husband's arm. Behind her, the sky had started to turn the faintest pink. "I put some griddle cakes and cheese on the table for you to eat later."

"Thank you."

It was not long before Eirik walked over to her, a slanted smile on his lips. In his arms, Finna had fallen asleep. "What did my parents want?"

She stood up and kissed him full on the lips. "To tell me how happy they are that I joined the family."

He let out a low growl and brushed his nose against her temple in a tender gesture. "They cannot be happier or more grateful than I am. I love you."

She smiled. It had become a jest between them to tell one another as often as they could of their love. "I love you too."

"Shall we open a cask of mead tonight?" he suggested. "I think I have one ready."

"Why? What is there to celebrate?"

He snorted. "Too many things, in truth. Being together. Being in love. Being parents to two wonderful little girls."

Indeed, what was worth celebrating more than that? "Perfect."

They walked back to the hut. After settling Finna in her cot, Eirik turned to face her again.

"Come here." With those words he sat on the stool and drew her onto his lap, her favorite place in the world. "There is something I would like to do with you, not immediately, but in a few months' time."

Her heart started to beat in an uncontrollable rhythm. Was this what she was thinking? It would be weeks before they could make love again properly. He had lavished pleasure on her these last few weeks and she on him, but her great belly had made it rather hard to enjoy anything more strenuous.

Was that what he was referring to? That they would soon be able to resume their fierce lovemaking? No. He'd said *months*. Surely he didn't mean to wait that long until he took her again?

"What would you like me to do?" she asked, unable to bear the wait any longer. She already knew she would agree, whatever it was.

"Take me to Denmark. Show me the place where you grew up. All my life I've wanted to go, and now I finally have a reason to. I want to go see the land of my father, and also meet your family."

A lump formed in Freyja's throat. She had not been expecting that, and a wave of emotion crashed through her at the idea of seeing her family again. She threw her arms around her husband's neck. How had she deserved a man who looked after her so well?

"Of course. We'll go as soon as Finna is old enough to travel safely, perhaps at the end of the summer, and stay over the winter."

Suddenly she couldn't wait to show her husband and her daughters to her brother, her sisters, her parents. They would be told about Finna's birth in a letter soon, of course, but that was not the same as meeting her.

"Staying there for the winter would be perfect, or even a ful year if you wish. I don't think I'd like to settle there, though," he added, as if worried she had misunderstood his intentions. "My life is here, and I—"

"I know. And we will come back. My life is here too."

It would be too odd to live with Eirik where she had lived with Arvid, having to be reminded of all she had endured. They were better off here, building their new family.

Which gave her an idea.

"But I would like you to father our next child on Danish soil," she whispered in his ear. "It seems fitting. Do you think you could manage that?"

"I think I can try, and see what happens, vixen," he growled when she captured his earlobe between her teeth.

Vixen. Mmmm. Freyja smiled.

Perhaps that would do for a special name.

EPILOGUE

A few days later, a banquet was given in honor of little Finna's birth in the center of the village.

The baby was two weeks old, and thriving. Freyja had never felt more blessed. Only a few months ago she'd thought her situation hopeless, her husband lost to her, her future filled with pain and solitude. Now she had a family, two healthy little girls, a new home, and a husband who'd restored her faith in life.

The day before, the two of them had gone to the harbor to ask one of the Danish merchants on his way back home to deliver a message to her parents, telling them she was happier than ever after the birth of her daughter. They could stop worrying about her, against all odds she had found what she needed by fleeing a situation she could not accept anymore.

Eirik had crafted a beautiful pot for them. The four members of the family, including baby Finna, had placed their hands on it, leaving their trace on the wet clay. Freyja had drawn patterns around the rim and written their names with the help of her trusted chicken feathers. She knew her parents would cherish the gift for the rest of their lives, the proof that she was loved and happy in her new home.

Eager to surprise them when the time came, in the letter they had not mentioned their intention of visiting Denmark before the year was over. The surprise on her parents' faces when they saw her would be worth the sacrifice.

The banquet was a resounding success, filled with laughter and delicious food.

As the sun started to disappear under the tallest trees, a cart was seen stopping by the bridge. All eyes turned in that direction in time to watch a blonde woman alight, wave to the driver and cross the bridge while the cart drove away.

Freyja leaned in to Eirik. "Who is that?"

It was obvious that most people knew the woman. The range of expressions on their faces made it clear, however, that she was not very popular. Moon was glaring at her. Aife had rolled her eyes in what might be exasperation and Torsten looked positively gleeful, as if he'd been handed an opportunity for mischief.

"It's my cousin, Edita," Eirik answered. Though she was family, he didn't seem particularly pleased to see her either. "My aunt Birgit's daughter. She lives far away, in Mercia, and gave no warning she might visit. This is definitely a surprise."

Yes, but apparently, not many people were delighted by this surprise. Who was this woman, Freyja wondered, and why was she provoking such strong reactions in Eirik's family, who had welcomed her so warmly?

Frigyth, in other words Edita's aunt, stood up and walked over to her.

"Heavens, this is unexpected. We never got word of your arrival. Is everything all right? What are you doing here?"

Edita demurred and allowed her gaze to wander over the assembled guests, as if to ensure all eyes were on her. They were, especially those of the men. Haakon, the goldsmith's son, and Arne, in particular, looked as if they would pounce at the first opportunity. She was rather pretty, Freyja had to admit, but the light lurking in her eyes made her appear petty. Without knowing why, she already knew they would not get along.

"I... Well, to tell you the truth, I was wondering if I could come live in the village," Edita eventually said.

"And what would your husband say to that, I wonder?" Aife said, when Frigyth appeared too stunned to react.

Eirik's sister had stood up and walked over to her cousin, Torsten following closely behind. When she saw her cousin's swollen belly, and little Thyra in her father's arms, Edita's eyes widened. For a moment she looked as if jealousy was consuming her.

Then, just as quickly, she seemed to recover.

"Oh, I don't have to worry about what Wulfric would say any more. He's dead."

Coming next
Haakon's Fate

ALSO BY VIRGINIE MARCONATO

Sons of the Wolf

Steinar's Gift

Torsten's Gamble

Sven's Promise

Eirik's Oath

The Welsh Rebels

A Husband for Esyllt

A Savior for Branwen

A Second Chance for Carys

A Rogue for Siân

A Lover for Lady Jane

A Scot for Bethan

The Noble Norsemen

Taming the Wolf

Soothing the Beast

Wooing the Devil

Baiting the Bear

Tempting the Saxon

Seducing the Warrior

Loving the Blacksmith

ABOUT THE AUTHOR

As far back as I remember, I have been attracted to the Middle Ages, to knights in shining armour and their ladies in spectacular dresses. Now I get to write about them, I feel like the luckiest woman in the world. Being French and married to a Brit makes each book I write extra special, as our countries share a long and sometimes painful past. But in the end, in life as well as in fiction, love conquers all!

I have published several medieval romances under my own name, including series, and also have a pen name, Judith Falcon, for spicier projects, still in historical romance.

Join my newsletter and check out my other books on virginiemarconato.com.

OLIVERHEBERBOOKS

A small press bound by the belief that every voice matters.

Sign up for our newsletter to learn about new releases and more.
https://oliver-heberbooks.com/subscribe/

Follow us on social media:

facebook.com/oliverheberbooks

instagram.com/oliverheberbooks

amazon.com/oliverheberbooks

youtube.com/@OliverHeberBooksPublisher